3/02

HESTER
AMONG THE
RUINS

HESTER AMONG THE RUINS

BINNIE KIRSHENBAUM

W. W. Norton   New York   London

John Toland, excerpts from *Adolf Hitler* (New York: Doubleday, 1976). Reprinted with the permission of Doubleday, a division of Random House, Inc. Tanya Bayard, translator, excerpts from *A Medieval Home Companion* (New York: Harper, 1992). Copyright © 1992 by Tanya Bayard. Reprinted with the permission of the author. **Art:** "Trabant, Legende auf Rädern" courtesy of Marianne Peltz/Trabant Pappe auf Rädern. "Reproduktion einer historischen Anisichtkarte." Copyright © Vertrieb R. Flügel. Photograph of two thatch-roofed buildings beneath trees courtesy of Landesfremdenverkehrsverband Mecklenburg-Vorpommern e.V. "Urlaub zwischen Meer und Bodden," from a catalogue published by Kur-und Tourismusbetrieb Ostseebad Zingst, courtesy of Tourist Information—Ostseebad Zingst. "Aus Umweltgründen Nicht Glanzfolienkaschiert" courtesy of Georg Tosonowski/De Beeke. "Bamberg, Dom, aussen, N-Seite, r. neben dem Fürstenportal: Synagoge, von vorn, etwa 1230–40" courtesy of Foto Marburg/Art Resource, NY. "Ruinen in der Innenstadt." Copyright © Sammlung Eickemeyer.

For information about permission to reproduce selections from this book, write to Permissions, W. W. Norton & Company, Inc., 500 Fifth Avenue, New York, NY 10110

The text of this book is composed in Berling
with the display set in Anisette
Composition by Molly Heron
Manufacturing by the Haddon Craftsmen, Inc.
Book design by Chris Welch
Production manager: Amanda Morrison

Library of Congress Cataloging-in-Publication Data
Kirshenbaum, Binnie.
Hester among the ruins / by Binnie Kirshenbaum
p. cm.
ISBN 0-393-04152-2
1. Americans—Germany—Fiction. 2. National Socialism—Fiction. 3. Women biographers—Fiction. 4. College teachers—Fiction. 5. Jewish women—Fiction. 6. Mistresses—Fiction. 7. Germany—Fiction. I. Title
PS3561.I755 H47 2002
813'.54—dc21   2001044488

W. W. Norton & Company, Inc.
500 Fifth Avenue, New York, N.Y. 10110
www.wwnorton.com

W. W. Norton & Company Ltd.
Castle House, 75/76 Wells Street, London W1T 3QT

1 2 3 4 5 6 7 8 9 0

FOR MY HUSBAND

Acknowledgments

Thank you—to those historians and biographers (and especially Patty O'Toole) who provided me with knowledge, material, and texture for this novel; to Jennifer Lyons, standout agent and pal; to my editor Jill Bialosky for her skills and wisdom; to Deirdre O'Dwyer for her assistance; to Richard Howard and to Maureen Howard, always.

And to Patricia Reimann, Wolfgang Balk, Olga and Ernst Mannheimer, and all my other dear ones in Munich—*danke* for their gracious hospitality, for their humor, and for their friendship.

People are trapped in history, and
history is trapped in them.
—James Baldwin

HESTER
AMONG THE
RUINS

Chapter One

They don't wear hats like that here

H is hair grows like grass in a cross breeze. This way and that. Blond and soft and no more than an inch long. I like his hair. A lot.

"*Kindchenschema*," he tells me. *Kindchenschema* is the word for it, but instead of translating he draws me a picture. On a blank page of my open notebook, he draws the head of an animal I don't recognize. A cross between a dog and a cat. A tuft of hair on its head stands up straight, with some hair leaning to the left and some leaning to the right. It looks like a hieroglyphic or a cave painting, a rendering of an animal extinct or of the imagination. "Young animals," he explains, "have short snouts and soft round heads which make other animals like and protect them."

Smitten with that idea, that his hair might have such an effect, he smiles, and his smile is a good one. Capable of charming the pants off, well, me, to name one.

When he is not smiling, he is still very handsome, but it's a different look altogether.

With one hand, he lifts his beer stein and polishes off the remains of his Helles. Then he asks me, "Do you want another?"

I've barely made a dent in mine, a Radler, which is a concoction of half beer and half lime juice in a stein as tall as my arm. To lift it, I hold it the way a small child holds a cup, with two hands to keep it steady. It's the same sort of stein with which Thomas Wolfe got whomped on the head, eventually, rumor had it, dying of complications from the injury sustained. "How about something to eat?" I say. "A snack."

He goes off to one of the four or five concession stands, and alone, without him to gaze upon, I look around at where I am.

I am in Munich. Munich, Germany. When I told people—friends, colleagues, my landlord—that I was going to Munich, I was asked, "Why?" as if I'd said I was going to someplace like Cleveland, Ohio, or Scranton, Pennsylvania. Moreover, Jews, even entirely irreligious ones like me, rarely put Munich on their holiday wish lists. And so I was asked, "Why Munich, of all places?"

"Professional reasons," I explained. "A new book." Which is the truth. Just not all of the truth. It's a talent of mine to tell truth in part and to omit the rest. And indeed part of the truth is that I am writing a history which demands I be here to study documents, to look at photographs, to conduct interviews, to understand the landscape, to ferret out secrets.

Munich is his city.

For the past twenty-two years now, Munich has been his home. Although he was raised largely in Frankfurt, he was born in Berlin in 1943 in an air-raid shelter during a blackout.

I am in Munich, smack in the middle of the Englischer Garten, a grand park designed in the tradition, untamed, of the Romantic English gardens. Hence the name. The hub of this beer garden is a Chinese Tower. It's a copy of the original copy, which was burned to the ground in 1944. The original copy, erected in 1789, was modeled on the pagoda in London's Kew Gardens, which leads me to wonder if the birds in these trees are copies of English birds from English trees. Fanning out around the tower are long wooden tables, row upon row of picnic tables arranged like barracks. Families and groups of friends and coworkers are gathered here at the day's end for dinner and beer. Some have brought food from home in baskets and some buy food—sausages or pretzels the size of Christmas wreaths—at concession stands fashioned like Alpine chalets. It is the first week of June, and they're going to make a night of it. A night that will end around ten because the city of Munich keeps tight hours. I can't say why, exactly, but this place, this beer garden, this horde of Germans drinking beer and eating sausages at the day's end, strikes me as folk motif. As though if I were to blink, I'd find them wearing, not suits and jeans and floral-print dresses, but animal skins and burlap, and many of them would be sitting there naked, as medieval peasants were wont to do in the summer months. Not an entirely pleasant image, but nowhere near as unpleasant as the other image involving hordes of beer-sotted Germans that can come to mind.

An hour or so ago, when he and I met up in front of my hotel, I was wearing a hat. A wide-brimmed black straw hat, capping off an ensemble of a black linen dress, patent-leather sandals and bag. Very chic, and I've been told that I look good in a hat, the way my hair—a profusion of black curls—is tucked underneath, unruly tendrils springing loose. Also, even though my skin is not the sort that burns, I don't like the sun on my face.

One look at me, and it was apparent that something about my person was causing him distress, which prompted me to look down at myself. Was my dress stained with gunk? Did I have a streamer of toilet paper trailing from my shoe? Then he made clear the problem. "Are you going to wear that hat?" he asked.

"Obviously," I said, "I was planning on it. Why? Is there something wrong with it?"

He hesitated, shuffled his feet, his eyes shifted away from mine. "They don't wear hats like that here," he said.

With any other man, I might've gotten snippy. I might've said, "I'll wear what I damn well please." But he isn't any other man, and his discomfort struck me as kind of cute, so I told him to wait while I ran the hat upstairs.

The reason I told him to wait outside, in front of the hotel, was the same reason why we met there in the first place. Over these last four days I have learned that if he first comes to my room, it proves impossible for us to leave. As if the door snaps shut, and we are, by some centrifugal force, pinned to the bed. For four days running, our plans to go to this beer garden went unrealized.

Just an aside, but yet another thing I've learned since I've been here: At the supermarket, they don't give you bags. I learned this yesterday, the hard way, having purchased a can of coffee, a box of chocolate, a wedge of Emmentaler cheese, a loaf of bread, a bunch of red grapes, a bottle of wine, and a six-pack of pilsner, all of which I had to carry back to the hotel in my arms and dangling from my teeth. But what is travel if not a learning experience? Later he told me that I could've purchased a cotton sack, reusable and environmentally friendly, at the cash register for a mere fifty pfennigs, but you have to request it, you have to ask.

When we got to this beer garden and found seats, he looked around in all directions and beckoned me to do the same. "See," he said. "No one is wearing anything like that hat of yours."

Now he returns to the table, a stein of beer in one hand and a plate in the other. He slides the plate before me. On it sits maybe a turnip or a rutabaga, a root I assume is edible because he passes me a salt shaker.

"What is this?" I ask.

"A radish." He seems genuinely surprised that I do not recognize it as such.

The radishes I know are small and red. This one is big and white. Moreover, when I asked for a snack, I was expecting to get chips or salted peanuts. I was not expecting a giant radish. I was not expecting a snack pulled from the ground, dirt brushed off, and dropped on a plate.

"It's good." He urges me to try it, and he is right. It is cool and sharp. There is a bite to it, but still my mind boggles. One giant radish on a plate is snack food.

His name is Heinrich Falk, but he goes by Herr Professor Heinrich Falk.

Falk is German for falcon. Falcon as in a bird of prey. Falcons have powerful wings, keen vision, and attack swiftly. In the Middle Ages, knights were falconers, skilled in the art of training their birds to hunt. (Genealogical inquiry? Is he descended from the order of chivalry?)

Officially, I am Dr. Hester Rosenfeld. Hester Rosenfeld is practically an oxymoron. An incongruity, unless you know that I was
named after Hester Street, on the Lower East Side of New York.
While Ashkenazic Jews, which is what my parents were, tradi-
tionally name a child after a deceased relative, there were too
many of those to choose from. My parents broke with tradition,
in that way and in most other ways too, and opted to name me
for a happy memory instead.

As is often the way with immigrants, my parents embraced
America, Americana, with the fervor of converts. We celebrated
no religious holidays, but we pulled out all the stops for the
Fourth of July. On Washington's Birthday, I got gifts, and every
Arbor Day, my father planted an apple tree. Trees that never did
grow strong and sturdy, but rather were stunted, bearing fruit
that was wizened and wormy. But still, he kept at it. My parents
didn't want me tethered in any way to the old ways of the old
world. I was their Hester, all-American girl, a Yankee Doodle,
swaddle-her-in-the-flag bundle of joy.

Dr. Hester Rosenfeld (not M.D., but Ph.D. in Colonial American History—what else was there for me?—Columbia University, 1989), only I rarely use the title. I am not with any
university. A choice made back when my dissertation, *Gender,
Wealth, and Justice in Buzzards Bay Country*, was published to
some commercial success. Centering on the plight of one Abigail
Muxon, a Puritan woman, who—because there was no statute of
limitations on sin—was tried thirty years after the fact for having had a little hanky-panky with a man who was not her husband. Significant double standards proliferated in the Puritan
courts. Leniency for the rich, the lash for the poor, the woman

was always to blame, and hapless hot-to-trot Abby made for kind of a juicy story too.

Every once in a while that happens—hell freezes and a scholarly work crosses over into the bosom of popular appeal, although they did change the title to *No Sin Goes Unpunished: The Abigail Muxon Story*, which the publisher's marketing division thought to be catchy.

The upshot of this was that job offers were lobbed at me from all directions. Instead of being yet one more newly anointed Ph.D. scrambling for a coveted university slot, I was a darling of the academy. I had my pick of suitors. And so what did I do? As if department chairs were swarms of bees, I ducked and ran for cover. Fear of making the wrong choice led me to choose none at all. I have more than my share of fears. Some rational, some not: heights, escalators, water deeper than knee level, electrical wiring, spontaneous combustion, squirrels, intimacy, commitment, and fear of anyone learning just how afraid I am. Consequently, I do not now have the solidity of position, the security of tenure, or so much as a regular paycheck.

However, when not a neurosis, fear is a survival instinct, which is how it turned out in this case. Instead of suffering interminable departmental meetings and faculty backbiting fests, I get to make my living as a guest lecturer. I do consultations for restoration projects and work with museum curators preparing exhibits on colonial life. I write articles and book reviews, and I have since written two other books. One centered around Francis Bale, whose income the town fathers of the Massachusetts Bay community deemed too meager to support a wife and seven children. Thus they ordered him to dispose of two of his children, that is, to send them into servitude, lest they become a burden on the public purse. My most recent book chronicled the redemption of Samuel Sewall, who sat as an *ad hoc* judge for the Salem witch trials. Not long after that fiasco, his beloved baby daughter died and Judge Sewall connected the dots. God had punished him for issuing mistaken verdicts, and I quite agreed.

All of this together, historian-at-large coupled with a small inheritance, and I don't want for much. I live in a cozy one-bedroom apartment on Ninth Avenue in what was once Hell's Kitchen but now is gentrified and called Clinton. I've got a clawfoot tub in the bathroom, and the sea-green linoleum kitchen floor, installed in the 1940s, is no worse for the wear. I can afford to shop in the food boutiques—Bruno's for fresh pasta, Wakim's for olives and figs, the Cheeze Wizard for feta and fontina. Most mornings, I would have a croissant and lattè at the Cupcake Café before heading off to the library or back home to work. Several nights a week, I'd eat dinner out. There has been more than an occasional lover, and I've got a closet full of nice clothes (albeit from the sale racks, but who cares). I buy all the books I want, and at dusk, the light on Ninth Avenue turns pale pink. It's an undoubtedly comfortable life and, until recently, I was quite content.

For more than ten years I had stuck by the colonies until the notion that one landmass and the scantiness of four centuries, give or take, was closing in on me. In the big scheme of civilization, America is a babe, and its short history began to feel like a short future.

The history I am writing now is his. *The Life and Times of Heinrich Falk.* True, his life and times are nowhere near my areas of expertise, but I can learn. Also true, he is neither famous nor infamous—although ask yourself how famous would Dr. Johnson have been without Boswell.

Let us now praise famous men, and our fathers that begat us.
(Ecclesiasticus 44:1)

HF does not make for an obvious subject, yet he is the subject I've chosen, the leap I have taken.

Conceived and born in the shadows of history, he was a war baby raised in the quagmire of defeat by a generation of murderers at worst or cowards at best. A German after the fact, he is the prototype of the everyman of a nation occupied, divided, and then put together again in a way that gives a kind of credence to the Humpty Dumpty story. These years of his could well make for a provocative document, and he is willing to open his life to me. No, amend that. It's something more than willing. This, being the subject of a book, tickles him pink, and he is participatory, translating documents, journals, and letters from German to English, bringing me photographs, drawing me maps, telling me stories, filling in the blanks.

Without a doubt, he is the most vain man I've ever met. Not vain in the arrogant sense. He is not the least bit conceited. He does not think he's all that and then some. Rather, it's that anything that has to do with himself delights him no end. He gets positively giddy when he is the center of attention. And I am not the first to note this. A letter dated November 26, 1944, reads:

Dear Frau Doktor Falk,
Your small one has grown. You will not recognize him. He is
dancing a lot because we watch him. Whenever he has an

audience, he is very much for it. He is a sweet monkey. (Signature illegible)

Professional reasons not withstanding, I have come to Munich to be his mistress, which is the reason above all others for having chosen him as my subject. I find him endlessly fascinating.

For love's more important and powerful than
Even a priest or a politician. (From "Calypso" by W. H. Auden)

Although HF and I haven't yet spent all that much time together, I notice I have already appropriated some of his language. Not German, but the way he speaks English. He speaks British, and I find I'm saying *holiday* instead of *vacation* and *pub* rather than *bar* and asking where is the *loo*, and I, too, am referring to my *panties* as *knickers*.

I lean in across the wooden table, and tell him that today I am wearing white lace knickers. "With a matching bra," I add. I know he favors white lace knickers, and black, but he is not keen on red ones. Pink, however, is good.

"Those you wore yesterday," he says. "Those pink ones. Your bum looked so round in those. You should've seen the knickers Bettina wore." HF laughs, and I write:

Bettina wore terrible knickers. Cheap nylon. Three for five Marks.

Bettina was his third wife and the one who worries me most. Even though he and Bettina are long since divorced, I'm wary where she's concerned. The other wives, them I sense that I can trust.

He has been married, all totaled, four times, thrice divorced, and he's now married again to his second wife, with whom he has two daughters.

In addition to those aforementioned two, he has yet another two daughters, as well. One for each marriage. Four daughters in all. "I always make girls," he says. He is proud of these girls, and he seems devoted to the concept that procreation is tangible evidence of sexual prowess. Proof to the world that he can hit the bull's-eye.

His wives all gave him babies. Blond-haired baby girls, and his wives cooked him meals, kept clean houses, offered to iron his shirts, an offer he has consistently refused because he prefers to look helpless and in need rather than neat. I am not going to be one of his wives, and I will do none of those wifely things. Instead of baking him strudel, I am going to give him immortality.

Today he has brought me photographs of his wives and daughters. He lays them out on the wooden table in two rows.

King Ludwig I of Bavaria commissioned the painting of portraits of thirty-six beautiful women, all of whom, it is believed, were his mistresses, including the flamboyant Lola Montez. The scandal of that affair cost him his crown.

None of the photographs are recent ones. His eldest daughter, the one he had with Konstanze, his first wife, is, to date, thirty-eight years old, but in this picture she is all of nineteen. A lovely-looking girl, vibrant, with spectacular golden hair.

"I made her a promise," he tells me, "that I would never have an affair with a woman younger than she is. She wishes never to be older than her stepmummy."

"You're cutting it close," I note.

"Yes," he grins, pleased, I suspect as much at getting over on a technicality as at having a mistress who is but three months older than his eldest daughter.

The pictures of his daughters from his second and current wife were taken four years ago, when the youngest of them was still in diapers. "While we were on holiday in Elba," he says. That wife, the twice wife, he refers to as his *now wife*. Her photograph, passport size, was taken shortly after they married for the first time. As best as I can tell, given this portrait in miniature, the now wife has a healthy glow. She is pretty, with cheeks like apples.

The colors have faded on Konstanze's picture, and the details of her features are blurry, which is to be expected from a Polaroid taken in the 1960s. All I can really make out is that she's wearing glasses and a blouse that looks as if it had been cut from an Indian-print bedspread. And that she looks entirely unlike me, although similar to the others insofar as her hair is blond and her complexion is porcelain-light.

They all ought to wear hats like the one I'm not wearing, because they've got the kind of skin that freckles easily and, unprotected, is prone to carcinomas.

Also, these women appear to be substantial in stature, whereas I am not. I am diminutive and dark. My hair, long and curly like bedsprings, is as black as a raven's wing, and so are my eyes. Indeed, it is difficult to discern the demarcation between my pupil and my iris, and my skin tone speaks of a desert tribe, which is where I suspect my nose—a shade prominent—originated as well as my difficulties with settling down. I have been described as striking, beautiful even, but never, ever pretty.

Because I don't miss a trick, I note that there is no picture of Bettina. He has told me that Bettina has an elegant face, a classical beauty, a Roman nose, but I'll have to take his word on that for now. There is, however, a picture of that daughter. "She's the prettiest of my daughters," he says. "She looks like her mother."

The other three daughters are the spitting image of him, and I do not agree at all that this one is the prettiest. In fact, in my opinion, this child resembles a marmoset. "It's curious," I say, "how the other three look exactly like you, but this one looks nothing like you whatever. Are you sure she's yours?"

"Yes. I'm sure she's mine." He rolls his eyes.

I make a memo in my notebook.

   ✳ *Further inquiry as to patrimony of daughter with B.*

And I roll my eyes back at him, and we're both up in a flash. We walk at a brisk clip, out of the park and to the hotel, where we take the stairs to my room two at time.

Liebste Hester, The weather is now sunny, cool in the mornings, warm in the afternoon, and balmy until late after dark. (There was a full moon last night.) The place where I have got you a room is in a small hotel on Hesseloherstrasse, near the park, about eight bicycle-minutes away from university. I picture you working there, going for walks in the park. The district is Schwabing, that historically has been a place for artists and intellectuals.

Bicycle-minutes? Which of us did he imagine riding a bicycle? Certainly not me.

Brecht and Mann and Ibsen lived there, and so for two years did Lenin. When I think of you there, I want to open your legs, kiss you on the pink spot, and push right inside you. It's a shame this cán't be done simultaneously! (Letter to the author from HF)

The urgency of desire is much like a whirlwind, and our clothes are flung here and there and my white lace knickers land like fringe on the lampshade.

One of the many nice things about sex is that, generally speaking, there is no place for conversation. I can express the deepest emotion without a coherent word spoken, and I have never been one to reveal little secrets postcoitally.

After he gets dressed, I walk him to the door, which is all of three steps from the bed. There we kiss, and it is definitely very sexy, this kissing HF while he is dressed and I am not, but one of us has to be strong, and so I pull away first and say, "You'd best be off now." The upshot of the commitment phobia is that I'm good at that, at pulling away first.

He starts to leave but, when he turns and sees me standing there at the threshold watching him go, he rushes back and we kiss some more, until I remind him that he really does have to leave me now, and I close the door behind him, which is also something I'm very experienced with, the closing of doors.

So, I say, smiling, to myself, this is what it is like to be a mistress. Your lover takes leave of you early in the evening to go home to his now wife and daughters, and you are left alone in your little hotel room, a garret really. It's got nothing to recommend it, this room, but it is not wretched at all. It is clean, and it has a full bathroom plus a sloped ceiling, narrow bed, kitchenette, and in the far corner is a table where my papers are spread out like playing cards in an abandoned game of solitaire. Stacked in two piles are my books, books on twentieth-century German history and, to learn a little more of what he knows, some on the Middle Ages. On one of the two chairs, I have set up my computer, a laptop.

It's not for everyone, this being a mistress, I know that, but I luxuriate in the longing, I'm thriving on the desire. To be loved with devouring passion, and then left the hell alone, that's what suits me, allows me room to breathe and time to dream. This is the way to true love, the way to keep it pure, fresh, and kicking.

. . . we find [Romantic love] quite apart from marriage when knighthood was in flower. . . . The troubadour argued that marriage, combining a maximum of opportunity with a minimum of temptation, could hardly engender or sustain romantic love; even the pious Dante seems never to have dreamed addressing love poems to his wife, or to have found any unseemliness in addressing them to another woman, single or married. The knight agreed with the poet that knightly love had to be for some other lady than his own wife. (Will Durant, The Age of Faith, Simon & Schuster, 1950, p. 576)

In the ways of love, it seems to me, the Middle Ages were enlightened times. Once, about ten years ago, I was supposed to get married, but I didn't show up at the wedding. It was an awful thing to do, to let a perfectly nice man stand out in the cold on the steps of City Hall on a wet October morning, the slick leaves huddled at the joints of the streets and sidewalks. Keeping him waiting, waiting for me to show up to marry him, but I woke that day to the stench of the imminent decay of romance. I smelled a kind of death, and the next thing I knew I was in the emergency room at Columbia Presbyterian Hospital being treated for severe anxiety.

After that, I kept my affairs brief, as if they were set to a timer, and I made no promises. There was no one about whom I was serious. Until now. Until HF. I can't stop thinking about him, I don't want to stop thinking about him, conjuring him up with an acute clarity that causes me to groan with pleasure. About him, I am serious. As serious as the disaster this affair could very well turn out to be. But, unlike the past, with which we can have a nodding aquaintance, the future is entirely unknowable. Therefore, not worth stewing over. As my father used to say, *The truth is in the experiment.* For now, I'll have a little dinner, the Emmentaler cheese and bread and grapes, and then I've got a stack of HF's letters to me in need of chronological order.

Chapter Two

From there to here

clear away some papers to slice off a chunk of the Emmentaler, and I really do have to laugh at myself. Munich. You would think if a person were going to spend an open-ended amount of time in a European city, such a person would choose Rome or Barcelona or Paris, even. But Munich? Home to breweries and oompah bands. Ah, life is full of little surprises, and I'm in Munich because, ignoring the caution to Lot's wife, I went looking over my shoulder, and beyond.

While in the throes of my historical wanderlust, questing for a new subject, I read and ruminated on a number of empires, and found myself drawn, pulled even, to the idea of capturing a life, an ordinary life from Middle Europe during the Middle Ages. For me, history is not with the powers that be, but with the common man, and so from there, I placed a call to Peter Bourne, a Renaissance scholar of my acquaintance, to see if he had any suggestions

for me. Peter Bourne wears off-the-rack Italian suits and bran-
dishes a Montblanc pen, the Meisterstück, the fat one, and it
doesn't take Freud to do the math on that. His wife is an anthropologist of the sort who goes native, wearing serapes and neck-
laces made of macadamia nuts. I also ought to mention here that
Peter Bourne has tried, on nine or seventeen occasions, to get into
my pants, which isn't all that flattering when you know that he
tries to get into the pants of any woman more attractive than a
gargoyle.

"For your purposes. Falk. Heinrich Falk. In Munich." Peter
spoke as if between rounds of blowing smoke rings. "Top
medievalist." As if the pauses lent weight to what he was saying.
"Give Falk a call."

*Heinrich Falk was promoted to Doktor of Philosophy in
Medieval History at the Albert-Ludwigs Universtät, Freiburg
(1967). His Habilitation was granted in 1970, and four years
later, he was called to be a professor of Medieval Studies at the
Ludwig Maximilian Universtät, Munich, where he has become
something of a big cheese in the field.*

I took down the necessary phone numbers, and then I asked,
"So, what's he like? This Falk." A routine question in regards to
any man whom I haven't met, but whom I might meet. Just for
the fun of it, to imagine, to toy with possibilities if there are any,
but Peter put the kibosh on fantasy. "Oh. Timid," he said. "A
timid, little fellow. Hunched over. Afraid of everyone," which led
me to picture this Heinrich Falk looking like Albert Einstein but
without Einstein's charisma. I imagined him as elderly, frail,

stooped, with two irregular puffs of white hair sprouting from either side of his head and from his ears too.

So tenacious was Peter Bourne's description of the timid, little fellow that prior to our meeting, having spoken to him only on the phone, I'd failed to notice his voice.

He has a voice that could seduce one thousand virgins.

I did notice that his English was excellent, and that his accent far nearer to British than to German. When I commented on that, he told me that he'd spent three years in England while researching and writing his *Habilitationsschrift*, a major expansion of the doctoral dissertation (from two hundred pages to six hundred, give or take) and a prerequisite to becoming a professor in Germany.

His Habilitationsschrift was titled The Society of the Nunnery at Exeter in the Year 1332.*

   *The nunnery at Exeter in 1332 was, like most nunneries of its day, closer in kind to a bordello than to a convent, which explains everything, as there is no way he could have sustained three years of interest in chaste women.

On the phone, in response to my request to discuss a possible subject for me, he posed a question. "What is it about the Middle Ages that captures your imagination?"

"The lack of personal hygiene," I said, which prompted him to laugh and to tell me an anecdote about a medieval peasant who journeyed to the city of Tours. "There, while walking past a row of perfume shops, he grew ill from the scent. He was revived when a peasant woman scooped up a pile of fresh feces and held it under his nose."

I laughed politely and counted my blessings, once again, for being outside the academy. Then he invited me to come to Munich for an upcoming conference, *The Role of the Rose Garden in Twelfth-Century Central European Medicine*. "It is to be a small conference. It will be mostly local scholars in attendance, but you might find it illuminating," he said.

People like me, and him too, eggheads, brilliant as we may be, often lack common sense. Only after I'd purchased my nonrefundable plane ticket—Tuesday arrival, Friday departure—and made my hotel reservation did it occur to me that I know no German. I suppose I should have known some German, a few words here and there picked up, but I didn't. Not a one. For me, this conference on the rose garden would be as illuminating as a blackout. Nonetheless, I went.

When he opened his office door to me, because I was fully expecting to be greeted by a troll, I was not the least bit prepared for him nor for the pulsating current which darted from my knees to my mouth, culminating in an electromagnetic discharge, whereby I said, "Oh!" as if it hurt.

He is over six feet tall. Six feet three inches to be exact. Broadshouldered. Slim. His hair is blond with touches of gray, and you'd likely guess him to be ten years younger than he is. And then there's this about his looks when he is not smiling: You know those movies, those Hollywood movies about World War

*II, and the scenes in the ghetto or in the camps, and how the
tension clamps around the insides tight like a fist when the
Kommandant arrives on the scene? He, that Kommandant,
appears to be carved from ice, and despite everything, you have
to agree that he is handsome. Well, that's exactly what Heinrich Falk looks like when he's not smiling. His mouth is full,
sensuous, and it is easy to think of it as cruel. His nose is
aquiline, and behind his hexagonal steel-framed glasses, his
eyes are slate gray. When his hair is cut short, even that stands
up straight.*

Wow. A pious woman would have said that he was the man
God chose for me. Our meeting had to be the endeavor of divine
intervention. Only destiny could think up an attraction this
intense and this perverse. Knowing that you must capitulate to
that which is ordained, what choice did I have but to give into it?

"Frau Doktor Rosenfeld," he said. "Please come in. I am putting
together for you a packet of articles that might be of interest."

*We were united first in the dwelling that sheltered our love and
then in the hearts that burned with it. Under the pretext of
study we spent our hours in the happiness of love, and learning
held out to us the secret opportunities that our passion craved.
Our speech was more of love than of the books which lay open
before us. Our kisses far outnumbered our reasoned words.
(Peter Abelard, History of My Calamities, 1139, chapter 16)*

Beyond that, forget any attempt to reconstruct what we dis-
cussed in the twenty minutes or so before we went to lunch. All I
heard was the deafening pitch of my heartbeat, the roar emanat-

ing from desire. My circulatory system was going ba-boom, ba-boom, ba-boom.

We, he and I and his two teaching assistants, Frau Doktors Schmidt and Frisch, went to a nearby restaurant where he had made reservations for four. There he regaled me with his courtly manners. Frau Doktors Schmidt and Frisch were all atwitter too, over the way he held the door for us, ladies first, and when he helped me off with my coat, I imagined the grace with which he would undress me. He pulled out the chair for me to sit next to him, on his right.

The restaurant was a typical Bavarian one, which means the waitress was dressed like a serving wench. In lieu of bread, we got pretzels in a basket. He translated the menu for me into English. The fare was all meat, a surfeit of pork, which posed a small problem because I am a vegetarian. Not that I was much hungry for food. It was another hunger which led me to wonder, what if I press my leg against his, would he like it if I lightly ran my fingers along his thigh?

Leaning in close to me, he was oh-so-close, my lips trembled, like a butterfly, to brush against his, and he placed his finger on a line of Gothic lettering. "Here. This. Asparagus with boiled potatoes," he said, and I was inching my foot toward his foot when he added, "My wife makes that very often because our older daughter is a vegetarian too."

When a man mentions a wife and a child thrown in to boot, the implied message needs no translation. He was letting me know that he was a happily married family man. In mid-inch, my foot froze.

A minor setback. Or maybe a major one. But not insurmountable. In love all things are possible. And this was love entirely unre-

lated to the contemporary level-headed version of the state. This
was the love of the poets and the gods. It felt as if I'd been searching all my life thus far, searching for I don't know what, not even
aware I was searching, and then finding it. As if I could have said,
Oh, there you are. I was looking for you. And although I had never
before experienced anything like this, I recognized it immediately
for what it was. Surely I would have once scoffed at such a notion,
but as would anyone who witnessed a miracle, now I believe.

On the last night of the conference, which I attended faithfully
despite my inability to follow any of it, I fell in with a large group
going for dinner on Prinzregentenstrasse. His group, and I was
desperate for a way to sit next to him at what was a banquet
table for twenty-four when fate maneuvered it for me, because
that's what happens when things are divinely blessed.

> *Queen Guinevere's chair is a canopied seat in the middle of the*
> *dais, at the elevated table of honor. The most important knights*
> *sit at the high table; there all guests are served double portions.*
> *King Arthur, however, refuses to eat until he hears of some adven-*
> *ture or marvel. (Madeleine Pelner Cosman, Fabulous Feasts:*
> *Medieval Cookery and Ceremony, Braziller, 1976, p. 15)*

He never did inquire as to why, not knowing the language, I
nonetheless attended every lecture. However, at some point well
into the meal, he turned to me and asked, "Did you notice the
woman who was sitting directly behind you this afternoon?"

"No," I said. I hadn't noticed anybody other than him, but I
didn't say that. Instead I asked, "Why? Should I have?"

"Up until four months ago," he said, "she was my lover."

Well, here was happy news indeed, to learn that he had strayed at least this once and was now free to stray again. "What happened?" I asked.

"I don't know," he shrugged. "I guess she didn't love me anymore, so she left me."

"I would never leave you," I said, flat out, a statement which resulted in as much self-amazement as anything else, because I meant it, and then I said, "Come outside. I want to kiss you."

And he did, and we did, and I had to stand on the very tips of my toes, and when the kiss ended, he pointed to a building across the street and told me, "Hitler had a flat there."

Hitler. The other history. "Really?" I mustered up an air of indifference and asked, "Is there a plaque of some sort?"

"No." As if the very idea were an Etch A Sketch that could be erased, he shook his head adamantly. "Absolutely not," and then we went back inside, and he told the others, "I was just showing Frau Doktor Rosenfeld where Hitler had his flat."

Liebste, This dinner-table situation (sitting with averted eyes in front of Frau Doktors Schmidt, Frisch, et al., because I had just kissed you and was secretly holding hands with you) was absolutely overwhelming. I felt like a teenager and I thought: This can't be true! I'm still completely in the dark why you did it. Will you ever tell me? (Letter to the author from HF)

When the dinner ended, it was already late into the evening, and my plane was leaving the next morning, but still we could've gone back to my hotel. Only we didn't. To delay that which could be had now was, on balance, not my custom nor, I was to learn, his. But delay we did, as if we both knew this was too much to hurry.

The next morning, in the minutes before the taxi arrived to take me to the airport, I called him as I'd promised, and he said to me, "I've been going crazy waiting for the phone to ring." Then he told me that already he had been to a travel agency and had, in hand, his ticket to New York for six weeks hence.

During those six weeks between my first trip to Munich and his to New York and then the five weeks more before my return here, we wrote each other letters. Old-fashioned letters. Written by hand, pen to paper. His came to me in dove-gray envelopes, *Luftpost.* "*Liebste,*" he wrote as a salutation, and "*Liebeliebeliebe.*" But he did not date them.

High treason is a question of dates. (Stanislaw Lec)

One, two, sometimes three letters a day he sent me. Now I squint to make out the postmarks, most of which have been obliterated by the elements or by my handling them because, again and again in those weeks, I took these letters from their envelopes and read them over and over. Now, I must, for the most part, rely on content and memory to paginate all 121 of them.

Liebste, I may be frightened and I confess to being shy (in a way) but I am not timid, and I shall not project any more

Eigenschaften* on you than I already have. I'll stick to the facts:
your face, your kiss, your lovely dress, and the feel of your bum.
I'll leave the rest to N.Y. By now there is a very strong longing
where there hasn't been anything for a long time and it hurts
rather good [sic]. (Letter #3 to the author from HF)
*qualities, attributes (Langenscheidt's Pocket Dictionary
of the English and German Languages)

Liebste Hester, I already feel like making plans for weeks when
we'll only be seeing us [sic] for what will seem a few hours. You
have in a very short time become rather important in my emo-
tional (im)balance. In fact, you are now an extremely attractive
de-stabilizing element in my life. Kiss you. (Letter #17 to the
author from HF)

His trip to New York is, in my mind, a blur of sex and Ellis
Island, although we must have taken meals. I do recall the waitress at the Cupcake Café, who had never before seen me breakfast with a man, give me a thumbs up. There was a slapdash tour
of the Guggenheim, and now that I think of it, we had a drink at
Fraunces Tavern, where, in 1783, George Washington bade his
officers a teary farewell before retiring to Mount Vernon. And as
long as we were in the neighborhood, I did point out Trinity
Church. Oh, and I took him to the Upper West Side, to 89th
Street, because he wanted to see where I was from. Actually, I'm
not from West 89th Street, but that is where I was conceived.

Hester Street was where my parents met, in 1940, in a store-
front turned classroom for English as a Second Language. My
mother was still a girl then, in years if not in life experiences. All

of seventeen, and my father was an older man of twenty-eight. They kept company, as my mother called it, for seven years, waiting for news and certainties before they married in 1947, which was when they took an apartment on West 89th Street.

After nearly fifteen years of trying to conceive a child, although grateful for the blessings she did have, my mother had to concede that a baby was not meant to be one of them. Consequently, she confused her first months of pregnancy with the onset of menopause. Surprise, surprise—I was the answered prayer, the very best thing that would ever happen for them—a station not easy to live up to. And so I was born into what would become the twilight of the American time of Camelot, amidst so much promise. A time when my mother wore the new-fangled interpretation of the tall conical hat—the pillbox—as if it heralded hope.

When my mother was in her seventh month with me, my parents set up residence in their new house, one of fourteen identical houses in a cul-de-sac in New Rochelle, which for my parents represented all that was right and good and American with the world. A house. A split-level house so new that it smelled of freshly cut wood. A house of their own with three bedrooms, two baths, a recreation room, a yard with a swing set in the back and a rose garden in front, and trees. One oak tree, one elm, and a hodgepodge of stunted apple trees.

Another thing about that cul-de-sac, ours was the only Jewish family there. That we were secular counted for nothing, as it never does. Eleven of the fourteen houses were inhabited by three denominations of Protestants—Methodists, Lutherans, Episcopalians—and two Catholic families capped the horseshoe.

"Isn't America vonderful," said my oblivious mother, with her unshakable faith in the nation, "how vee all lif togezzer in harmony like music." Harmony like music. Yeah. Like music. Like song. Singsong. Singsong like chanting, like when all the other neighborhood kids circled around me in the Crawfords' backyard chanting, chanting *Christ-killer, Christ-killer,* while I, all of six years old, wept, "I didn't kill anybody. I didn't kill anybody." Instinctively I knew not to tell my parents about that, the same way I knew not to tell them when Jack Wade and Thomas Leary threw pennies at me and when, some years later, that same Thomas Leary pulled me behind a row of hedges, where he stuck his hand under my sweater. I didn't tell my parents any of this because I had to protect them from the hurt it would have caused, and moreover, I somehow knew they could not protect me from any of it, and I burned from the shame of it all.

My parents believed, because they wanted to believe, that the house in New Rochelle was a home where we could put down roots. The way my grandparents had tried their best to belong to Europe, my parents tried to belong to America. You would think that they would've thought twice before trusting any nation, any state, any village. But they didn't. Their faith, like all faith, was blind and deaf. Moreover, their emphasis on all things American—automobiles, schools, system of government—being best rendered them, my parents, by definition, something less than first-rate. I knew I did not belong in that cul-de-sac, and I could not hightail it out of there fast enough, away from that place where all the girls were button-nosed and pretty and nobody else had weird parents who were old and spoke with accents.

When my father died, a year after my mother, I sold the house against the advice of the real estate agent, who thought I should have held out for a better offer. The truth was I would have given the place away just to be rid of it.

Yet, as my parents tried to make a new life for themselves, I did too. I entered the world as an adult as if I had no past, and like them I too embraced my new world with appreciation, but without the obsequious gratitude. In other words, I got it right and felt beholden to no one.

As HF and I waited for the light to change on the corner of West 89th and Broadway, he asked, "Where do your parents live now?" and I told him, "The other side. They're dead," and I said no more. I rarely, if ever, spoke of my parents to anyone, because their lives aroused pity and questions I did not want to answer. I certainly wasn't going to discuss my parents with him, and he grabbed me and kissed me and there we were, a pair of orphans making out like teenagers on the corner of West 89th Street and Broadway as if we had no ties to anywhere.

But what memory highlights of his trip to New York is the sex and Ellis Island.

I can't yet bring myself to discuss the sex.

> *Liebeliebeliebe, You really must teach me more about this con-*
> *cept of "parameters." Teach me about the dialectics of freedom,*
> *love, and fences! Let me kiss your lips, catch [sic] my tongue*
> *between your thighs, and take me, if you want to. (Letter #46 to*
> *the author from HF)*

Aside from those few forays out into the world, he and I remained holed up in my apartment, mostly in the bedroom, for all the days and nights, and it was like nothing else. Not ever. For the time being, let it suffice to say, he and I, we crossed boundaries. Points from which there is no turning back. Without discussing it, without so much as making mention, we both seemed to know where we wanted to go, and we went there, and after I said, "You've done all this before?"

"No," he swore. "Never. Nothing like this," and when I got up to go to the bathroom, my legs fluttered and I crumpled to the kilim on the floor beside the bed and it seemed as if it were a magic carpet. I laughed and laughed until I wept, and he came next to me and kissed my eyes and drank my tears.

To go to Ellis Island was his idea.

He was amazed, a little shocked even, that I, an American history scholar who perhaps even had family—a cousin thrice removed or an uncle or two, maybe—who might have come through those same gates like cattle unloaded, had not yet visited the Ellis Island site and museum. But it was newly restored and had not been open to the public all that long. I simply hadn't gotten around to it. So it seemed like an okay thing to do on that, our second-to-last, day together.

> *Liebste, I think of you at the Battery Park where we waited for the ferry boat to Ellis Island. You were shivering in my arms and no wonder. It was ever so sweet of you to go without knickers just for me, but I was so worried you would have [sic] a cold. (Letter #87 to the author from HF)*

Ellis Island overwhelmed him, the hope of it, the promise of a new life in a new world, and there beneath a photograph of somebody's *bubba*, he broke down. I hustled him off to the cafeteria, where we sat at a corner table, and then I started crying too. "What will become of us?" he asked me. "What are we going to do?" and then I said, "I'll come to Munich," clearly meaning not for a few days, but for an indefinite stay. And why not go to Munich? There was nothing tying me to New York. No job, no boyfriend, no cat, not even a plant. Just an apartment easily sublet. It was time to dare something new, to take a chance, because while indeed I was content with my life thus far, I wasn't happy. And so without considering any of the consequences, I said, "I'll come to Munich."

> *When the cartographers of the Middle Ages came to the end of the world as they knew it, they wrote: "Beware: Dragons Lurk Beyond Here." (William Manchester, A World Lit Only by Fire, Little, Brown, 1992, p. 27)*

"But Hester, you are so American," he worried. "What will you do there?" *So American?* Was *so American* a euphemism for Jewish? Although he did, in two or maybe three of his letters to me, write the word *Jewish*, he still has yet to speak it. Nor has he broached the subject—Germans and Jews—that sits squarely before us, a subject of elephantine proportions. Instead, he maneuvers around it, deftly sidestepping, it as if it were a booby trap.

> *Ah my sweet Liebste, I wanted to write you a long involved letter about love and Germans and Jews and language and the frailty of man but it all boils down to one simple thing: I want to be in the same room with you and pull down your knickers. (Letter #38 to the author from HF)*

Certainly *so American* could've been a catchword, but I wasn't about to go looking for encumbrances, and so I said, "I'll be your mistress," which seemed a perfectly European way of doing things, a way for us to be together without wrecking anything. "I'll be your mistress and"—then, because I knew I would also need an additional occupation, it came to me, inspired, a splendid idea—"and I will write your history."

"My history? Why would you write my history? I am not famous."

"I never write about famous people," I told him. "Kings and generals are of no compelling interest to me. I write micro-histories. Community chronicles. Kitchen-table accounts." I aim to capture the times through the narrow prism of the eyes of one of the earth born. One of the people. A man, or woman, of the street. These days, it's a trend in history, to look at how the common life was shaped by the events of history and, vice versa, how history was shaped by the social fabric of common life.

"Still," he says, "I do not see how I am worthy of such an endeavor." The modicum of modesty got lost in the expressions of jubilation. "What is there to write about my life?" Sparkle in the eyes, broad grin, a glow like moonbeam, he jiggled in his seat.

"Maybe there will be nothing," I conceded, "but I suspect otherwise. Every life has story. It's simply a matter of finding it. Your times are still fresh. The bones have not yet been picked clean. Think of it. The defeat, the shame, the guilt, the Berlin Wall." I took his hands in mine. "More books have been written on the Third Reich than on any other subject in history," I reminded him of what he was bound to know. "But what of the next generation? The generation that had to clean up the mess? Your generation.

You!" I discovered I was genuinely excited, that more than simply an excuse to be with him, the idea really did grab me, but being with him, let me not kid anyone, excited me to no end too.

Here was the solution, the perfect solution, the proverbial two birds with one stone.

"Yes," he concurred. "You are right. This could be an important book. My generation needs to be explained. Understood. We are the ones in power now. Chancellor Schröder has my years. He was born in 1943 too, or maybe '44," he said, and he pulled my hands to his mouth and kissed my fingers, and I was happy and didn't think that maybe it's not always smart to go snooping into the life of your lover.

> *Liebeliebeliebe, You've broken through my defenses (I'm not telling you how!). My need to love you and be loved by you is far greater than my fears. But I promise: I'll look for treason and flippancy in every little fold of your flesh. (Letter #16 to the author from HF)*

And snooping into the life of a German, well, it's not unlike turning over rocks after a rain. There is likely to be something unpleasant there, but I waved away that thought as if it were nothing more than a hint of sulfur in the air.

Chapter Three

No more talk of Nazis for now

T o be born, as he was, in Berlin in 1943 demands the
question that, unpleasant as it may be, I do have to ask
if I'm going to write a reasonably honest history.
When he joins me in the hotel breakfast room—six tables for
four and two posters of the Alps tacked to the white walls—
where I have just finished with my boiled egg and poppy-seed
roll, I pour us both a cup of coffee from the faux Meissen-ware
pot on the table, and I come out with it, "Your parents," I say.
"Were they Nazis?"

He looks around the room to see if anyone has overheard, is
anyone listening in, but there is no one else here. We are alone, and
he says, "No. No, my parents considered the Nazis to be riffraff."

As is a most effective interview method, I say nothing. Instead,
I wait. Expectantly, as if, without a doubt, there is more to come,
and I'm not wrong.

"Not that they might not have shared some sentiments," he confesses, "but Nazism rose from the shopkeepers, taxi drivers, pimps, ex-soldiers, policemen, out-of-work workers, and *Hausmeisters*. Janitors, custodial crews," he translates, and then adds, "My parents would never have aligned themselves with those sorts."

Yet:

"My father's sister was a Nazi with a low number. She had four daughters." He smiles broadly, almost lasciviously, at that, at the four daughters. "She gave all of them those Germanic names. Brunhild, Kriemhild, Hiltrun, and Gudrun."

His four daughters were not given those Germanic names. His eldest daughter, the one he had with Konstanze (wife #1), is named Rebekka. The two daughters with his now wife are called Barbara and Kristina, and Angelika is the one he insists is his and Bettina's child.

> *Before and during the war, his father's sister, a Nazi with a low number, this indicating that she joined the party early on, had been a schoolteacher. But after the war, Nazis were forbidden to teach school, and so this aunt was reeducated to work on a potato farm; to be a potato breeder.*

"I used to go to that farm every year for a month in the summer until I was fifteen or so," he tells me.

"Why did your parents send you to stay with a Nazi?" I ask. "Weren't they concerned about what she might teach you?"

"Former Nazi," he corrects me, as if that made any kind of difference. "It was all over by the time I went there, but mostly I think my parents just wanted to be easily rid of me for a month. My mother was a real career woman." Again, he scans the room to be sure we are alone still, and with his mouth open ever so slightly, he kisses my mouth, and he places a hand on my breast. I groan, and we go upstairs to my room, and there is no more talk of Nazis for now.

Yet:

Can a case be made for these bedroom games we play?

It's time for him to go to university. (To university. No article.) I will take a walk through the narrow and crooked streets of Schwabing. Further attempt to get a feel for the lay of the land. Late in the afternoon, he and I will meet at a café on Leopold-strasse.

There is no denying that Munich is a pretty city. Oh so pretty. Sweet to the eye, like spun confection, a plate of petit fours, a wedding cake with scalloped white icing and pink cream rosettes. And it is so clean, and so many people ride their bicycles. Twice already this morning I've mistaken the bicycle lanes for pedestrian crosswalks and come within a hair of being clipped. Also, I'm pretty sure I was cursed at.

At Odeonsplatz I slow down to look at the Leuchtenberg Palace and nearby some frescos of landscapes, and next I meander over to the infamous Feldherrnhalle, where on the 9th of November 1923, the procession from the Beerhall Putsch met up with state police, and on both sides blood was shed. During the time of the Third Reich, in remembrance of the aforementioned bloodbath, all who passed by here were required to give the Nazi salute. Those not inclined to *Heil!* took a side street, which earned the nickname Dodge Down Alley. Here now, it is easy to picture that, passersby saluting like wind-up toys, and now and again some plucky paladin ducking down the alternate route, because, from where I stand, it is only the cars on the road which disclose the decade.

The Hofgarten is a manicured public park which used to be the court's vegetable garden, where the Ludwigs grew radishes and beets, and there I sit on a bench wishing I knew the German words for "coffee to go," because I wouldn't mind having one now, on this bench, in this garden. There is a café handy across the street, but I'm not altogether sure "coffee to go" is a done thing in Munich. I've yet to see a Starbucks or a paper cup with a sip lid anywhere.

For the record, I suppose I ought to come clean on the question of authorial objectivity on my subject. How objective can I be when I am in love with him? Admittedly, my take is going to be somewhat slanted, but objectivity, pure objectivity, is, frankly, dull stuff and overrated, and likely never to be possible in any rendering anyway, except perhaps in a chronology of dates, and even those are often fudged. As I see it, the historian's mission is not simply to put forth the facts, but to put the facts in context, to offer a perspective, to take a stand.

In his Untimely Meditations (double-check source) Nietzsche identified three approaches to history, which he labeled "the monumental, the antiquarian, and the critical." That last one, "the critical," is the way that we judge history and condemn the guilty.

Historians and biographers respond to their subjects—no matter dead or alive—with ardor. Condemn or praise, we judge. And as we go along, we become either their disciples or their detractors or we fall deeply in love with them. So I got that one out of the way before I began as opposed to further down the road. But to be in love is not the same as to be entirely stupid. And I must make clear: I do not have an agenda. I am not the child of Holocaust survivors. By the time the ovens were fired up, my parents were long and safely ensconced in New York. My mother even had some cousins and an uncle in California. Yes, there were other relatives who never made the crossing, and they died as a result of it. And they might have had husbands and wives and children who also were murdered in that way, but not that I know for sure.

As I scarcely speak to anyone of my parents, my parents seldom spoke of their lives before coming to America. All of Europe was referred to as the old country. My mother pronounced *old country* as if she were saying *old shoe*. My parents were isolationists, although the results of their immersion into the American culture often were comical, sometimes heart-wrenching, and, especially during my teenage years, entirely mortifying to me. My father, a frizzy-haired, rumpled high school chemistry teacher, lost in the world, adrift in his own mind, experienced rapture in his BarcaLounger bopping his head and finger-snapping to the Delta Blues on the hi-fi, which was what he called the stereo, a hi-fi. To the exclusion of all dining pleasure, we ate only what my mother deemed American food—Kellogg's Sugar Frosted Flakes, Campbell's Soup, and Rice-A-Roni, a dish she truly believed was the haute cuisine of San Francisco.

Liebste, I want to explain why this sweatshirt* you give [sic] me is so important. In the fifties, when I was a teenager, we had a huge cultural revolution. The authorities (Parents, Teachers, Priests, Boy Scout Leaders, etc.) all wanted us to wear "Hosen" or rather "real Hosen," that is, shorts, Lederhosen, Bundhosen (breeches), Knickerbockers, or trousers. (Skirts, Dirndls, etc. for the girls). We didn't want that. We wanted to be something other than what we were and what we had been. We wanted BLUE JEANS! And SWEATSHIRTS! These things were sexy, they were connected with Rock 'N' Roll. Wearing them was our rebellion against the fathers who had lost the war and the old Nazis who were not willing to accept defeat. Of course such American clothings [sic] were not easy to get. (Letter #99 to the author from HF)

*A New York University sweatshirt, white with purple letter-ing, purchased on a whim and given to him upon his arrival at Kennedy Airport. "This way you'll pass for a real New Yorker," I joked, as if he could ever be mistaken for anything but what he is.

Despite the atrocious Norman Rockwell prints adorning nearly every room of the house, there were innumerable dead giveaways to expose my parents as un-Americans: the inability to master the backyard barbecue grill, which invariably gave off great clouds of black smoke and charred the hamburgers to ash; that I was forced to take violin lessons because, and I quote, "A girl who can play ze violin vill be popular at all ze parties." My mother with her poodle haircut, tight curls in the shape of a shower cap, never wore pants like the other mothers in the neighborhood. My father had one pair of blue jeans, an off brand, which he ironed as if they were dress slacks, and there was no getting around the accent. Theirs was not an accent that could ever be heard as sophisticated like a British one or sexy like the Italian. Their accent begged for mockery. Somehow, it never dawned on them, in their bubble of happiness, that they were outsiders, excluded from neighborhood fêtes, even from informal gatherings for iced tea on summer nights. They were too old to be parents of an American girl my age, and, granted through no fault of their own, they made people uncomfortable.

When both my parents had died, I was secretly more than a bit relieved to be done with these little people who shrank as I diminished them. And such a secret was shameful too.

Given their emphasis on the grand stature of America, it is no wonder that when I chose my field of study, there wasn't a history for me save for the American one. I have no personal relationship to any of Europe except by degrees of separation. I knew a girl at college whose live-in grandmother had survived Auschwitz, and we all, and especially me, felt sorry for her, the girl, for being saddled with such a grandmother, who was a nervous wreck. The girl was always having to call home every twenty minutes to assure her grandmother that nothing bad had happened to her since the last call home. For me, it was nowhere near that extreme. My mother did not imagine the Gestapo lurking in doorways. She did not fear deportation from Westchester County. She trusted in the security of my father's position as the chemistry teacher at New Rochelle High School and hers at P.S. 22. Still, she worried for me, for my safety. Danger was everywhere, which was why I had to wear a sweater well into the summer months (*A draft can get into your lungs*), why I had to carry a packet of crackers with me at all times (*Suppose you should get hungry*), why I was not allowed to join the Girl Scouts (*Nice people don't wear uniforms, mine Hester, and what do they do anyway, these Nature Girls? Schlep through a forest that is filled with bugs and snakes and rodents with rabies?*).

At night, when I was supposed to be sleeping, I would hear my parents whispering in their mother tongue, which I didn't understand, of things not for me to hear. Things kept from me. When I was young I did ask questions, which were met with a heavy silence. Soon enough, I quit asking. After my father died, I found, on the top shelf of a closet in my parents' bedroom, a box of old photographs and papers from their former lives. Looking through that stuff was like seeing my parents naked.

Shortly after HF's father died, some nine or ten years ago, the woman with whom his father was living sent HF a package. A box the dimensions of a gift box for a shirt or a sweater, which HF put away in a drawer without opening it.

> HF doesn't know if his parents ever legally divorced. Therefore, he does not know if this woman with whom his father lived was his stepmother or not. Deliberate ignorance? Why? (Look for divorce decree.)

In a drawer, under reams of old papers and notebooks, he keeps this box, unopened. HF insists he's not interested in what the box might contain. He insists he's not the least bit curious.

I make a note:

✳ *Ask again about the box.*

The sun has shifted. I stand up from the bench, and I walk over
to the Staatbibliothek, the big library, where I ask for a history of
postwar Munich, the reconstruction. The librarian says for that I'd
be better off at the Stadtarchiv on St.-Jakobsplatz, but instead of
going there, I take a long and winding route back to Schwabing, all
side streets. I'm enjoying the weather and the scenery, the houses
painted light blue with white trim, the flower beds, neat rows of
rose bushes in bloom, when I first hear, and then see, a gang of
boys. A pack of them, twenty or so, only they are not boys, but
young men. Their heads are shaved and their faces are painted the
same colors as the flags they wear draped over their shoulders like
prayer shawls. They are singing, and the song carries belligerence
in its tune. I look around to see if anyone else is disturbed or
frightened by this, but no one else is on this street. It's as empty of
people in the late afternoon as it would be late at night. Bad
things could happen here, and so I sidestep into the first shop I
come upon, a lamp store, a forest of floor lamps, and from the
ceiling hangs a stilled rainstorm of crystal chandeliers.

Peering out as if from behind a curtain, I wait by the door for
this time to pass, for the coast to clear before I venture back out
onto the street.

At the appointed café on Leopoldstrasse, HF is waiting by the
door, which he holds open for me. It is perfect weather for sitting
out of doors, but he rejects the sidewalk tables. Inside it is dark
and too warm to be comfortable. The Germans, I have noticed,
don't seem to go in for air-conditioning. He claims he doesn't like
sidewalk tables because of noise, sun, wind, whatever, but really it
is because he fears meeting up with someone he knows, someone
who will see us together and draw conclusions.

Although I will have to, at some point, I have not yet asked questions about his now wife and their marriage. I assume she's been through plenty with him, and he doesn't want to put her through more by being discovered at a sidewalk table with me. So I go along with sitting inside a dark and stuffy café, where I drink beer and eat *Kaiserschmarrn*—chopped-up pancakes smothered in applesauce and raisins—and tell HF about the young men I saw. I describe them with words like *skinhead* and *fascist* and *thug*.

"Soccer fans," he tells me. "You saw Croatian soccer fans. The Croatians won against the Rumanians."

Apparently I overreacted. Which leads me to something which I haven't yet mentioned. It is this Jewish question. This question of why my being Jewish in Munich feels different from being Jewish in New York. In New York, being Jewish by way of cultural definition was just there, like my thyroid or appendix. A section of myself to which I rarely gave thought unless it was going to give me trouble, which, since childhood, it has not. I've never been one to suspect anti-Semitism of lurking in the hearts and minds of all Christendom. But here I am finding that I experience the occasional pang of heritage. Germany acts as a daily reminder. Tweaks *Jew* and twinges *Jew*, a pinch here and there *Jew, Jew, Jew.*

"There are a lot of Croats living here in Munich," HF is telling me. "And we don't much like them," he adds.

"Why not?" I ask.

"Well, they were quite Hitlerites," he says, which prompts me to smirk and say, "And you all weren't?"

"Yes, of course. But we're trying to forgive ourselves. We like to

believe that the Germans have changed but the Croats have not."
He acknowledges the absurdity and adds to it. "If I had my way,
all skinheads and neo-Nazis and fascists would be shot on sight,"
he says. Then he smiles, that killer smile, and he continues, "I suppose that sort of statement renders me something of a fascist too.
Everyone does have tendencies. Even my generation, who believe
we have nothing in common with our parents. Even intelligent
and sensitive people harbor the occasional coarse idea. However,
we know not to act on it, which is really what separates the
decent people from the rubbish."

He is not all wrong here, and I admit, although not to him, to a
modicum of prejudice toward the German people. I know it is
wrongheaded to reduce the city of Munich to oompah bands,
breweries, and Nazis. Still, I do it.

But then he tells me, "My first father-in-law was *Einsatzgrup-
pen*. Killing police," he translates, although there is no need. This
word I know. My beer goes down the wrong pipe, and I have a
coughing fit. When it quells, when I've assured him twice that I
am fine, he says, "I used to get him so angry, this father of Konstanze." His eyes sparkle when he says this, as if getting a murderer angry were an especially fun prank. "You know in those
days, I was very much a Communist. We were all Communists,
those of us from the sixties, and at dinner with him I would go on
and on about the virtues of Marxism, and he would get so mad,
and his face would go all red and his teeth would grind together."

"You sat down to dinner with him?" I ask. "You broke bread
with a man who murdered children and women and old people?"

He pulls back. Clearly, he has never thought about it that way,
about what it meant to grace the same table with such a man,

and he asks me, "You think I should not have done that? You're right. I should not have. You wouldn't have, would you?" He bestows me with moral superiority, but there's no way of knowing if I am deserving or not.

Who can say, with absolute certainty, what one would have or would not have done? We all like to think we would always do the right thing, the humane thing, the courageous thing, but when confronted with the realities, we don't necessarily take that route, and I include myself in that assessment. I have been a coward at times. Plenty of times. Often, in fact.

We do what we do, and then we figure out a way to live with it.

Konstanze, his first wife and the daughter of a murderer, holds a Ph.D. in Germanistiks,* but she has become an expert on Israeli literature, which she doggedly promotes under the auspices of her position with the Kulturreferat.** She is especially active in a healing group where children of Holocaust survivors have therapy with children of Nazis. Konstanze is over the top in her philo-Semitism. While she doesn't exactly keep kosher, she won't mix meat with dairy, as if keeping cheese away from the burger were penance. When, at the age of thirty-eight, she had a child with her second husband, she had the baby boy circumcised, a tidbit of information she tells anyone who will listen, much to the chagrin of the boy, who is now sixteen.

    *German literature.

    **Arts Council of Munich.

To himself as well as to me, HF tries to explain away his quiescence regarding Konstanze's father. "When I found out about him, what he had done," he says, "she and I had been lovers for a few months already. We were in a café when she said something about her mother, something unimportant, but it dawned on me, at that moment, that she had yet to mention her father. So I asked about him, and she broke down crying and told me he was just out of jail and why he was there in the first place, but all I could think about was that she was crying. This woman I loved, or thought I loved, was crying, and I wanted to comfort her. I was thinking about her, about how sad she was. I wasn't thinking about her father, and what he had done." His eyes are moist. HF, he cries easily, at the drop of a hat.

I place the palm of my hand on his cheek, and I say, "Come on. Let's blow this popsicle stand," which confuses him utterly, so I translate. "Let's go to my room."

Now, he wants it to be all soft, gentle, tender, as if the other reproaches him, and he whispers, "I want to give you a baby. Oh, my Hester. My sweet Hester, I want to give you a baby girl."

From the get-go, he started in on me with that. A baby. We should have a baby together. A baby girl. A boy and, given his track record, he would doubt it was his. This itch of his for us to have a baby has nothing to do with me personally. Whenever he and I are out and he spies a pregnant woman carrying her load and feet splayed, he goes into paroxysms of pleasure. He looks at all pregnant women as if he had some part in it.

Somehow he [Martin Bormann] managed to convince his wife, whom he kept almost permanently pregnant, that his infideli-

ties were for the greater good of National Socialism. In one remarkable letter she suggested he bring his latest mistress, M., to their Berchtesgaden home and then expressed the hope that Bormann see to it that "one year M. has a child and the next year I, so that you always have a wife who is mobile." (John Toland, Adolf Hitler, Doubleday, 1976, p. 739)

He is sweet on the idea of making babies, is all. I don't take it seriously. I can't take it seriously. How could I, a person who panics at the prospect of caring for a geranium, consider a child?

On August 1, 1943, Doktor Goebbels issued a call urging civilians to evacuate Berlin. All children, however, by order of the Führer, had to leave the city, and the schools were closed. HF's mother took him, an infant a mere three weeks old, to a small town on the Baltic, far away from the bombings, and left him there at a children's home, where she paid a fee in exchange for his care.* As her job with the gas company was a government position, she was not exactly a civilian, and so she returned to her job and to her husband in Berlin, where she remained until their flat was destroyed. Frau Doktor Falk did visit her infant son at this children's home whenever possible. Near the very end of the war, she went and got her baby back, although what with moving and scarce housing and lack of food, HF was periodically returned to that children's home for months at a clip until he was six, and then came to stay with his mother more or less for good.

*Well-to-do women rarely nurse their own children. The wet nurse is chosen with care, for all manner of qualities may be

imbibed with her milk. . . . As the baby grows bigger, she will chew his meat for him (Joseph and Frances Gies, Life in a Medieval City, Thomas Y. Crowell, 1969, p. 61).

"Yes, a baby," he says again.

"Enough," I say, but still he goes on. "I want a black-haired baby. Yes, a dark baby girl. And your belly will swell. Oh so pretty."

Black-haired? Dark? A new twist on the now familiar theme of baby-making. Black-haired? Dark? Jewish? What gives?

But even with this new twist—black-haired, dark—on the otherwise familiar plea, HF manages to maintain his moratorium on the word *Jew* and all its configurations. Oh, every now and then, as if intrigued, he has come a bit closer, but then, as if equating the words with chunks of sky about to fall on his head, he ducks, and runs for cover.

But *black-haired, dark*, does indicate a slight shift nearer to the center of his discomfort. A penance of *his* own making? If Konstanze can have a circumcised child, then he can have a dark-haired one. Is his yen to make, specifically, a Jewish baby an apologia in the form of attempt at repopulation? "Darling," I say, "surrender the master plan, would you please. It's far too ridiculous."

Chapter Four

No one should ever go hungry

॰ॐ॰

When the whimpering subsides, and I've gotten myself together again, I say, "I don't understand this. I really don't get it."

He doesn't get it either, but he sure likes it that he causes me to scream and to weep and to whimper. And I like it too, except when I am afraid of it, afraid that I might die, or that my faculties are leaving me and I will be unable to retrieve them all into one basket.

One of his letters, instead of the usual *xoxoxoxoxoxo*, had this for a salutation:

(((((((((((((O))))))))))))))) (Me licking your sweet cunt.)

He waits on the edge of the bed while I freshen my lipstick, and together we walk the one block to the U-bahn station at

Hertie's, a department store much smaller than Macy's but about equal in banality. There he buys me a ticket good for five rides. "You should always buy your tickets this way because it is easier and more economical." He assumes that, thus far, I've bought my tickets the other way, for one ride at a time, and I say, "Okay." I do not tell him that, thus far, I have not bought tickets at all. It's something of an honor system that they've got here. You don't need a ticket to board, and there's no turnstile as there is in New York. Instead they have random spot checks to keep you honest, but I have yet to encounter one. Thus far, I've been riding the Munich subway without paying, and I intend, as an act of civil disobedience, to continue cheating the system, because I don't think I should pay to ride a train in Munich.

As we pull into the Universität station, he stands and tells me he'll come by to see me again around four in the afternoon. I stay on the train until Marienplatz, where I ascend the stairs just in time to witness the 11-a.m. clocktower show. The *Glockenspiel*. Forty-three bells chime, and mechanical figures emerge from the recesses of the neo-Gothic town hall to reenact the knights' tournament during the wedding feast of Wilhelm V and Renate of Lorraine. I stand there and watch the song-and-dance doll act. It is the stuff of nightmares.

It really is quite something, the way Munich is such a pristine place, as if they believe they could scrub away more than just dirt. I walk the streets made of cobblestones that veritably glisten, the immaculate medieval footpaths, and into a courtyard café that is an idyllic and romantic spot, even if it is in Germany.

For the first time since my arrival, I am singularly struck by the force of how alone I am in Munich, how my being here is the mirror image of how it must have been for my mother when she first arrived in New York, having found herself in a city where the language was foreign and everyone was a stranger.

> *Liebeliebeliebe, my sweet Hester. You are a lonely girl, aren't you? I love you for that. (People have told me I was rather lonely too, and I suspect they are right.) I'll take you in my arms and hold you and keep you warm when it is cold. And I don't feel lonely anymore since I met you. (Letter #29 to the author from HF)*

It's true. I am lonely. I've always been lonely. There are people I refer to as friends, but really they are only acquaintances with whom I pass time, over dinner or cocktails or bed. Mostly I've kept myself to myself. I let no one get too close, which resulted in a kind of quarantine perfected to such a degree that rarely was I aware of the ache of emotional isolation. It's been twenty years, not since I was a teenager, that I last wept because I was lonesome. Here in Munich—except for HF and the two sisters who run my hotel—no one knows who I am, or even that I am. Yet, while being alone here is highlighted and pronounced, my existence somehow seems less lonely overall.

I order a coffee, black, and an *Apfelstrudel*, inordinately proud of my mastery of the word. Pride before the fall. The *Apfelstrudel* is heavy, industrial. One bite, and I push the plate to the far left corner of the table, and I retrieve my notebook and a pen from my bag.

> *His mother was no spring chicken when, on the 13th day of July 1943, she gave birth to him. His father was her second husband. HF has a half brother who is thirteen years his senior.*

I skip two lines, and I note:

✗ In 1943 his brother was already a teenager and doing what with himself in 1944–45? (Ask.)

Ivy climbs along these courtyard walls, and I picture it here at night, how the full moon would be suspended over the church spire and how footsteps on cobblestone would echo. I wonder if HF could get away one evening, to come here with me, ostensibly for dinner but really to kiss, to kiss beneath the moonlight.

Here is where pity is likely to be aroused for the mistress because her lover goes home to his wife and daughters for dinner. But, let me reiterate, it would be pity misplaced. I spurned a professorship because I could not cope with the commitment of tenure track. Why would I want to be his wife?

I don't want to be any man's wife, and love him though I do, I especially don't want to be this man's wife. His wife is an altogether different role than that of his mistress, and rest assured, I'm not waiting in the wings for her part.

She said: "We consider that marital affection and the true love of lovers are wholly different and arise from entirely different sources. . . ." (Andreas Capellanus, The Art of Courtly Love, Columbia University Press, 1960, p. 171)

It takes a patient woman to be his wife, and bless her for it. He needs her, and I need her, and I'll forgo the dinners and the moonlight because he and I have something else entirely.

And pleased to the point of smug with what we do have, I turn my attention back to the work at hand.

Having earned herself a Ph.D.—unusual for a woman of her day—in economics—very unusual for a woman of her day—his mother was not your run-of-the-mill Hausfrau, and her advanced education turned out to be fortuitous indeed. Widowed after four years of marriage, she now had a young child (HF's half brother) to support, and these were the years of desperate economic straits nationwide. Although the time of runaway inflation—the 30-million-Reichsmark postage stamp, the 32-million RM potato—was over, Germany had not in any way recovered from the defeats of the First World War. Her husband's death—the indirect result of a blow to the head, which apparently, in and of itself, is perhaps not a remarkable way to die here (see Thomas Wolfe)—came as a surprise to all involved parties, but the circumstances of his demise were, well, the stuff of slapstick.

What I desperately need is more coffee, and I look around for the waiter. Also, it is time for lunch, and I am getting hungry.

Marienplatz is tourist central, rife with souvenir shops, postcard racks, tourist information booths, signs in seven languages requesting you do not litter, but the menu in this café is in German only and my waiter speaks no English. Between us and my pocket dictionary, we work out the second cup of coffee but no more than that, and so I eat the *Apfelstrudel* after all. Its texture is gummy, and the aftertaste is not a good one. However, it quiets my stomach long enough for me to finish this much.

This late husband of hers was the director of a theater in Berlin, the same city where they lived. One part of his job was to decide which plays were produced and which were not. Hav-

ing read one in particular which he considered god-awful, he scrawled Mist* across the title page. When that copy of the play in question was, mistakenly, returned to its author, the author, as one might expect, was not amused. He confronted the director. A scuffle ensued and came to a conclusion when the author, with his walking stick, whomped the director on the head. The director went home, where his wife put a cold compress on the bump, and that would have been the end of that except ten days later, the director died of pneumonia. There was some talk that this author was a Jew. After the death of her husband, rather than return to her family in Saxony, his mother opted to remain in Berlin, where she got a position with the National Gas Board making propaganda.** There she met her second husband, who quite possibly was some other woman's husband at the time. He, her second husband, HF's father, was definitely married at some point before they met, because HF has two half sisters his elder as proof.

    *dung, manure; (Langenscheidt's Pocket Dictionary of the English and German Languages)

      **"Making propaganda" is HF's phraseology. I would've called it writing ad copy.

Having settled up at the café, I head in the direction of the open-air market, but I take a wrong turn and find myself at the Hofbräuhaus. History has been written here. On February 24, 1920, some absurdly mustached, little-known political agitator delivered his first speech to a large audience. I step inside. The main room is cavernous and tumultuous, the din vibrates, and busty dirndl-clad waitresses barge past, hips jutting this way and that, with five or seven liter-sized steins gripped in one hand, plates piled high with food in the other. It's a tourist trap, this Hofbräuhaus. They all want to eat and drink at the place where Hitler gave a speech. Only I wonder if they know they are in the wrong room. Hitler spoke in the ballroom upstairs. This room is called the *Schwemme*, which, I discover when I consult my dictionary, means *trough*.

On the other side of St. Peter's Church (built in 1368), the Viktualienmarkt blazons into view. The stalls and stands are bright with fresh flowers and ripe produce—green and yellow and the red of the tomatoes, cherries, and strawberries—and bushels of potatoes and wedges of cheese and ropes of sausage and loaves of bread and pyramids of those giant radishes that I now know. The open-air food market makes for a picture-perfect postcard, and I like this, to buy food from the farmers and millers, the way food was bought in the centuries before supermarkets and takeout.

I stroll and survey the goodies, deciding what it is I would like to buy to eat, and I am drawn to the tomatoes. I choose two fat, ripe red ones, and I hand them to the vendor to be weighed. I smile at him, and it seems to me that in return, he scowls. He wraps my tomatoes in paper folded like an origami cup, and he says, "*Fünf.*"

"*No sprechen zee Deutsche,*" I say. I don't know enough German to properly articulate that I speak no German, but I figure I'm close enough that he'll catch on. I smile again, broad, friendly, helpless.

"*Fünf!*" he barks. "*Fünf!*"

I reach into my pocket and pull out a jangle of coins, which I hold out to him. He is positively sneering now, and he sifts through my money as if paying special attention to not touching my hand. He extracts a five-mark piece. Five. *Fünf.* I get it now, and then with both his hands operating like flippers, he motions me to leave the area of his stall.

Backing away, my efforts concentrated on keeping tears in check—I refuse to cry over some vegetable vendor's insensitivity to tourists—I don't look to see what is behind me, and I collide into a burly man who is leaning against a counter. He is eating a red sausage. Not with a knife and fork, and the sausage isn't wrapped in bread either. Just a greasy sausage gripped in a bare hand.

> *Spoons were used for soups and puddings; . . . But all else was picked, balanced, and conveyed . . . [by] the hands. (Madeleine Pelner Cosman, Fabulous Feasts: Medieval Cookery and Ceremony, Braziller, 1976, p. 17)*

"*Pardon*," I say. In French. I'm thinking that maybe *pardon* is universal, but apparently it is not, and, oh damn it. My tomatoes have split open and they are leaking through the paper, onto my hands and my dress and dripping down my leg. I toss the whole mess into a trash can, and I brush away my tears with the back of my hand.

> *After everything was destroyed, we didn't have much, and then what we did have, those things of value that we'd managed to save—the family silver and jewelry—we bartered for food. I learned one thing from all of this. Hunger is demoralizing.— (From a pamphlet* titled "Making Soup from Common Grasses" by Frau Doktor Charlotte Falk)*

In 1951, Frau Doktor Falk got a new and very important job as chief adviser to the German Commission on Consumer Policy, an agency established to teach hausfraus the art of home economy, how to make do with less and with nothing. She gave speeches and compiled pamphlets on how to whip a spoonful of meat into a meat pudding for a family of four, recipes for making soap from mortar, mouthwash from camphor, gold from flax. She devised a method for washing dishes in a thimble of water. (It's all in the scrub brush.) Frau Doktor Falk was a government-sponsored and glorified Heloise of "Household Hints" fame.

Unfed and wiping slippery tomato seeds from my hands and clothes, I board the U-bahn (no ticket—fuck them) back to my hotel, where I shower and wait for HF. I tell him about the tomato vendor.

"Well, you see," he tries to explain the tomato vendor's bad behavior, to rationalize it even, "you don't speak the language. They don't know what you are. What you need to do," he advises me, "is not to say that you don't speak German, but immediately establish your superiority by asking if they speak English."

"How does that immediately establish my superiority?" I ask, having recovered from the sting of it enough to wedge my tongue in my cheek.

"For one thing," he says, in all seriousness, "it announces that you are either British or American. And it will put them on the defensive because everybody who is anybody here speaks some English. If they don't, they are inferior."

My love is something of a snob.

Before the Great War of 1917 ruined everything, his mother
was accustomed to life in the style of the grand bourgeoisie. Her
parents owned a number of factories and paper mills in Saxony. Everyone in the family attended university, and also they
all learned to play the piano, although none of them played
particularly well.*

> **An ethnocentric date. For the Europeans, it was the Great
> War of 1914; for me (the author), an American, it was 1917,
> when we got into the act.*

There is something to this episode with the tomato vendor
that he is not saying, and so I say it for him. "I was treated badly
because he thought I was a Turk or an Arab. Isn't that so?"

"Yes," he admits. "It is like that," and he professes a disgust for
his countrymen. Then he says, "So you haven't eaten anything all
day. Are you hungry?"

"Yes," I say. "What about you?"

He says he is not hungry. He always says that he is not hungry.
His relationship to food is a funny one. Peculiar. He positively
refuses to own up to hunger. As if there is a lack of virtue to it, a
weakness. He represses appetite for food the way Josef, his half
brother, has repressed his appetite for sex. When Josef and his
wife failed to produce a child, they quit having sex. "But," HF told
me, "my brother never took a lover. Instead he became repressed
and took to patting the bums of neighborhood children."

Always HF insists he is not the least bit hungry, and when we
go to a restaurant, he orders food, he says, only to be polite, so
that I don't eat alone. Then he devours every morsel and he even
licks his plate clean, and invariably he eats what I have left over
on my plate.

In those very lean years after the Second World War, there was
so little food to be had that his grandfather finally starved to
death. Once, during those same years, somebody, a neighbor,
gave HF a cup of molasses, which was an extraordinary treat.
But he was just a small boy unaccustomed to such riches. He
could not finish an entire cup of molasses, and so he dumped
most of it away, into the dirt beneath some shrubbery, which
was a dreadful thing to have done, to have wasted food while
his maternal grandfather was dying from hunger.

My mother's cousin Alfie told me about that too. He was one
of the cousins born in California. He had a suntan and knew
movie stars because he was an entertainment lawyer. I used to
wish that I lived in California under sunshine as opposed to
under a pall. In California, I'd have had movie stars' kids for
friends instead of no friends, but mostly I just wished that Alfie
were my father. Whenever Alfie came to New York on business,
he took us—my mother, my father, and me—out to dinner to
hoity-toity restaurants, and I would wonder if he was embarrassed by my parents too. It was over one of these lavish dinners
that Alfie told me about how, at the tail end of the war, he was
drafted and then stationed, during the Occupation, in Munich.

"An American GI. A real GI Joe," my mother said in the same
reverent voice usually reserved for *Ph.D.* and *concert pianist.*

My father also was in service for the United States military at
that time, but not as a GI Joe. My father was stationed in Brook-
lyn, at the Navy Yard, where he sat at a desk and translated documents, which is not all that different from what HF claims his
father did during the war. "He typed," HF said, but, of course, I
can't take his word on it. I'll need corroboration.

Alfie told me about Munich after the war, about how the city was in ruins, and how the people had no food, how he routinely came upon old women and children picking through the garbage outside the mess tent, about how he gave them coffee and his second helpings and the ubiquitous chocolate bars. "It wasn't right," he said, "that old women and children should have to pick through garbage for food."

I looked to my parents, and they were nodding in agreement. "No one should ever go hungry," my mother said. "You see, Hester, vy you should to hev ze crackers viz you. Tell her, Alfie," she prodded her cousin, "about how it is to hev ze hunger."

Other than the kind that emanates from the heart, I have never gone hungry. Going hungry as differentiated from being hungry. Going hungry is to be starving, dying from it. Being hungry is the hunger that strikes between meals, the kind of hunger I have now.

HF insists we go to the supermarket, where he chooses for me a huge bread, a jar of yogurt, a dairy product called quark, beer, and chocolates. While he is at the cheese counter, I wander off to look at the jams in pretty jars and then at the schnapps, marveling at the variety. When I look back at the cheese counter, I don't see him there, and then I spy him across the store, his head turning this way and that looking for me. I want to call out to him, to tell him I'm here, in the aisle of schnapps, but I can't. The same way the word *Jew* gets trapped in his larynx, I cannot call out *Heinrich*. I cannot even whisper *Heinrich*. I can barely write *Heinrich* on paper, and even then it is infrequent and only in the confines of objectivity. When I wrote letters to him, I began them with *Dear Love*. With him, I refer to him as *Darling*. Yes, darling. No, darling. Like that.

I wave frantically across the supermarket, but he doesn't see me, and so I call out, "Darling," and I go to him.

He has bought for me, along with the aforementioned goodies, a cotton tote bag and three different kinds of cheese. I put the beer and the dairy products in the mini-fridge before going to the bed. This bed is a single, designed for one person sleeping alone. And so we are on our sides, facing one another, when I ask, "Is there a diminutive for your name? A nickname like Rick or Ricky or Rich?" I am thinking of names that sound American. Not so in-my-face German. "Yes," he tells me. "Heinz. Heinz is diminutive for Heinrich," and he slips his hand between my thighs, touching me, and my breath goes short and I gasp, "Oh," I say. "Oh, darling."

Later, we share a beer, and I eat some chocolate. He has to go home early today to help his youngest daughter "with her maths because she got a four."

So he goes, and I close the door and go to the table, and open my notebook, picking up where I left off.

At a time near the end of the war, his mother returned to her hometown in Saxony because their flat in Berlin had been bombed to smithereens. His father stayed on in Berlin, at his job with the National Gas Board, where, instead of encouraging the use of gas, the wartime aim was now to get everyone to conserve all energy. To this end, his father created a cartoon character named Kohlenklau, Coal Thief. After the war, back in Saxony, his mother started up a little factory of her own with six women and six looms on which they wove blankets, which his mother, when successful, traded for butter and eggs and bread. His half brother, Josef, got work on a farm; a lucky break, because although he got no pay, he did get fed. Currency *was pretty much worthless anyway. In the West, where the British and the French and the Americans had set up camp, there was some food. The Americans especially had food, and they shared it. But in the East, winners and losers went hungry alike. HF saw his grandfather for the last time on November 18, 1946. "I saw him sitting in the kitchen eating the seeds from a pumpkin.* There was no pumpkin. Just some seeds. An old body could not be kept alive by a handful of pumpkin seeds." A week later, HF's grandfather died from the effects of starvation.*

> **It is not entirely plausible that HF really remembers seeing his grandfather with the pumpkin seeds. More likely, he was told that he had seen such a thing, and from the telling, the memory took hold.*

My stomach grumbles at me, and I remember that I've eaten nothing other than a few bites of chocolate since that gummy *Apfelstrudel.* I unwrap one of the cheeses, a Gouda, and slice a hunk of bread from the loaf that is as big as a pillow and as heavy as guilt.

Chapter Five

Ah, women!

Postretirement, Frau Doktor Falk set about writing her memoirs. Fifty-seven pages into it, and then her death—the result of a sudden heart attack, which, because it is brutal and swift, HF contends is a man's way to die—brought her rememberings to an end. HF presents me with both the original—typed on onionskin paper, the ink already faded and bleeding—and his translation, laser-printed.

"My mother thought hers was a life of significance," he tells me.

"It was," I say. "All lives are significant."

"Yes, but she thought hers was especially so. And," he adds, "she was a notorious liar," he says of his mother. He has said the same of Bettina too, that Bettina is a notorious liar, that you can't believe half of what she says either.

In periodic fits of distress, I make myself sick with the idea that Bettina is the love of his life, the way he is the true love of mine. I worry that, try as he might, he can't shake her hold on him. I suspect this because, other than his mother, she is the only woman in his life of whom he speaks ill. Although somehow the ill he speaks of his mother is loving. It is with amusement that he refers to her as grandiose, and he is grinning when he cautions that I read her memoirs "with both eyes open." His voice chokes on affection when he tells me how she was self-important like nobody's business.

In letter #18 to the author, HF made first reference to his mother as "dead since 1987, but still going strong."

When he says his mother was a notorious liar, his countenance softens, but when he said the same of Bettina, no pleasure was in evidence.

Except to say that Bettina is a classical beauty, he has no kind words for her. Rather, I have heard how she is manipulative, conniving, and selfish, and worst of all, how he'd imagined she was someone very special, only to discover she was a run-of-the-mill small-town girl with medium-size ambitions. Such loud denouncement, protests too much and all that, leads me to consider that he loves her still, and I can't bear it. I can't bear the thought of him loving someone else the way I love him. The pain grips me from the inside out.

Jealousy is a passion which eagerly seeks that what causes pain. (German aphorism)

I clutch at my stomach as if there were the part that hurt, and I beg of him, "Tell me you love me. Tell me you love me."

"Oh Hester." He kisses my eyes, my lips, my neck. "Yes, I love you. I do love you," which proves to be insufficient to quell the torment of the thought that I am simply one pearl on a strand and there are pearls before and pearls after and a pearl is a pearl and you can't really distinguish one from the next.

As he goes to leave for work, I pull him back to me and ask him, "Why? Why do you love me? Why me above all others?"

He considers the question, and he concludes, "I suppose I love you because *you* chose me."

Then there's this: Yesterday we went to a nearby café for coffee. After we were seated, he looked around and said, "I have been here before once. With my family."

"Which family?" I asked, and he said, "I don't recall." Most men, women too, would have lied, would've said one family or another for the sake of appearances, and never mind *handsome* or *intelligent* or *charming*, the laundry list of attributes we tick off as a means to justify love. *I don't recall* is why I love him. That he can be so entirely without artifice, without guile, that it doesn't occur to him to lie to me.

Not that I lie to him. But there is much I don't tell him. Some things I have deliberately chosen not to tell, and some seem not worth the effort of telling, and therein lies the difference between my past love life and his: Mine is a revisionist's version, as if all romantic entanglements before him have been eradicated, and my history with men is a clean slate, a big load of insignificance. Boyfriends, lovers, one-night stands, the almost-husband, poof! Gone! Never mind. Oh, for most of them I can recite the names, places, dates. But they've left no mark on me, no story worth telling, which could be construed as the American way, the opportunity to begin anew, start over, from scratch. But in Europe history is thick like muck, which could be one reason why his former girlfriends, his ex-wives, his lovers past, are stuck to him still. A kind of static electricity. As if every woman who has ever touched him has lasting significance by virtue of having been a woman in his life.

Of the men in his life, he has spoken of only four, including his father, who, he contends, didn't make much of an impression. His relationship with his half brother, Josef, is no more than cordial. Josef, seventy years old, busies himself with his garden, and he acts in amateur theatrical productions, where he is most often assigned the role of the butler because he is so tall. Also Josef and his wife keep a lot of pets. Not dogs and cats, but guinea pigs and rabbits. HF thinks this is especially pitiful, but I disagree.

His son-in-law, Rebekka's husband, was mentioned with a gesture of indifference. He has spoken of only one friend, an old friend from childhood named Eckie.

Oktober 1951
Liebe Frau Doktor Falk, Eckie will wear the shirt* of Heinrich
with special joy. Heinrich will be unforgettable for Eckie. What
a shame Frankfurt** is on another star.*** Sincerely, Irene
Bader (Letter to HF's mother from Eckie's mother)
    *A hand-me-down and parting gift. Eckie was an undersized
    boy, and HF had outgrown the shirt. Times were still hard
    enough that a hand-me-down shirt was a gift of significance.
      **Frau Doktor Falk's new and fancy job with the German
    Commission on Consumer Policy necessitated she live in
    Frankfurt-on-Main. This time, she took her husband and
    her son with her.

***A star, seemingly close yet impossible to reach, was a metaphor for the West from the East.

Just before the wall went up, in his one and only deed of der-ring-do, Eckie fled from Nossen to Hannover, where he is now a civil servant. HF used to visit him there once every couple of years, but stopped because, as he explained, "We had nothing to talk about. Eckie was bitch-ridden."

"What?" I asked. "He was what?"

"Bitch-ridden. You know, when the wife is boss and the hus-band wears the dress."

"Henpecked," I told him. "We call that henpecked, although there is an archaic term *witch-ridden*, but that is more like an experience with a succubus. You mean henpecked. Bitch-ridden." I shook my head at the wonder of it. "That is rich," I said, and then I turned to the back of my notebook and headed a section *Nutball Stuff He Says*. Beneath that I wrote: *1) Bitch-ridden*.

That HF has confided in no one about me, about us, is not entirely due to the absence of a comrade. Our affair would be a covert matter even if he were one of the boys.

Liebste, You are my accomplice in the secret crime of love (love being criminal since it doesn't submit to the laws of third par-ties, society, etc.). Letting anybody know about you would be treason. I don't want people to know that you are my escape hatch to another world. I don't even want them to know there is an escape hatch. (Letter #111 to the author from HF)

To tackle the subject of his women is the sort of task for which

I ought to roll up my sleeves. First, I should list them, these women. Or at least the ones I know of thus far.

1) Wives: Konstanze, the now wife (round 1), Bettina, and the now wife (round 2)

✳ *now wife's name???*

HF and Konstanze were students, nineteen years old and virgins, the both of them, when they met, which might explain why they have such a fondness for one another still, why it seems as if they are more like brother and sister as opposed to ex-husband and ex-wife.

Unlike most young men of nineteen finding himself in such a predicament, he was overjoyed to learn that his girlfriend was pregnant. This was wonderful news. Yes, he wanted to get married and have a child, be a good family man. The only possible fly in the ointment might come from his mother. His formidable mother might not be quite as overjoyed to learn that he stupidly knocked up some little tramp. At his request, his mother took the train from Frankfurt to Freiburg. On his way to meet his mother at the station, he caught his jacket on a fence and tore the fabric near the pocket, which his mother spied right off. Frau Doktor Falk was the sort of woman who came prepared for any kind of emergency. As soon as they were seated in the restaurant, she took her sewing kit from her purse and motioned to him to give her the jacket. She ordered lunch for the two of them, and then while his mother sat, hunched over, repairing the tear in his jacket, the needle and thread looping in

and out and over, he came out with it. He said, "Mother, I got a
girl pregnant." His mother's mouth set square, and she did not
look up from her task. Sewing his jacket so that the tear would
be imperceptible, she asked him, "What do you intend to do
about it?" Summoning all his courage into one breath, he said,
"I intend to marry her," and he sat back and waited. After the
proverbial interminable minute, his mother said, "Good," and
from there they went on to discuss his studies, and even though
it was a ways away, she wanted to know what thought he'd
given to the subject of his doctoral dissertation, because she had
some ideas on that.

Further contraposition to general expectations, it comforts me
to share him with Konstanze the way it does to share him with
his now wife. This is not to say that I'd go for something like
polygamy. Rather, it's because Konstanze fills his need for sister
and mother, yet more jobs for which I have no aptitude.

. . . love the person of your husband and keep his linen clean. . . .
of the relaxations, delights and pleasures she will have waiting
for him: to seat him before a warm fire, to wash his feet, to have
fresh shoes and stockings for him, a good meal and fine drink. . . .
And on the next day clean undergarments and shirts. (Le
Ménagier de Paris [1393], ed. Baron Jérôme Pichon, Paris,
1846, Tome Premier, p. 168, author's translation)

He is the one who blurs lines, especially when he goes on
about that baby business, when he coos, "Oh, Hester. That's how
I want you. All swollen. Yes, my Hester. Yes, with a big belly and
big tits."

He is the only man I've ever known who considers my breasts to be small. They are not small. They are bigger than average, a plump B cup, which leads me to conclude that his other women must have breasts like cow udders.

"Some do," he concurred. "My mother had enormous breasts. My second daughter got those. Enormous breasts with nipples real big and red. Bettina has huge ones, but she has no good bum. My first wife, Konstanze, hers are small like yours, but when she was pregnant, oh, they grew so big."

✳ *how does he know that his second daughter's nipples are real big and red? (Ask? Don't ask!)*

✳ *put "no good bum" in the* Nutball *section.*

His face broke open like an egg when he said that, about how Konstanze's breasts grew big when she was pregnant.

2) Daughters: Rebekka, Barbara, Angelika (?), Kristina

When his first daughter was born with a shock of blond hair the exact same shade as his mother's, he was such a proud papa. What a man! He did this, he made a precious baby, all systems go! But Konstanze, a student, a wife, and now a mother too, was up to her eyeballs in work and responsibility, and something had to give. She had time for only so much, and soon he began to feel a little bit neglected. Needing more attention than he was getting, feeling so terribly sorry for himself, as if he were all alone in the world, is how the stage was set for the first Sabine to enter.

This is the pattern with him—love, baby, lonely, new love—

and maybe one encoded on his DNA, as repetitious as an Escher print, and I'm not about to step into the pitfall.

3) Lovers: The first Sabine,* the two subsequent Sabines, the Tick Girl,** the Yugoslavian, the Canadian, the East German who was probably Stasi, the one who was the wife of his colleague who had the office next to his, Beate, Friederike, the two in England, and Bettina. (Do I count her twice?)

> **Before she was his lover, the first Sabine had been his Gymnasium sweetheart back in Frankfurt. They had kissed and touched each other's soft spots, but nothing more because, although she was willing, he was not sure exactly what to do, which led him to do nothing.*

> ***The lover who preceded me, the one who sat behind me at the conference, and I never did get a look at her. The name, Tick Girl, is derived from an incident when, while driving to a conference in Heidelberg, they pulled off the road to make love in a field. Later, they discovered they'd been attacked by ticks, and they had to go to the hospital for tick removal from private parts and for inoculations against early-summer encephalitis.*

He has somewhere a picture of the first Sabine, and he has promised to bring it to me even though he says it is truly awful to look at because the first Sabine resembled a ham. The subsequent Sabines were insignificant. Casual flings of no substance, memorable only because of the repetition of the name.

He met up with the first Sabine in Freiburg, where she too was a student, and he was now a man of experience who knew exactly what to do. There is no way of knowing for how long he would have carried on with the first Sabine had Konstanze not taken him by surprise. Had she not—one Sunday night, shortly after the baby had been fed and put to bed, when he, in their bed, turned to her to make love—said, "No. No. You can't make love to two people. Not for long." Practically in flagrante delicto, he was caught off-guard and he got that awful sick feeling which accompanies getting found with one's hand in the cookie jar. Respecting his wife's intelligence too much to lie to her or maybe he just couldn't think fast enough, he asked simply, "How did you find out?" and Konstanze asked, "How did I find out what?" Konstanze had been referring to herself. She was the one who could no longer make love to two people. For some months now, she'd had herself a lover, and she had come to the point where she didn't like cheating on her boyfriend. Given the circumstances, what could they do but laugh? The parting was amicable.

4)Others: Nannies, housekeepers, two aunts, four cousins, schoolgirls on whom there were crushes, two half sisters, his secretary, Frau Doktors Schmidt and Frisch, the Little Bonn Girl,* the woman who cuts his hair, and the homeopath who treats his headaches by massaging his feet.

> **A reputedly brilliant student at the University at Bonn with whom he was having a flirtation which was intended to go well beyond the flirtation stage, but then he met me.*

5) Mother: the one and only.

I've exhausted myself with this list, with its limitless potential for tragedy. Also, I need some chronology, some dates, so I call him and ask if he can meet me for lunch.

"Sure," he says, and he names a place where, I happen to know for a fact, he and Bettina used to meet for lunch, back when they were lovers and still married to other people.

He was married for the first round to his now wife when he took up with Bettina. She was, at that same time, married to another professor, one of mathematics. Bettina worked, and still does, at the university in the Press and Public Relations Department, which was where and how she and HF met. She was putting together a press release announcing the publication of his monograph "The Economic Growth Factor of Taxation on a Select Populace of Bamberg 1352–1355." Over the weeks following, he popped by her office on one pretense or another. She came to see him to clarify this or that. Another lunch at the Gastätte Goldener Adler, and they were all over each other like sticky-tape. The Gastätte Goldener Adler became their place, their special somewhere.

"Not there. Definitely not there," I tell him.

It is too easy to dismiss him as a mere womanizer, a cad. It is too easy, and it is wrong. It, he, is more complicated than that. All these women, he loved them. Still does love them in a fashion of his own. He needs them, appreciates them, adores them all. The love is genuine, and who can wholly resist being loved, which is, of course, why he is successful.

Rule XXXI. Nothing forbids one woman being loved by two men or one man by two women. (Andreas Capellanus, The Art of Courtly Love, Columbia University Press, 1960, p. 186)

Because he equates mortal women with goddesses, believes that each and every woman is a Diana, an Aphrodite in her own right, he desires to do her bidding. A mere man cannot refuse a goddess. Women are to be worshiped, and also he's a little bit afraid of them, and I can't fault him for any of it. Some women might fault him for it. Some women, I presume, would be rigorous in their condemnation of him, furious at his attempt to please so many women, which results only in his displeasing that many more. Women make his head spin and confuse him entirely, and he loves them for that too.

Out on the street, I do, as I always have, make an attempt to be a good guest in foreign lands. I make it a rule to learn the words for *please* and *thank you*. I abide by local custom as much as is possible for me. I am respectful of the faiths of others. I rarely complain about the quality of toilet paper, but as a stranger, you can't be expected to know everything, and in a hurry to see him, I cross Theresienstrasse just as I would've crossed 14th Street; that is, against the light because no cars were coming from either direction. When I reach the other side, a woman of middle years and shaped like a fire hydrant is planted there waiting for me. She starts in, shouting I don't know what and wagging her finger in my face in reprimand, and then I understand, *"Der Kinder, der Kinder."* I look back to see a gaggle of schoolchildren now crossing the street with the light, and I realize she is chastising me for having set a bad example.

And I might have been sorry about that if I didn't have the distinct impression that *der Kinder* were but an excuse. What really pissed her off was my disobedience, that *I* crossed against the light. *I* broke a rule.

> *Most of them [the denouncers] were ordinary citizens, not Nazi enthusiasts. A certain self-important type, who liked gossip, snooping and flitting around authority figured frequently, tarting up malice in the guise of bounden duty to the national collective. . . . Parties of schoolgirls scoured the quarters of Ostjuden seeking cases of open "miscegenation," while Nazi Women's Organization members patrolled the streets armed with cameras to record the evidence. (Michael Burleigh, The Third Reich: A New History, Hill & Wang, 2000, p. 304–5)*

Because I don't know the words for it in German, I give her the finger instead.

So much for my being a good guest, respectful of the ways of others. Because that's the truth too. I'm not respectful here.

When I arrive at the restaurant, he is already seated at a booth and reading the newspaper, a short beer in front of him. He looks up to see me, and folds the paper neatly, putting it away in his briefcase. I go to slide into the seat across from him, but he says, "No. Sit here," his hand square beside him, and then this same hand snakes up my thigh, his fingers probe.

> *His hands. They're huge. Perhaps twice the size of an average hand. His fingernails are bigger than quarters or the 2DM piece. The thumbnail has got to be the size of an apricot. His are hands of remarkable proportion. Such big hands, and you might expect them to be clumsy but they are not. The way an elephant is incongruously a dainty creature, his enormous*

hands are delicate, poised, almost feminine. His feet too. Big feet. Very big feet, but shaped so sweetly. Toes the color of seashells and nestled in a row like pigs-in-blankets. Big, big hands and big, big feet, and worth mentioning, yes, the myth of correlation of size is, in his case, no myth at all.

Alas, he needs both his hands to cut his meat, which looks to be pork. I take a few bites of a leaden dumpling in brown gravy before I push my plate away and turn to a fresh page in my notebook. "When," I ask, "did Bettina go from lover to wife to ex-wife, and when did the child come into the picture?"

Bettina gave birth to Angelika while she was still married to the professor of mathematics. They divorced when the child was three years of age. As far as the mathematician knows, Angelika is his daughter. (Can a mathematician count backwards from nine?) When he left, in autumn of 1991, Bettina wanted HF to take his place, to marry her. Oh, how he wanted to do just that, but however great was his love for Bettina, the pangs of conscience were greater still. When Bettina issued an ultimatum—marry me or it's over—well, he was something of a coward. As winter neared and the days grew shorter and colder, he tried to resign himself to a life without her. He tried to be a good husband to his wife, an attentive father to Barbara, and more or less, he managed until only a few days before Christmas of that same year.

"I was out shopping," he tells me, "for a stereo for my wife. I had promised her that. A stereo for Christmas. The store was very, very crowded. Christmas carols were piped in over the loudspeaker system, and I was standing in this long line that seemed to never move, holding a stereo that grew more and more heavy by the minute. My arms ached, and the next thing I knew, tears were streaming down my face. I was sobbing."

It was this profound unhappiness at the height of the Christmas season, or perhaps more precisely what Henry David Thoreau named "quiet desperation," which prompted him to leave the stereo right there on the floor as if to hold his place in line. To leave behind the stereo and the Christmas carols and to run. To run from Marienplatz to the Isar Tor and to cross the river on the Ludwigsbrücke. Sprinting along Rosenheimer Strasse until, perspiring profusely, and his heart beating the way wings flap, he knocked on her door, prepared to drop to his knees to tell her he loved her madly and couldn't live a day more without her and yes, he would marry her gladly. Only Bettina was not at home. She was out doing some Christmas shopping of her own. At least that's what the man said, the man who answered her door, the man who was her lover, her other lover.

"She was cheating on me. Are you getting this down?" He glances at my notebook on the table, and then reaches for my plate, and proceeds to eat the dumpling weighted under the sludge of the brown gravy congealed. "All along," he says, "she was cheating on me." He says this with neither the indignity of how-dare-she nor the irony of well-what-could-I-expect. "I went all to pieces," he says. "I went home to my wife crying and shaking, and I told her everything. Oh, that was an awful Christmas. I was so sad."

"Your wife probably wasn't any too happy either," I say. "Did you ever get her the stereo she wanted?"

"For her birthday. In March," he tells me, and then he checks his watch. He has a lecture to present at 15:00, which is 3 p.m. real time.

Indeed, he is a pip, but because the self-centeredness is so pure, so unadulterated, it is rendered innocent. There isn't anything mean about him. He is ever so sweet, really.

I walk with him to the university, where he points out to me, with solemnity, the square dedicated to Sophie Scholl. He is proud that the resistance is honored, and then he steers me to look up to the balcony where Sophie and her brother Hans hid the antifascist leaflets, which resulted in their expedient arrest, interrogation, trial, and execution by beheading. Beheading. What a medieval way to die. I try to imagine Sophie Scholl, twenty-one years old and so very brave, her bones broken by the Gestapo but not her courage.

"But," I ask, "why is she so honored and not her brother?"

"Because," HF explains, "she was a girl. She stirs the imagination in a way he cannot."

Is this fixation on women perhaps not limited to HF, but now a national collective consciousness, the result of fathers dead, in prison, shamed? Has there been a generational and national shift from Fatherland to matriarchy?

Back in my hotel room, I sit at the table to work. The window at my back is open, and the air cools with an oncoming rain. I need to return to the beginning. I've gotten ahead of myself, caught in Bettina's web and spun there. I need to go to the beginning before Bettina, or Konstanze even. Back to the beginning when his mother, his Mutti, was the only woman of significance in his life.

The pile of papers on my right are his letters to me, which, despite the time they were written, do not constitute the beginning of anything. We, he and I, are an end. I tell him always, "I'm your last lover." I say, "There will be no lover after me." I say to him, "I am the last of a line."

Although these letters will not now take me where I need to be, I look through them again simply for the pleasure of them, and I am rewarded with this gem.

> *Liebste Hester, Today I took my youngest daughter and her two little friends to a carnival. I did not want to do this, but Kristina wept and said that if I did not take them then her two friends would go to the carnival with Lotte, who is Kristina's sworn enemy. Ah, women! (Letter #102 to the author from HF)*

Ah, women! Indeed.

Chapter Six

My mother had Jewish blood in her

harlotte Stadler born 1901 in Nossen (Saxony). Earned her Ph.D. in Economics from Humboldt Universität, Berlin (1926). Married Georg Haushofer (1926). Bore one son, Josef Haushofer (1930). Widowed (1932). Employed at the National Gas Board (1932–1945?). Married Klaus Falk (1942). Bore second son, Heinrich Falk (1943). Appointed Head Adviser to German Commission on Consumer Policy (1951–1968). Divorced (?). Died (1987).

Dates alone don't tell us much about a life, but they do provide a framework, a way to contain, to place, and there's no getting around it: The life of Charlotte Stadler Haushofer Falk was shaped by war.

In the course of time there will be days that enter history. They need not be the real beginnings of decisive developments. For me, the Second World War started just after Pentecost, 1939. After a conference, Klaus* and I stayed on in Vienna for a day, and so we were in a hurry to get back to Berlin. We took turns at the wheel of my old Stöwer** as we drove through the Bavarian woods. It was in the middle of the night when we got to Jüterbog, where we had to pause for a large column of military vehicles to overtake us on the road. The last of the convoy trucks had passed when I saw a white shape that looked like a ghost in front of our car. It was a young woman and her thin nightgown barely hid the fact that she was pregnant in her seventh month. Her arms were stretched out toward the full moon. She had obviously come from a nearby farmhouse and had managed to get around the military column without being harmed. Now she stood in front of our car and sang, "I see war, I see blood, I see death." If Klaus and I both had not seen this sleepwalker, I would have thought it was a delusion. Klaus told her to step away from the car, but she stayed in front of the wheels. Suddenly, she seemed to get a fright. She swayed to one side, and Klaus stepped on the gas pedal and swerved to the other side, and we were on the open road. We did not talk until we got to Berlin, and we did get to the office on time. That summer, butter was rationed. (From the memoir of Frau Doktor Falk)

     *Klaus Falk, who would become her husband and HF's father.
     **A make of car that went the way of the Edsel.

And if a picture doesn't lie, his mother was no beauty either. Tall and angular, all elbows and knees and colossal boobs. Eyes set too close together and a beaked nose, she could have been an anthropomorphic ostrich. Because this photograph is in black and white, the fact that she ostensibly had golden hair that shimmered in the light is more or less lost on me. HF has mentioned her hair on several of our otherwise intimate occasions, how when unpinned it cascaded glimmering down her back, how the texture was like the richest silk threads, and the smell, he rhapsodized on the smell of the rosewater she used to rinse this golden hair of hers.

The way he speaks of his mother's hair could raise a few eyebrows. And that's not the half of it.

When he was fourteen, his mother took him with her on a business trip to Amsterdam, a city where she had been before but only once. After dinner, she proposed a walk, and strolling without aim, they found themselves in Oudekerk. Mother and son walked, at an even pace, from one end of the famous red light district to the other, neither of them remarking on any of it. Rather, they walked those streets as if at the windows there were nothing but curtains and shades as opposed to prostitutes. When they got back to their hotel, where they shared a room, his mother was so tired. So very tired. Aches from the stress of Frau Doktor Falk's very important job, and her lumbago was acting up again, and wouldn't he be a good boy and rub his Mutti's back, but wait one minute and let Mutti first take off her blouse* and shoes.

*That's right. Her blouse.

It's my opinion that they, the whole lot of them—this family—were kinky. Kinky and each of them with a Ph.D. too. Not so kinky as to actually engage in incest, but, repressed beneath the surface of decorum, there bubbled some seriously strange cravings, and it didn't end there with mother and son.

Take as your spouse whomever you please, whether it be godparent, godchild, or the daughter or sister of a sponsor, and disregard those artificial money-seeking impediments. (Martin Luther)

HF has told me how he and his eldest daughter, before she married, would meet for dinner and regale each other with recounts of their sexual peccadilloes. It's a rare father who would relish the tale of his daughter screwing a Portuguese businessman on a billiard table in a pub in Marseille, nor would most fathers be so sorely disappointed to learn that their daughters are monogamous in their marriages, but he made a face and said, "She's all for one man now." And then there is that bit about his next daughter's nipples, but I really don't want to investigate that any further.

And back to his mother. In a fit of amateur psychology, I trace the path from his relationship with his mother (never a stretch) to his need to have, at all times, and concurrently, a wife and a mistress.

Liebste, You have no cause for worry. I am monogamous in my adultery. (Letter #55 to the author from HF)

His adored mother. Big Mutti. Tall (coming in at six feet herself) and erect and strong with a backbone of iron. Driven and

successful and intelligent and dominant, and she was domineer-
ing too. "My mother was her own woman," he has said. "Not
bossed by anyone. No one would dare." A woman to reckon with,
for sure, and he loved his mother ever so much, and such a good
little boy he was. Such a good little boy to make a mother proud,
but first remember there was the war raging at the time of his
birth. The war, which necessitated that he, a mere babe, an infant
only weeks old, be plucked from his mother's breast, and sent
away.

> She knew that I should be utterly an orphan with no one at all
> on whom to depend, for great as was my wealth of kinsfolk and
> connections, yet there was no one to give me the loving care a
> little child needs at such an age. . . . I often suffered from the
> loss of that careful provision for the helplessness of tender years
> that only a woman can provide. (From The Memoirs of Abbot
> Guibert of Nogent, 1115)

True, HF was sent away for safekeeping, but no baby could be
expected to understand the concept of *for your own good*. Thus his
fear of abandonment, of being left behind, dumped, is to be easily
understood in this context. And it didn't end there. After the war,
there was pandemonium. No place to live, arrests, releases,
hunger, and the migration west. No, in those postwar years he
could not rest easy, he could not trust that the days spent with his
mother were infinite, because, in fact, they were not.

> Near the end of the war, after their flat in Berlin had been
> bombed to such a degree that it was no longer inhabitable, his
> mother went to stay with her parents in Saxony. His father

remained in Berlin, sleeping here and there for the duration.
After the war was over, when the first layer of dust began to set-
tle, his mother wanted to leave the zone occupied by the Rus-
sians. She wanted to return to Berlin, but to the American zone,
only housing was pitifully scarce. Families were doubling and
tripling up, but Frau Doktor Falk was a determined woman
and she instructed her husband to find them a place to live.
And so he did. Two rooms on the third floor of a building where
the fourth and fifth floors and the roof had been destroyed.
When it rained, they got wet. The other rooms to this flat were
owned and occupied by his father's mistress and her children.
When his mother returned to work, little HF was left in the care
of the mistress. Eventually his parents got a flat of their own,
and then because there was no one in Berlin to watch over him,
HF was again sent away, shuttled between relatives in Saxony
and the children's home on the Baltic. HF remembers his last
day in Berlin. "I remember being outside, in front of the build-
ing. We lived in the Charlottenburg section. I was playing with
a little girl. Maybe she was the daughter of my father's mistress.
I don't know. I was five years old, and I bit the girl to the quick.
She really bled. I don't know why I did it. Just for the fun, I
guess. I liked hearing her scream."

(At this point in the telling, HF gave me, the author, that look, and I gave it right back because he also likes making me scream, and I like it too.)

Then, finally, in 1951, when all that war mess was swept
under the carpet and life in West Germany, at least, was more
or less good again, Mutti landed her very important job in

Frankfurt, and HF went there to live with her. Just the two of them, except when that interloper father of his was around. HF was ever so proud of her, of his important Mutti, and yes, maybe a teensy bit resentful because she had to travel so much. Okay, maybe an itty-bitty part of him was even angry, furious, enraged because the bitch was never at home. That fucking oh-so-important job took her to Brussels and Paris and London and Amsterdam and once even to New York, and although she brought back for him a red plastic ViewMaster with slides of the Statue of Liberty and the Empire State Building, he wanted, needed, ached for his mother's love and attention far more than for any toy.

Fast-forward, and what do we get? He is irresistibly drawn to strong and intelligent women. Women like his Mutti, in the hopes that these women will, in this version of things, be all that Mutti was and all that she was not. But, and he knows this as well as anyone, such a wish must go unfulfilled. Should he finally dominate the dominant woman, all would be lost.

His now wife echoes those parts of his mother's makeup which allowed her to ignore his father's infidelities, which allowed her to live in the same flat as his mistress, which instructed the housekeeper to set a place at the table for breakfast each morning for a man who might or might not have slept at home and dinner too, so that often they ate, he and his mother alone, across from a clean plate and silverware untouched. His now wife, who for sixteen years minus his one year sabbatical with Bettina, washes his socks and makes him dinner. She has eased his heartaches and turned a blind eye, so that he is more or less free to pursue the remainder of what will make him whole. Wife plus Mistress equal Dream Mother. At least that's the idea. Oh, how he wants to be loved. He needs to be loved. He begs, *love me, love me,* and that vulnerability is also part of what makes him so hard to resist. But, in fact, no woman nor any combination of women will heal the wounds, will assuage the fear of abandonment, will compensate for what he then did not get. But still, he tries and he tries and he tries.

Actually, he washes his own socks. Each and every night he peels off his socks and washes them in the sink by hand, as if he had but one pair. This, washing his own socks, is something I witnessed when he was in New York. I'd asked him why he did that, but all he said was, "I do not know. But I have always done it."

The next photograph I look at shows Frau Doktor Falk standing beside her sister, the one who became a doctor and saved the infant HF from a likely death in a Berlin hospital during wartime. She was short and plump and very pretty. She's blind now, this aunt. She lives in utter darkness. To view the two sisters in this picture is to conclude that their mother must've done the milkman.

I'm sifting through the papers looking, looking for I don't know what, when the phone rings, which is a surprise because it's Saturday. HF spends the weekends with his now wife and their daughters, and who else would be calling me here? The little communication I have with those from home is through e-mail. I haven't sent so much as a postcard, and I left no forwarding address or phone number. Coming to Munich necessitated I live in another kind of exile.

Often on Saturdays, and Sundays too, HF and his family go on hikes. Long arduous walks in the mountains. This is their idea of fun, but today, HF tells me, his now wife and their two daughters have gone to Marienplatz. "Shopping," he says. "For I don't know what. Women's things, I imagine." HF wants to know what I am doing today, and I tell him, "I'm trying to get a grasp on your mother."

"She is too big for one person," he says, and then he offers, "Let me help you with her."

We have sex twice in an hour, and he is ever so pleased with himself. "I performed quite well, didn't I?" he asks. It's silly, really, the emphasis he places on the completion of the act. Orgasmi-centric. My sweetie must spurt to be happy, as if no orgasm negates all the niceties that came before it. I inquire as to why this is so, and he tells me, "It is proof to myself that I am a man," to which I say, "Oh, your mother really did a job on you."

And with that subject, the specter of his mother, evoked, I slip out of the bed to bring back some papers and pictures, and he sits up so we can look together.

He's got the photograph I'd been looking at earlier, the one of his mother and his aunt. "They look like a pair of Jewish sisters, don't you think?" He has startled himself, and now that he has done it, spoken the word *Jew* aloud, he waits as if to see if God will smite him. When it appears that there will be no repercussion, he feels safe to go on with it. "I've always suspected that my mother had Jewish blood in her."

"Ridiculous," I snort. "Besides, you can't be part Jewish," I bristle as if I'm wanting to keep this, Jewishness, for myself. As if something would be ruined if we had that in common. "You're Jewish or you're not. And, trust me, your mother was not."

"But if she was, then I would be Jewish too."

In one frantic swoop, he's gone from speaking the word *Jewish* to an attempt at appropriating the whole shebang, and I note, "You sound as if you want to be Jewish."

"Of course I would want to be Jewish," he says. "Wouldn't everybody?"

"No," I tell him. "Definitely, definitely not," and I turn my attention back to the papers at hand.

After she retired, Frau Doktor Falk moved from Frankfurt to Munich to be near her sons. Then, as required by law, she registered, with the authorities at the Einwohnermeldamt München, her address and her religion. As this is a matter of public record, I availed myself of the bureaucratic services, which entailed filling out forms in triplicate, paying one fee to look at the records and another fee for photocopies of them. Frau Doktor Falk was registered as a Protestant. Her baptismal and confirmation certificates—courtesy of HF—back that up. HF is registered as an atheist, which is officially known as *without confession.*

> *When he was four years of age Little Heinrich asked me,*
> *"Mummy, if God is the father of Jesus, then who is Josef?" I hes-*
> *itated because I was not sure what to tell him, and during my*
> *hesitation, he said, "Oh, I know. Josef is Maria's friend."**
> *(From the memoir of Frau Doktor Falk)*
>   **Worth noting: Four years old and already he was wise to the*
>   *concept of "friend."*

Religion is registered here because there is a church tax, or at least that is the official reason given, and you have to register your address so that the authorities can find you if need be. But

such practices reverberate, and all things considered, they ought
to give that up.

Despite this evidence that she was a Protestant through and
through, HF still insists that his mother, whose mild distaste for
Jews might have been nothing but a ruse to deflect suspicion,
could very well have had a Jewish parent or grandparent. "I
always had this feeling," he says, "that she was hiding something."

"Maybe she was hiding something," I say, "but not that." From
the pile, I pull a piece of paper at random, like pick-a-card-any-
card, and I've picked this one:

> *The first of September was one of those days history remembers.
> It was early in the morning when the voices on the radio said
> there was shooting in Poland. The managing director of the gas
> board who was Blutordensträger* and SS-Sturmbannführer
> with a very low party number gathered the workforce into his
> office to announce the beginning of the war with appropriate
> pomp. But I suddenly saw the misery that was coming. The
> managing director's words triggered a spasm of crying.
> Although I tried very hard, I could not control my sobbing and
> when the dutiful "Sieg Heil" was shouted, I cried more. Every-
> one was giving me poisoned looks, but they did not reach me.
> (From the memoir of Frau Doktor Falk)*
>
> **An honor bestowed on those who took part in the 1923
> Putsch.*

"What bullshit," I say.

"What?" he asks. "What is bullshit?"

"That while everyone else was *Sieg Heiling*, she alone was
weeping. That's what is bullshit."

"Maybe," he concedes. "But it is possible that it is true. You have to understand that after the First World War, the people were terrified at the thought of another one. All evidence shows that it was only following the initial victories over Poland and France that the people supported the war. When Poland and France fell, they became convinced this one would turn out better. But at first, it was very frightening. I believe she cried."

"Just her? No one else?"

"Oh well, that's just my mother being self-important," and suddenly, without warning, he springs from the bed, and infused with invigorated intentions, he steps into his trousers. "Come on, come on," he says. "Get dressed."

He refuses to tell me where we are going, and he leads me to the U-bahn, where he buys me another one of those tickets good for five rides. Two stops later we get off at Nordsomething-or-other, and at a kiosk just outside the station, he purchases a bouquet of white and pink carnations. Then he tells me, "Okay, now we'll go watch Mummy turn over in her grave."

The cemetery bears the same name as the U-bahn stop, Nordfriedhof, which he translates for me as North Court of Peace. A brick wall surrounds the grounds, and the pathways are lined with what he says are linden trees. Shade trees with heart-shaped leaves.

HF points out a wide plot with two or three stones and tells me, "This is for the victims of air raids, people who could not be identified."

The other graves are close together, in neat rows like good soldiers, and remarkably well-tended. The gardening is formal. Some of the plots sport topiaries and little picket fences. The only other people here are old women, widows with watering cans. HF explains that you can either pay a gardening fee or you can weed and plant yourself and save the money. Also, you don't buy a cemetery plot here, but you rent one for ten years at a clip.

He comes to a stop at a grave where pansies and well-groomed miniature rose bushes blossom with artistry. "Here we are," he says. "Meet Mummy."

If you think you can't tell much about a person by her gravestone, think again. This stone is tall, maybe three and a half feet high and pink marble. An obelisk, shaped like the Washington Monument (could you get any more phallic, and in pink, no less) and engraved with her date of birth and date of death and her name. Doktor Charlotte Falk, the *D* of Doktor twice the size of the other letters and ornate, an Albertus Italic *D*. On her headstone *Doktor* is engraved. I don't believe I've ever encountered *Doktor* on a headstone before. *Doktor*. But she is not alone in that pomposity. There are other Doktors here too, and some Professors, and even a *Professorwitwe*, which HF tells me is a professor's widow, which has a prestige of its own.

"My brother"—he gestures at the plants, the pansies circling the roses on and around the grave—"my brother comes here every Sunday, and at Christmas he puts up a little fir tree with decorations. My brother is still devoted to her." He places the bouquet of carnations at the headstone, and I say, "And you're not still devoted to her?"

"Not in the same way," he says. Certainly his devotion does not express itself as tangibly as his brother's does. The carnations, in comparison to the pansies and roses, look shabby, and yet I have the feeling that if his mother were alive, she would be far more pleased with his meager contribution than with the pains his brother takes trying to win her love.

"You were her favorite, weren't you?" I ask, and he pretends to ponder this for a moment. "Yes, I suppose so." He tries to hide his satisfaction, but there's a rosy glow to his cheek. "How did you know?" he asks.

"Because your brother is competing with you, and you do not compete with him. But you remain in love with your mother nonetheless."

"My mother was the sort of woman whose dominant presence was not easily escaped."

"Your father managed," I point out, and he shrugs as if to say maybe, maybe not.

Not so much a boy anymore, but not yet a man, HF was six-teen, old enough to take care of himself while his mother was away on yet another one of her business trips. It was to Brussels this time, when a letter arrived for her at home. It was marked URGENT. It was marked URGENT in his father's handwrit-ing, and fearing an emergency of some kind—illness, accident, dire straits—HF tore open the envelope and read his father's letter to his mother, the letter which stated that he was not com-ing back to her, the letter which asked her for a divorce. HF was hurt and indignant on his mother's behalf, but he claims not at all on his own behalf, because, he says, he never had any use for his father and was glad to be rid of him. Given the Oedipal quality of his affections for his mother, this statement is credible. He considered burning the letter, keeping it, and the pain it would inflict, from her, but when she returned home, he handed it over and said, "Do not give in to him. Do not give him the divorce." His mother slipped the letter into her pocket, kissed her son tenderly on the back of his neck, and set about making dinner. Nothing more was said on the subject. Not by either of them, not then, not ever. Which is why he never learned if his parents did, in fact, divorce or if they merely remained estranged until death did them part. His mother died first. In her will, there was no mention of a husband. She left all she had, property and an amount of money not unsubstantial, because she was a success and something of a miser, to her two sons and a nest egg for her first granddaughter, the one who got her shimmering golden hair.

✳ *It is very puzzling how HF could rip open an envelope clearly addressed to his mother, but when his father's widow (or whatever she was) sends him a package, he's not the least bit concerned with what it contains.*

I suspect his mother's bequest to her first granddaughter, while leaving nothing to her second one (Barbara had been born the year before her death), had to do with more than hair color and the shimmer factor. "Did your mother not like your now wife?" I ask.

"Not so much," he says. "My now wife didn't go to university, and because she was my second wife. My mother's loyalties were with Konstanze."

So his now wife is the lone exception to Ph.D. rule of thumb in this family, and if I had to put my money on it, I'd bet she's the most normal one of the bunch.

"Would your mother have liked me?" I ask, and he says, "No. She was never a real anti-Semite, but I sensed that being around Jews made her uncomfortable. I still think that's because . . ."

I cut him off and say, "If I weren't Jewish, would she have liked me? After all, I am a Frau Doktor too."

"Yes," he says, "but still no. You are too sexy. She would not have approved of that. She was a real feminist, my mother."

We walk back the way we came, and he tells me about his mother's funeral. Many important persons were there. All the seats were taken, and there was even a telegram from the Minister of Agriculture, which his brother kept because HF was never a fan of the Christian Democrats. "I gave the eulogy," he says. "It was really more of a speech, and quite inspiring, if I dare say so. I spoke on feminism, the history of modern feminism, and my mother's role in that. It was a most impressive talk. I cried."

I gave the eulogy at my mother's funeral too. I didn't want to give the eulogy, but there was no one else to do it. I stood before the rows of folding chairs, nearly all of them empty but for my father in the front row, five neighbors from New Rochelle clustered together in the middle, and behind them were two former colleagues from Public School Number 22, where my mother taught second grade, a thankless job. Who ever remembers their second-grade teacher? First grade is when you learn to read, write, add, and subtract. Third grade brings you into the big leagues: multiplication, division, script, no more pencil but writing with a pen. Face it, second grade is a lost year. My mother worked not because she was a feminist (*feminist, schmeminist* is a direct quote) but because she believed fervently in the public school system, and she liked little children. Probably in part because little children didn't make all that much fun of her accent the way fifth- or sixth-graders would have done more cruelly. When I was in the second grade, my friends asked only, "How come your parents talk funny?" and I told them it was because they were from California, and it was left at that. A year later, when the children grew wiser and the California accent could no longer fly, I said, "They're from Belgium," figuring Belgium was a place no one knew much about, and therefore they wouldn't ask questions.

As if it were that easily done, I once tried to rid my parents of their accent. Seating them side by side, I sat in a chair across from them, the little speech pathologist, the little tyrant. "*Th*," I said, the tip of my tongue jammed in exaggeration against my front teeth. "*Th. The. This. Those.*"

"Ze. Zis." My mother was sure she was repeating after me.

"Zem." My father was somewhere else.

"*The. This. Those. Th. Th. Th,*" I was making sounds near to hissing and spitting. "*Th. Th. Th.*" My arms flapped as if I were preparing for flight up from the chair, out of the room, away from my parents forever.

Soon after that, I simply quit inviting anyone home, which did not escape my mother's attention. "Vy, mine Hester," she asked, "you don't invite your friends to ze house? You are embarrassed of your parents?"

Never could I have said yes, yes I am embarrassed, embarrassed that my parents were old enough to be my grandparents, embarrassed that they spoke English like Dr. Strangelove, embarrassed that, until I was sixteen, my mother insisted on cutting my meat into bite-sized pieces for me, lest I choke. But mostly I was embarrassed by who they were and why they came to America. I was embarrassed that they were chased from their homes, pushed out. I saw them as the weak, the picked-upon, the losers.

I saw them the same way I saw Joel Bingham, a pale and frightened boy in my class who, daily, was relieved of his lunch money and whatever else of value—a yo-yo, a purple Magic Marker, a comic book—he had on him. After a while, those pint-sized school-yard barbarians didn't need to beat him up. Joel would see them coming and empty his pockets first. And although Joel Bingham did nothing wrong, he was the one who suffered shame, the shame of being the object of derision, the shame of his inability to fight back. I saw that same helplessness in my parents' eyes.

Every day my heart broke for my mother and father, because I loved them nonetheless, the way Joel Bingham's mother must have had a broken heart too. And because I loved them, never could I say, "Yes. I am embarrassed by you," and so I said, "Really, Mama. I prefer to be by myself," and, in time, that came to be true.

Other than my father and me, there were no relatives at my mother's funeral. Her cousin Alfie did not come in from California for it, but he sent a fruit basket.

When my father died, I didn't bother with a funeral service. Not one person, other than me, would've been there. Instead, alone, I went to the cemetery, where I threw a handful of earth on the coffin already in the ground. Then I went home.

I don't mention any of this to HF. It's all too pitiful. I have told him next to nothing about my parents, and bless his self-absorption, he doesn't ask. He is not very curious about me unless it has to do with him and me.

Near the U-bahn, I look up to reference where we are exactly, and I see the street sign on the post. Ungererstrasse.

Ungererstrasse. I know that street. I once read it on a document that was otherwise written in Hebrew. Five or six lines of

Hebrew and then Ungererstrasse 217. A document I found in that box in the closet in my parents' bedroom after my father died. A box filled with papers, a few photographs, and an old toy from my mother's childhood. A mechanical bear, its fur patchy and bald in spots. Glued to its head was a to-scale Bavarian cap made of green felt. Its paws held a tiny wooden beer mug, and when I wound the key in its back, in jerky mechanical motions, that sorry bear brought the beer mug to a spot near its mouth.

I remember this particular document only because it was partially written in Hebrew. The Hebrew stood out. Hebrew, a language which I could understand no better than I understand German, but at least with German I'm able to read the alphabet. Ungererstrasse 217. I tell HF, "I think I'm going to take a walk."

"Where to?" He pivots to follow me.

"You have to go home now," I remind him. It is already late in the afternoon and the shops at Marienplatz close at four on Saturday. His now wife and their two daughters will be home soon.

He wavers, but says, "No. I'll walk with you."

I warn him that he is playing fast and loose with our happiness. "Your wife is no fool. If you're not at home when she gets in, she'll ask questions. She'll know. Go on," I insist. "Go home. I'll be fine. I just feel like walking." After we kiss, I wait for him to descend the stairs to the U-bahn, and then I walk off in search of Ungererstrasse 217.

I pass an air-raid shelter and then a square of allotment gardens—cabbage patches for city dwellers to keep them connected to their roots as peasants—but there's nothing where 217 ought to be. Nothing but an expanse of open space. I am about to give up and go back to my hotel when I spy a small road, Garchingerstrasse, flanked by meadows on either side, like a garden path. I follow it to the end, where I hit a wall.

White stucco walls joined at right angles that are far too tall for me to look over, to see what it is they protect, but on the eastern side there is a gate of iron grillwork. A concrete arch adorned with a gold Star of David caps the gate, which is locked, maybe because today is Saturday, and although I can see in from here, there is nothing much to see other than some linden trees. Behind the foliage I can make out two small buildings, white stucco like the walls, but there is no indication of what purpose they serve.

It is at another gated gap in the wall that, with one eye closed the way you look through a telescope to the stars, I see a cluster of headstones. Five of them. Black marble, clean as a whistle, the engravings in Hebrew. On one I can make out the year of death. 1956.

Conclusions ought not to be drawn until all the facts are in, but I come to some conclusions nonetheless: 1) There once was a Jewish cemetery at Ungererstrasse 217. 2) Some relative of my mother's, her mother perhaps, was buried there. 3) The Jewish cemetery at Ungererstrasse 217 was either destroyed or severely desecrated during the time of the Third Reich. 4) After the war, the Jewish cemetery was moved here, some yards away, to Garchingerstrasse, where it is hidden and protected. 5) This, what I am doing, poking around in the not so distant past of this nation and its people, is going to unearth more than I'd bargained for.

Of course it is possible that this change of address is for a reason entirely innocent. Maybe the Jews themselves, needing more space, up and moved around the corner. It could easily be something like that, but it is difficult to believe anything but the worst.

Rather than taking the U-bahn, I walk. I walk and I listen because it's my experience that cities speak to me. When I walk city streets, I hear voices. Not the way a schizophrenic person hears voices, but rather I hear the past echoing back at me. I hear the stories the buildings tell, and the sidewalks. The older a city is, the more it has to say. Since the first day I got here, and every day since, Munich has whispered to me, although I've been trying my damnedest not to listen. Until now.

I get out my notebook and make a list.

Reasons I Hate the City of Munich

—*You don't get water with your meal*

—*No air-conditioning*

—*Bicycles*

—*No bags with grocery purchase*

—*Sausages that are white and look like giant maggots*

—*No crossing against the light even if the next oncoming car is still in France*

—*No one wears black sunhats*

—*Tampons without applicators*

—*You don't get bread with your meal*

—*And then if there is bread, Germans slather on the butter, or worse, pork fat, an inch thick and tear it ferociously with their teeth the way an animal tears flesh from prey**

—*They eat pork fat*

—*Despite the advanced technology and engineering, I often get*

the feeling that it's 1226, as if the smell of donkey dung were
wafting in the air
—*Despite that it's not, I often get the feeling that it's 1939*
—*No one smiles much here*
—*No one smiles at me*
　Last week, when HF and I were having lunch, he looked
　around and said, "Now I remember why I hate restaurants.
　All these people eating where I can see them. Shoveling food in
　their mouths. It's disgusting. What's next? Public shitting?"**
　(To be filed under the subsection: Nutball Stuff He Says)
　　**Now that I think of it, I wouldn't be surprised if public
　　shitting were a done thing here.

I finish with my reasons to hate this city except for one: This is
the city that turned my mother out, spun her like a top, from
a teenage girl into a refugee. If you've ever seen pictures of
refugees, you know they all have eyes that are pools of fear and
bafflement, that these are people lost and confused, and try as
they might, they never fit in anywhere.

My mother was from Munich. A fact I've been dodging like
falling debris since I arrived here. Until today, I've avoided all and
any possible connections, never imagining her walking these
streets, never wondering if she frequented that little café on Wilhelmstrasse that I like, never venturing near the train station
where she said goodbye.

Some years after my mother's mother died, her father, my
grandfather, liquidated, at ten percent of their value, whatever
assets remained, and bought for her, his daughter who was not
yet seventeen years old, documents and passage out. From

Munich she took a train, taking with her the one small suitcase allowed and, although too old for such a thing, a mechanical toy bear. This train wasn't like any train we know. It was one car, isolated for emigrants. The windows were painted over so no one could see out or in. The car was bolted shut from the outside, as if this train were a test run for the trains that were to follow. It stopped often, but who knew where because no one was allowed off. It took nine days to get to France, where my mother disembarked long enough to board another train, which took her to Spain and from there to Lisbon, where she boarded a freighter for America. That was early in 1940, which in many regards is lifetimes ago, but for historians 1940 is practically yesterday, and also it's practically yesterday when it comes to your own mother.

1940. Dates alone can't tell us much about a life, but they do provide a framework.

Chapter Seven

And then there was the father

M y body clock has been reset to run on child time. Asleep by ten or, as they insist here, 22:00. This change in sleep pattern has nothing to do with jet lag. It's simply that nights in Munich are different for me from nights at home. At home, I made social rounds—dinner, a party, the movies—but here I have no life like that. Here at night, I eat dinner, bread and cheese, at my table. I brush away the crumbs and do some work. Then I get into bed with a book, *Marriage and Family in the Middle Ages* or maybe *The Face of the Third Reich*. I'm having something of a monk's life here except, of course, when I'm with HF. Then, it's nothing at all like a monk's life.

Asleep by ten means awake at the ungodly hour of six with the chickens. After making a pot of coffee at the kitchenette counter, I go to my table, and take a look at what I've got, thus far, on HF's father.

It's not much. A few photographs, a residence registration, something that looks to be a fishing license. HF has not brought me the package I requested. The package the size of a shirt box, the one he has squirreled away unopened. "How could you not be curious?" I asked. "Who knows what's in there? It could be filled with money." I tried to tempt him.

"Not likely," he said. "I'm sure there's nothing in there except cheap sentiment." Where his mother is concerned, he is all cheap sentiment, soggy as a wet hankie. For his father, he apparently has none. When it comes to his father, he is dismissive and abrupt. Naturally, I suspect he is covering up something. "I detested my father," he told me. "He was either absent or useless. Soft and . . ."

"Wait. Hold that thought." I scrambled from the bed for my notebook on the table and a pen.

Soft and old and led around by the nose. The only thing I ever learned from him was fishing, and I rebelled against it. But it wasn't just him. It was that whole generation. They followed some idiot, they slaughtered innocent people, and quite a few got killed or maimed in the process. They got caught, they lost the war, they brought shame over all of us. They were not available when our mothers were bombed by the Allies and raped by the Russians.

I interrupted him here to ask, "Your mother was raped by a Russian?"

"I don't know for sure," he said. "She claimed that one tried, but she fought him off. As children the only people for us to look up to were our mothers."

Yet, he is his father's son, and the similarities are not confined to physiognomy. No matter what he says, he learned plenty more than fishing from his father.

He does look like his father. Exactly like his father. Three generations now, that I know of, with this face. His mother may have worn the pants in the family, but his father's genes are clearly the dominant ones. The same spark in the eye, that playful I'm-up-to-no-good grin. He's a looker too, Herr Doktor Klaus Falk.

Clipped to the back of a studio portrait of Klaus Falk is a certificate of marriage. Klaus Falk and Charlotte Haushofer tied the knot in a place called Spreewald in October 1942, which would render HF legitimate by a hair, if he indeed was born when he says he was in July 1943. His birth certificate, along with who knows how many other possibly incriminating German documents, no longer exists. Reams of paper, files, certificates, and evidence were incinerated during the war, especially during those last few days. Instead of a birth certificate, HF has a document stating that his birth certificate got burned to ash and that his mother has attested and sworn to this day in July 1943 as the day of his birth. Easily enough, his mother could've fudged a few months to cover up a small scandal. Maybe his brother will know.

Born in the dawn of the twentieth century (exact date unknown) in the Sudetenland, now part of the Czech Republic but then a part of the Austro-Hungarian Empire populated with a substantial German minority, Klaus Falk was raised in the picturesque spa town of Marienbad. There his father was a medical doctor treating a myriad of ailments with sulfur water. In 1918, at the tail end of the Great War—encouraged by

Allied victories and German defeats—the peoples of Bohemia, Moravia, and Slovakia issued a formal declaration of independence and together formed the nation of Czechoslovakia. Less than a year later—January 1919—the Allied and associated powers, one of which was the newly established Czechoslovakian Republic, convened in Versailles, where they stuck it to the Germans but good. Nothing about the Treaty of Versailles sat well with the Germans, and Klaus Falk—who had escaped military service in that Great War by having been a scant few months too young—then, in a spasm of nationalism, decided to attend university not in Prague or Vienna, but in Berlin. He would join the nation of his people. In Berlin, he completed his studies (Ph.D. in Engineering Sciences) and he married (who? name? year?) and together they had two daughters. At some point in the late 1930s, he took up with the widow Haushofer, whom he met at the National Gas Board, where they both worked in the department of propaganda. He divorced (at least that is the assumption, but when?) and married Charlotte Haushofer. Shortly after, they had a son, our Heinrich. During the Second World War, Klaus Falk, a lover and not a warrior (his maxim: Better to be a long-living dog than a dead lion), managed to avoid military service until fairly late in the game (1944 or '45), and then he was not an infantryman, but a typist (typing what? Could be anything from Eichmann's list of the doomed to requests for toilet paper). At the end of the war, he was arrested by the Russians for allegedly working for the Ministry of Propaganda under Josef Goebbels, but apparently this was a mix-up, Falk being a fairly common name, and six weeks after his arrest, he was released. Nonetheless, this experience left a deep impression and resulted in his fervent desire to get as

far away from the Russians as possible, which is one of the rea-
sons why he moved his family in with his mistress and her fam-
ily. The flat of his mistress was in West Berlin, but even West
Berlin was too close for his comfort. When his wife landed a
fancy job in Frankfurt, he went with her, although it is evident
that, by that point, the marriage was not much more than in
name only. It is not known how many lovers he had during
those years in Frankfurt. It is known only that some nights he
came home, but most nights he did not, and then in 1959, he
left for good. At age sixty-five he retired from his job at an engi-
neering firm ("I have no idea what he did there," HF said.
"Probably nothing much. He was fairly useless.") and with a
woman (name?), the one whom he either married or not, but
with whom he did live out the rest of his days, he moved to
Gimmeldingen, a village on the Rhine.

The breakfast room opens at eight, which is now only minutes
away. I stand up from my seat at the table and stretch. There is
only one window in this peculiar little room of mine, and it faces
the front. Hesseloherstrasse is a small and narrow street, not
much trafficked except when the theater across the way, a fringe
theater, lets out. The play running there now is about vampires.
Or at least that's what the marquee poster leads me to believe.
There isn't much to see from this window other than the
weather.

The thing about Sundays here is how quiet they are. On Sundays, this city closes up like a clam. It is by now my fourth Sunday in Munich, and so I know that I will not get an egg at
breakfast. For some reason, there are no eggs on Sundays.

The brown-haired of the two sisters drops a basket of rolls on my table. "*Grüss Gott*, Frau Doktor Rosenfeld," she says. That is the only way to tell these sisters apart, the hair color.

> *Dearest Hester, I was there to make final arrangements with the two matron [sic] sisters who run this hotel. You'll never know how much I worry about your quarters in Munich! If the worse comes to the worst, you can always go and work in the library of the Amerika-Haus. I love you. (Letter #76 to the author from HF)*

Grüss Gott. Go with God, or something like it, and she says it in a way as if she believes that usually I go with Satan. I could suspect these sisters of anti-Semitism, but the truth is that they, I am confident, would hate me regardless of my religious affiliations.

The previous Sundays here were interminable. Days that stood still. Not even a breeze to move the air or time. Like a dead zone. The poppy-seed rolls in the basket are from yesterday, and they are stale.

"*Kaffee*, Frau Doktor Rosenfeld." The blond sister slides a pot of coffee to me. They, these sisters, know my habits. Pretty much all of them by now, and they don't think much of them.

> *Liebste, Whow! [sic] Shall we try that phantasy in reality? It's very inviting. Oh no, now I got hard again. (Letter #63 to the author from HF)*

They, the sisters, no longer leave a piece of candy on my pillow after making the bed.

I wonder what HF is doing today.

On alternating Saturday nights, he and his now wife play cards with Konstanze and her now husband. On Saturday nights and not on Friday nights because Konstanze observes the Jewish sabbath. She proclaims to spend her Friday nights in contemplation of her father's sins. When HF told me about that, I made a face and asked, "What good does that do anybody?"

Her Jew-o-philia aside, because frankly, I don't know what to make of that, I have a hunch I might like Konstanze. There is much she could tell me, and then I have to laugh at myself. Laugh at how if I'm not on my toes, I could stumble head-on into his personal gynaeceum, his hothouse of sorts, and I laugh again at how he'd like that, all of us under one roof tending to him, to his many, many, many needs.

Without buying a ticket (naturally), I board the U-bahn #3 bound for the Olympic Park. The train will arrive in two minutes. Exactly two minutes, unless my watch is off, which is more likely than the possibility of this train running late. The trains here run on time and according to schedule, which is a good thing but also a little bit creepy.

The other thing about the subways here, there are no crazy people in them. No seats taken by the great unwashed. No one is talking to himself or to demons. Everyone seems clean and sane. Where are the crazy people? Where have they gone?

The train, like pretty much every place else in Munich, is not air-conditioned. I fan myself with my hand. A grandmotherly woman sitting across from me is dressed as if coming from church. I smile at her, and she grips her purse to her chest.

Once an old military training ground, then the site for the 1972 Olympic Games—where the Israeli athletes were taken hostage and murdered—this is the place where HF lives with his now wife and two daughters.

The Olympic Park and Village stand in stark contrast to the rest of Munich, which looks like a place where old ladies go for tea, three sugars and a sweet. Here I find myself at a model village, the sort that city planners create first in miniature complete with little plastic trees and little plastic people. Night never comes and the seasons never change. Under glass domes, these model villages are shown at exhibitions beneath banners that read *City of the Future*.

One set of residential buildings suggests it houses students, because much of the outer walls is painted with amateurish murals. Also a library and copy shop are featured in this complex. The other set of buildings—where I assume HF lives—sports balconies laden with plants and flowers and some even have fir trees. The overall effect—a wall of foliage—is broken up by striated slabs of concrete painted orange and lime green.

The business district is something like a small town's Main Street, although not the least bit quaint. Actually, it's nearer to a suburban shopping center, a strip mall. Two rows of shops—three pubs, two bakeries, a bank, a post office, a bookstore, a hotel, a greengrocer, two supermarkets, a chocolate shop, and a beauty salon—on each side of the walkway.

And then there is this: Every fourth person here is in a wheel-chair. State-of-the-art wheelchairs. Motorized wheelchairs, three-speed. It would appear that this complex includes housing for the physically challenged, and I ponder how that includes my love. True, he is a near-perfect physical specimen, but, as I have noted to him more than once, "Oh darling. You do need time on the couch."

He owns two of these Olympic Village apartments. One where he and his family live, and, as an investment, he'd bought a second one—one room, kitchenette, and bath—which his now wife uses as her office. She runs a clipping service, which she started up on her own after she tired of her job as a full-time *Hausfrau*. Before that, she'd been his secretary.

On the other side of the walkway, behind the U-bahn station, is the Olympic Park with its indoor skating rink and swimming pool, trampolines built into the ground, the stadium, an ampitheater, winding walkways where children are roller-blading and biking, and a lake where there are geese and one swan and rowboats for hire.

At a vendor's cart, I buy an ice cream cone. I give the man a ten-Mark bill, which is all I've got on me. He gives me back eight Marks in clear plastic rolls of ten-Pfennig coins. Eight rolls of coins. Ten coins per roll. I take this as an insult.

These insults loom large and entirely eclipse the contrary. With vision skewed, I am on the lookout for bad behavior. I expect these people to be hateful; I want them to be hateful, because if they are hateful then the world makes sense, and when they are something other than hateful, when it happens that someone here is pleasant or friendly, I am disillusioned by the experience. I make excuses for their kindness, as if it were all some silly mistake. I rationalize that the nice man at the kiosk where I buy my *Herald Tribune* must be a Turk.

Near the lake, under the shade of a tree, I sit and eat my ice cream, a scrumptiously creamy pistachio—no skimping on the milk fat here—and I scan the area. Some yards away—is that who I think it is?—I spy HF with what must be his now wife and youngest daughter. I get up and scoot behind the tree, where I imagine myself to be hidden from their view. I am thrilled like a rabbit.

The way an anthropologist observes, I watch him play with the blond child, tickling her as she rolls around in the grass and the dirt. I watch his wife, and although I cannot see her face, I imagine her expression is serene, radiating the warmth that contentment brings on this sunny Sunday afternoon as she watches her handsome husband delight their adorable child. I imagine she is enjoying a kind of agreeability that I have no desire to know firsthand. One man's pleasure etc. etc. Yet, bearing witness to this snippet of family happiness sends a shock wave of anger through me. My sense of justice is aggravated. It's as if I'm thinking that no German family should enjoy such innocence. I try to remember if my father tickled me like that while I rolled around in the grass. I have no such memory.

The blond child is grabbing fistfuls of grass and leaves and showering them over his head. It occurs to me that while I do not envy his wife, perhaps I do envy his daughter.

Fascinating though all this may be, I really should go before he spots me. I'm looking to map out a route from here to the U-bahn station which would preclude the likelihood of being seen by him. For a man who has spent pretty much his entire adult life in a state of adultery, he is sometimes clumsy about keeping cool. I trust myself to walk past them without so much as a backward glance, but I can't vouch for him. He is likely to fluster and panic, which would be the same as a confession.

> *The man who wants to keep his love affair for a long time untroubled should above all things be careful to not let it be known. . . . (Andreas Capellanus, The Art of Courtly Love, Columbia University Press, 1960, p. 151)*

No good could come of that.

> *His affair with the first Sabine ended within days of the end of his marriage. For one thing, without the excitement generated by intrigue and secrecy, there wasn't much allure to a girl who looked like a ham.*

Maybe it's possible to backtrack around the ice cream vendor's cart, and then I see him and his family stand up to leave. I freeze, stilled by grand indecision: to run, and in which direction, or to hide? Only my eyes move, darting frantically in search of cover, and then I see that this family I've been spying on is not HF, his now wife, and youngest daughter. It's some other family. One that could have been his, but isn't. The man is far too short to be HF, and the child is too young.

It's a relief that I won't be discovered, but also I'm disappointed. A secret glimpse into his family life would have been invaluable.

When HF was twelve, still a boy, and his mother was yet again away on a business trip, he went for a hike in the woods with his father and the housekeeper. They are hardy people, the Germans. Hiking, skiing, swimming, biking. Great fans of the out-of-doors. At the end of the three-hour traipse through weeds, mud, and up and down hills and between trees, his father begged off. He'd had enough fun for one day, he said, but HF and the housekeeper forged on. Late in the day when they got back to the flat, they discovered neither of them had the keys. The keys were with his father, who was not at home. Who knew where he'd gone to or when he would be coming back. He often disappeared for stretches of time, hours, days, weeks even. But the housekeeper knew. She wrote an address on a piece of paper, and told HF to go there and get the keys from his father. The housekeeper was an older woman and stout and too pooped from the hike to do anything but sit on the front steps and wait. HF went to the address given to him, a small single-family house made of brick and mortar, and when he knocked on the door, a woman answered. "I'm here to get keys from my father," he said. The woman nodded and beckoned him to follow her, and he did, through the kitchen and into the living room, and there was his father sitting in an easy chair watching television. His shoes were off. It was early television. HF didn't even know what programs they had then. Newsreels, he guessed. He didn't have a television. His mother wouldn't allow one.

Although highly improbable, it would almost seem as if these entanglements with women were a genetically predisposed condition.

HF did not inform his mother in a timely manner of the fact that his marriage to Konstanze was over. It wasn't until he was living in London when his mother called him there, and a woman who was not Konstanze answered the phone, that his mother realized the truth, to which she said, "Well, you've turned out to be just like your father."

It came as quite a blow to HF, that at least in this way, he was indeed a chip off the old block. "It was devastating. I never wanted that," he told me. "I had all intentions of being a very different man from him."

Now it is up to me to find out just what sort of man his father really was.

Chapter Eight

Every reason for fear

क्ष

A s so often happens with the best of plans and good intentions, something goes awry. Well in advance and while I was still in New York, I'd carefully selected gifts to give him on his birthday. I wrapped them in blue paper, and I brought them with me to Munich. Now it is clear that one did not survive the trip. I hear the sound, the tinkling, of broken glass.

I hand him that package first, and I say, "I'm sure it can be fixed, but it's broken for now."

Having given birth to him in the hospital's air-raid shelter dur-
ing a blackout, his mother then kept him, not in a crib or a cra-
dle, but in a laundry basket with handles. That way she could
transport him easily when the sirens went off, which they did
every night, to the basement which doubled as the air-raid shel-

ter for their building and the neighboring ones. It might very
well have been the damp basement air which was responsible
for his contracting a respiratory infection when he was a mere
few days old. His mother and his aunt, who was a physician
but not a pediatrician, took him to the clinic at the hospital.
The doctor in attendance advised leaving the baby there, where
such things were better treated, he said. But his aunt knew all
too well that babies admitted to the hospital in Berlin in 1943
had a way of dying in the hospital. Berlin in 1943 was no time
or place to be a sick baby. His aunt shook her head at the doc-
tor in attendance, and said shame on him for suggesting that a
baby with a cold take up precious space in a hospital when the
brave soldiers wounded fighting for the Fatherland were in need
of the good medical care. She would take the baby home and fix
him up herself.

HF carefully peels away the paper and picks out the shards of
glass, placing them on the nightstand. Then he looks at the photograph in the frame.

"It's Ellis Island," I tell him. "An aerial shot taken on a foggy
night. I'll get the glass replaced and you can hang it in your office,
can't you?"

"Yes," he says. "Thank you." He kisses me before turning his
attention to the second gift. "Oh!" he exclaims. "Oh!" If he were a
teenage girl, he'd be squealing. "Oh, this is wonderful. Oh, I hope
it fits," and wearing nothing else, he slips on the denim jacket
from the Gap.

When he was in New York, he admired those denim jackets
from the Gap as if they were something really special, and now

he is beside himself. "Oh, this is perfect," he fairly gasps, and he dashes to the mirror to admire the figure he cuts. "Oh thank you, Hester. Thank you."

I make a mental note: From now on, buy him clothes.

> *One year for his birthday Konstanze, his now wife, and Bettina each gave him a yellow shirt. Yellow shirts of varying cuts and qualities, but yellow shirts nonetheless. Apparently, yellow shirts were all the rage that year. The one from Konstanze was the nicest of the three. One hundred percent cotton and Hugo Boss.*

I make another mental note: Never buy him a yellow shirt.

Not that it was likely that I would have bought him a yellow shirt, as I think yellow is a fairly atrocious color for clothing.

He kisses me on the mouth and on the neck, and then he kisses me on the forehead, which is like the period at the end of a sentence. "Come on." He takes me by the hand and pulls me up from the bed. "We need to get going. Put on your jeans and your hiking boots."

"Jeans? Hiking boots? Going? Going where?"

"For a hike. You don't have hiking boots? Okay then, trainers will do."

"Trainers?"

"Jogging shoes." He translates from British to American, although there is no need. I know what trainers are. I just don't understand what they have to do with me. "Have you ever seen me in jogging shoes? Or jeans, for that matter?"

In lieu of jeans, which I don't have either because I am not given to casual wear, I put on a skirt, but not a slinky one, because we are going for a hike in the woods. This is how he wants to spend his birthday. Schlepping through the forest.

His car is parked out in front of the hotel. It is a Mitsubishi, a hatchback. He places his gifts on the back seat. As he drives onto Leopoldstrasse, he speaks of a German tradition, how it is customary for married couples to go to the mountains or to the park to walk and discuss things, plans and problems. "Usually, they do this on Sundays," he says.

I tell him that is a Jewish custom too. To walk while discussing matters of importance. How I know this, I don't know, genetic memory or osmosis, maybe. But I speak with authority, as if I were raised with Jewish customs. The longer I stay in Munich, the more I imbue the ways and means of my forebears. It's as if I'm walking backward, which is not an entirely safe way to go. "But our Sunday walks are not limited to married couples." *Our*, I say *our*, the collective *our*, and I tell him Jewish tradition dictates that all weighty discussions on history, theology, politics, be held while walking.

When I was a small child, on Sundays my father and I would drive to a point along the Bronx River where he would park the car. Then he and I would walk the path flanking the river, which wasn't much of a river at all. More like a brook or a stream. There we would feed the ducks. My father, in his three-piece tweed suit, would fling bread crusts into the water, fling them the way a little girl would, because my father knew no sports, not even how to throw a ball. Then when the bread was gone, he would say something weird. Something like *All things are alive, a quote from ze great Spinoza* or *Ze same sun shines everyvhere.* Just something weird and sad like that, and then nothing else, after which we would walk back to the car and drive home. Except for those walks on Sunday, my father drove everywhere. One time my father drove from his parking spot in front of the bakery to another parking spot, two rows down the shopping center lot, to a spot in front of the Baskin Robbins. When he realized what he'd done, that he'd gotten back in the car and driven a matter of a few steps, he nearly exploded with pride. "Look at zis, Hester. Your papa is all American now." He was so happy, and I was so mortified. At what, I wonder. His happiness? Or at that which made him happy? Now when I remember this, I smile too.

"What's so funny?" HF wants to know, and I say, "Nothing. I'm just happy. So," I ask, "is that what you did on Sunday? Take a walk and talk with your wife?" Yet one more thing I haven't told him is how on Sunday I was at the Olympic Park, spying on a family that wasn't his, but could have been his.

"No," he says. "My wife and I have neither plans nor problems to discuss." He so rarely speaks of his now wife, and I am reluctant to raise the subject of her lest I upset the balance. Still, there are things I will need to know, although this question might not be one of them. "Is she at all suspicious?" I ask. "You leave early in the morning. You come home late at night. Isn't she wondering why? Maybe you ought to skip some days with me."

This suggestion is met with an outcry. He accuses me of tiring of him, of wanting to be rid of him. It takes some doing to convince him that this is not at all the case. "Not even a little bit. I'm just concerned about your marriage. Do you think your wife has any idea that something is up?"

"Maybe," he concedes. "If she is aware of anything, it is that I am in a good mood. She would notice that. Bettina," he tells me, "thought my now wife was weak. Spineless."

"Bettina was mistaken," I say, and he agrees. "Yes. It is not like that." His now wife is not at all weak. Rather, she is some kind of saint, and saints are as solid as the marble which memorializes them. Martyrdom is not for the faint of heart. Patient, sympathetic, sagacious, a comfort, and above all, a stoic. Consistently and ridiculously forgiving. An ethereal woman who is all-merciful. A saint. I have to believe this, that she wears Birkenstocks on her feet and a halo over her head. For one thing, saints, for all their lovely qualities, are not dynamos in bed. Also, if she were not a saint, I would then have to conclude that she loves him madly, deeply. Why else would she put up with him? And it is that possibility with which I cannot cope. In that way, I am possessive. Very possessive. I believe, I have to believe, that no one loves him or has ever loved him or ever will love him the way I love him. For our love to go where it has gone, to be what it is, and to maintain its proportions, it has got to be singular. So I anoint his wife a saint, which leaves only Bettina as nemesis.

When Bettina's live-in lover, the one who'd arrived in time for the Christmas season, reneged on his promise to marry her and moved out, HF moved in. He divorced his wife and married Bettina, and theirs was a marriage based on mutual suspicion. He never did trust Bettina. And apparently she never quite trusted him either. Each expected the other to cheat, and as if infidelity were a race, Bettina got there first. According to HF, Bettina is wildly ambitious and competitive. It might very well have been that she simply wanted nothing more than to beat

him to the punch. What she said when she left was that her
new lover was better than HF. "You don't please me sexually,"
she said, "and he does."

"She had to be lying," I conclude. "It's not possible that you
didn't please her in bed." I'm basing this assessment on my own
experiences, although I do warm to the possibility that it is with
me alone that he is so lovely.

"It had a terrible effect on me. When she said that, I lost all
confidence."

Confidence lost, spirit broken, humbled, and head in hand, he
returned to his second wife and made her his now wife. His
now wife neither wounds his pride nor inflates it. Rather, she is
there offering a kind of absolution. They have sex once or twice
a week and never talk about it; not any of it, neither the sex nor
what happened with Bettina.

She does put up with a lot, his wife. A lot more than I'd put up
with, which is all the more reason to be mistress.

Beyond the city, in a suburb, HF drives us to a shopping mall,
which is pretty much identical to the shopping malls of America.
As a rule, shopping malls give me the willies, but I find I am
nearly overjoyed by this one, so happy to see Eddie Bauer,
McDonald's, The Body Shop, as if all the way over here, across
the ocean, I've run into, if not friends, then acquaintances from
home. I imagine darting from store to store to hug the merchandise, to bring familiarity to my bosom.

At a sporting-goods shop, HF is jabbering away in German with the store clerk, and then he asks me, "What size shoe do you wear?"

"Thirty-eight." I know my European size because at home I buy shoes imported from Italy. Pretty shoes with pointed toes and high heels. Not jogging shoes.

I take a seat to try on the sneakers HF has picked out for me. I feel like a child with him picking out the sneakers, and then he gets down on one knee to lace them for me. They are pink, the sneakers. Pink, and they are that fat kind too. I hate them. He adores them. He pinches the toes for fit. "Oh Hester, they're perfect," he says.

"Oh darling, they're ridiculous," I say, but I wear the pink sneakers out of the store. The socks too. Thick socks, black. My slingbacks are in my bag. It wounds my sense of honor to look at my feet so impossibly swaddled.

With one hand on the steering wheel, and the other between my legs, he drives like a cowboy. One hundred, one-twenty, one-forty, one-sixty on the speedometer. I've got one hand between his legs too, and when we've had about as much as we can take, he takes the next exit off the autobahn. Beyond an *Allee*—which is a tree-lined road, the trees tall and thick so that the leaves form a canopy—is a clearing, where he pulls over and stops. The grass is dotted with daisies and thistles. He gets out of the car, and I go to do the same, but he tells me to stay in the car and move the seat all the way back.

When HF and Bettina were married to their previous and respective spouses but having their affair with each other, he

*would drive to a prearranged corner near where she lived. There
she and their (her?) baby would be waiting for him. Bettina did
not bring the baby along so that the supposed father and daughter could bond. At that time, he didn't even know the child was
his (if it indeed is his), although he claims he did know, just not
officially. Bettina brought the baby along because the baby was
the ruse. "I'm taking the baby for a walk," she would tell her husband, and then bundle the kid up and plunk her in the pram,
which she would then push to the appointed spot of rendezvous.
The pram went in the trunk, the baby went in the backseat, and
HF would drive at 160 km per hour to some secluded spot where
they would fuck in the front seat of the car while the baby
screamed the whole time from the back.*

You would think that as an American girl who was born and
raised in the suburbs, land of automobiles and bored teenagers, I
would have had sex in cars dozens of times. But in fact, I have
never had the pleasure because during my teenage years I kept
pretty much to myself, and I'm not so sure I want to start having
sex in a car now. "Let's go over there." I point to a bed of pine
needles between two fir trees that actually looks comfortable, but
because of the incident with the Tick Girl, he categorically
refuses to have sex in the out-of-doors.

Sex in the car is cramped—my pink-shod feet up on the dash-
board—and hurried, but not half bad either, and from there on
we take alternate and scenic routes.

Crossing the border from Germany to Austria is the same as
crossing from New York to New Jersey, as if Germany and Aus-

tria were still one country. We have only to pay a toll, in schillings or Deutschemarks, no matter.

The mountains, the Alps, loom in the near distance, and they are, I have to admit, majestic. Many of the top peaks are snow-capped even now in July. The light reflects pale yellow and shades of lavender as if the rendering of a paint-by-numbers oil set.

Just beyond one of those cutesy Alpine villages where the houses look to be constructed from gingerbread and gumdrops is where we will begin our hike. At the base of the trail, rules are posted, as rules are posted everywhere in Germany too, only these rules are in the language of pictograms: a boom box in a red circle, a red slash cutting across on the diagonal. No boom boxes allowed here. Also no fires. No littering. No dogs. No camping. And then there's a new one on me: In the same red circle as the others, behind the red slash, is a picture of a shoe, a high-heeled pump of the sort I favor. "Look," I point to that one. "No Jewesses allowed."

I have made him uncomfortable. He does not know whether to laugh or not. He is not ready for jokes about Jews. Looking off in the distance, he says, "Ready?" and I say, "Not really," but we set out anyway.

The path winds between the trees. The trail is clearly marked, which is good because this isn't a place where I'd like to get lost in the forest.

Hiking seems not unlike sex in the car. Although I far prefer to do my walking on pavement, this isn't the worst experience. After a while, we come upon a clearing, and only now do I realize we are on a mountain. I look up and up and up, and then I look for a way to keep calm.

I fix my eyes to the ground. My pink sneakers are rimmed with mud. Admittedly, aside from the slight strain on the calf muscles, this, walking up a mountain, doesn't feel like going high up the way, say, taking the elevator to the top of the World Trade Center does. As long as I keep my gaze steady on my feet, it seems as if we are walking along rolling hills, gentle inclines and declines too, and I can live with that. HF walks in front of me leading the way. Then he stops as if he were waiting for me, only he is looking, not behind him, but straight ahead, his hand shield-ing the sun from his eyes, as if he has spotted something other than dirt, rocks, and weeds. Something worth looking at.

I come to his side. "Isn't it beautiful?" he asks, and there, at my feet in pink sneakers, is a fifty-gazillion-foot drop, at the bottom of which is a lake. I am acrophobic. He is soaking up the view, while my legs go so weak as to be unable to support me. I slide to the ground and pull into a fetal position.

HF, somehow, and a marvel all its own, seems oblivious to my condition. As if I were merely taking a rest instead of quaking all over, he urges me onward. "Come on," he says. "Get up. Let's go."

I'm not going anywhere. I'm going to stay put, curled in a ball, and wait for the rescue team to come and get me down from here.

Now that HF is beginning to understand my panic, it amuses him. "There is no rescue team," he says. He crouches beside me.

"Suppose my leg were broken? How would I get down then?"

"I suppose in that case, I would have to go to hospital and get an ambulance and medics with a thingie. A bed on sticks."

I tell him to go then and get the medics with the stretcher.

After much cajoling and many assurances and promises to

hold my hand the whole way down, I eventually stand up. What seemed like rolling hills on the incline is steep on the decline. I take baby steps for fear of losing my balance and tumbling the rest of the way down like an avalanche.

Only when we reach the base of the mountain unharmed do I relax to the point where I can cry. I cry and I make a fist, pommeling him on the arm. He finds all of this, my fear and its release, precious. "Oh Hester." He pulls me to him and hugs me, rubbing my back and kissing the top of my head, as if I were a doll-baby.

But I don't think any of it is cute, and, angry, I pull away from him. "I was scared. Fear is not funny. It was cruel of you to take me there."

"Oh my beautiful Hester," he says. "My beautiful dark-haired Hester. Do you think I would ever let anything happen to you?"

And that question comes between us, as surely as a curtain drawn, and I have to wonder, what if HF and I were to step into an H. G. Wells–type time machine, if we were jettisoned backward sixty years, would he have let anything happen to me then? Would he have kept me safe concealed behind a false wall or hidden away in the root cellar? Or would he have turned me in to the authorities? Would he have renounced me in a heartbeat, and then would he have wept, wept copiously, "Oh my beautiful Hester, my beautiful dark-haired Hester"? And so I tell him, "I don't know." I say, "I don't know if you'd let anything happen to me or not. What would you have done?"

He understands that I'm no longer talking about falling off the mountain, and he says, "How could you ask such a question?"

How could I not ask such a question is more like it. How

could I be in this country, day after day confronted with that past and these people—they're not all dead—and given who I am and given who he is, how could I not wonder? "I was scared," I say, and he says, "I know. But you have no reason for fear."

But he is wrong. Very wrong. There is every reason for fear.

On the way back to Munich the traffic is thick, and so is the tension between us. The cars go slow and stop and start, but mostly stop. I change shoes, the pink sneakers go in the bag, the slingbacks on my feet. He is cursing the traffic with a frenzy and slapping his palm against the steering wheel as if that will get things going, and he shouts, not at me but at the situation, "Oh for fuck's sake! Move!"

I am on the verge of telling him, so for fuck's sake, we are stuck in traffic, what's the big deal, when it occurs to me. The cavalier attitude about time spent with me has been for my benefit. His wife's finding out about us worries him more than he lets on. His family, no doubt, is expecting him home. It's his birthday, and they probably have plans. He likely arranged to be with them at a prescribed time, which doesn't allow for a standstill on the autobahn. So profound is the standstill that he turns off the ignition. Why waste gas, why pollute air to go nowhere? I do give them credit there, the Germans. They really are Green, taking care to pollute as little as possible, and they recycle in a way that could be considered mass obsessive-compulsive disorder. Eighteen trash bins per household. I've seen them peel apart the paper backing from the foil on a gum wrapper because foil goes in one container and paper in another. Their tampons are without applicators, not even the cardboard kind. And, as mentioned, no bags with purchases and no air-conditioning. So we sit here baking in the car, in an uneasy quiet.

By the time we reach the city limits, I can barely breathe from the heat and the contention between us, so I say, "Why don't you drop me off right here? I'll take the U-bahn back to the hotel."

As if relief were a beam of light, it washes across his face. My hotel is in the opposite direction from the Olympic Village. "Are you sure you don't mind?"

"I don't mind," I promise him. I wish him a happy birthday, and he says, "Hester, I love you. You've got to believe me."

"I do," I say, and I do believe that he loves me. Love was never at issue here. Gathering my things—pocketbook and sneakers—I get out of the car on Schellingstrasse, which is a reassuring place to walk if only because it is pavement.

Number 50 Schellingstrasse is where the National Socialist Party was headquartered until 1931, and there over the doorway the carved eagle remains, albeit without its head and swastika. Next I pop in at the Schelling Salon, another Hitler hangout. It seems that the way *George Washington Slept Here* up and down the Eastern Seaboard, Hitler parked his butt all over Munich. Only there are no commemorative plaques indicating this because the good Germans fear the making of shrines. They fear that neo-Nazis and old Nazis alike would make Hitler's places into holy places. Therefore, where Hitler lived and worked and spoke and played and ate and shat and died is unacknowledged but common knowledge fully documented in the history books and guidebooks too.

Also unacknowledged is this: Like HF, but not at all like HF, my father was born in Berlin. It is likely that I am the only person alive who knows this, but I keep that bit of history to myself, where it sometimes burns, as reproach is wont to do. Other than their birthplaces and a few stories, I know so little of my parents' lives before they came to America. Was my mother, as a young girl, a member of the *Blau-Weiss* club, the Jewish version of the *Wandervogel*, that German back-to-nature youth movement? Did she ever tra-la-la through the Alps? Sing songs around the campfire like other Bavarian girls? It's impossible to imagine my mother reveling in the out-of-doors as it is impossible to imagine her as carefree. But she must have been carefree at one time. Of my father's youth, I know only this much: Attempting to solve Schrödinger's equation—the quantum mechanical picture of the atom—in application to carbon, my father was a favorite student of Fritz Haber, the chemist and Nobel laureate, at the esteemed Kaiser-Wilhelm Institute for Physical Chemistry. Haber, a Jew, applied for "retirement" in 1933 and strongly urged his Jewish colleagues to emigrate. In the hope that his learning precisely how the carbon electrons are distributed would be merely a dream deferred, my father eventually found his way to America, where he rose to the rank of high school chemistry teacher, which, I suspect, was not a dream deferred, but rather the bitter disappointment of a dream defeated.

Almost no daylight remains, and I am tired, but I make my way over to Königsplatz for a gander at the Führerbauten. The massive pair of neoclassical buildings were designed as National Socialist headquarters and were built to last the same thousand years as the Reich. Although the Reich fell short some 988 years, the buildings still stand. I walk up to the one on the right side of Königsplatz. I am surprised to find the door is not locked.

The former Nazi headquarters is now the Hochschule für Musik und Theater, and perhaps because it is summer and the students are away or because it is evening, it is deserted. All alone, I stand in the lobby, dwarfed by the sheer size of the place. Front and center, I am faced with a brown marble staircase that leads to two tiers of balconies so that Nazis could step from their offices, as if from the summit, and look down at whomever was coming up the steps. Thirty-six steps. I count them as I ascend, but slowly as if headed for an appointment I am reluctant to keep. There is a chill in the air here, and the landing at the top of the stairs seems higher up than any mountain.

The office doors are oak. It is very possible that behind one of these oak doors my grandfather once stood, trembling most likely, with all the necessary papers in hand, papers that needed a stamp of permission in order to get his daughter, my mother, out. Permission that could be granted, or denied, on a whim.

I hurry down the stairs and out the door. It is dark now, and if I didn't love HF so much, if I were able to remain angry with him for longer than two hours, which I'm not, I don't know that I could last five minutes more in this country.

There is every reason for fear.

Chapter Nine

Those three monkeys

A t the branch library on Hohenzollernstrasse, on a metal chair at a beige Formica table, I sit flipping through pages of a book I can't read, looking at the pictures of Freiburg, HF's alma mater: rickety streets paved with cobblestones, medieval fortresses refurbished as classrooms, dueling students (apparently some kind of fraternity ritual).

⚔ *Ask K: did HF play Zorro with the other boys?*

After checking my watch yet again—it's 12:19—I return the book to the librarian at the front desk and head out to interview my lover's first wife.

Even though HF has assured me there is no reason to be, I'm as nervous as aspic.

Interviews I Will Need to Conduct

In Munich:

1) Konstanze

2) Now wife (her name?!)

3) Bettina

4) Josef and his wife (her name?)

5) Two eldest daughters

   a) Rebekka and her husband (his name?)

   b) Barbara

6) Frau Doktor Schmidt

7) Frau Doktor Frisch

8) the quack who treats his headaches

Elsewhere:

1) His father's widow or whatever she is (is she still alive?)

2) Eckie

3) the Nazi aunt's daughters*

4) the blind aunt

5) Ulrike (the blind aunt's daughter)

6) the first Sabine

7) the Tick Girl

   *One of the Nazi aunt's daughters lives in America, in Texas, he thinks. When HF and his mother (and his father too, in a fashion) lived in Frankfurt, that cousin came to stay with them for the purpose of marrying an American GI, but first she had to meet one. It was far more likely that she would get herself an American in Frankfurt, which was occupied by the American forces. The potato farm where she lived with her mother and sisters was in the British zone. To camouflage

what she was up to—husband hunting—she took HF along to the pubs frequented by the American servicemen. "The kid wanted to see the soldiers," she shrugged to imply that she was indulging the kid, and then she flirted up a storm with anything in khakis, all of which resulted in decided conflict for HF, who was not so much of a kid, but thirteen years old. Hormonal flare-ups left him longing to kiss his cousin himself, rather than stand around with his hands in his pockets while she necked with American soldiers. On the other hand, those Americans represented everything that was cool, and one of them, a private named Duffy who looked like one of the Seven Dwarves, only taller, invited them to the Idle Hour Cinema, the movie theater inside the compound where Germans could go only as a guest of an American military man. The film showing was Abbott and Costello Meet Dr. Jekyll and Mr. Hyde, and popcorn littered the floor like bits of rubble in the aftermath of the bombs. His cousin whispered to him to say nothing of this, don't mention the mess the Americans made with their snacks for fear of offending Herr Duffy. On Christmas of that year, the daughter of the Nazi aunt invited her American GI to the Falks' flat for Christmas dinner, to which he brought a gallon of ice cream. Three stripes, one each of vanilla, chocolate, and strawberry, which was an unheard-of thing in Frankfurt in 1956, and marveled over for many years after.

HF set up this interview for me, made all the arrangements. "I told her you are a Jewess," he said, "so she'll be on her very best behavior. I told her you are a Jewess writing a book on postwar German men, and she is very excited to meet with you."

Anxiety has resulted in my being early for this appointment, and I am hungry too, and so I pop into a shop on Ameliastrasse to buy a chocolate bar. Savoring the chocolate, I let it dissolve on my tongue as if it were a lozenge. To kill time, I window-shop at bookstores, and I people-watch. Students and tourists and old ladies riding bicycles with the aplomb of witches on broomsticks. Having finished the last bite of the chocolate, I look around for a trash can. But I don't see one anywhere, so I put the empty wrapper in my purse because I suspect littering here gets you a trial by ordeal—fire or water.

Our point of rendezvous is, to my utter bemusement, Munich's kosher restaurant, which explains the decor. Or rather, the lack of decor, which is clearly inspired by public school cafeterias except there are cloth napkins on these tables. It's as if they used the same decorator as the kosher restaurants in New York, which also have the cozy warmth of industrial feeding zones. The surprise here is that there is a kosher restaurant in Munich and it is crowded.

Konstanze tells me that she was lucky to get us a table. "But I am known here," she adds, as if this dump were Lutèce. Then she asks me, "You are kosher?"

Without thinking I say, "No," only to witness a profound falling of countenance for which I have no desire to be responsible. I aim to fix the damage done. "I am vegetarian," I tell her, "which many Jews believe is the step beyond kosher. That it is more pious." That this is not the reason for my vegetarianism I keep to myself because her rosy expectation has been restored, and it is critical to a successful interview that she be comfortable and off-guard.

Even now, sitting down, it is evident that Konstanze is taller than I am. Her figure is stocky. Solid like a gymnast's. Her face is broad, as is her smile, but her eyes, a watery pale blue, reflect some sorrow and are lined with crow's-feet. She and HF are the same age, but she hasn't held up as well despite that she dyes her hair to cover the gray, which is obvious because she is in need of a touch-up.

I did bring my tape recorder, but this restaurant is too noisy for it to be of any use. I'd wind up with tapes of nothing but the sounds of dishes clattering and a general din. I place my note-book and two pens on the table, and right off, as if to rid herself of the weight of it, she says to me, "Do you know about my father?" Or is it, rather and perversely, a kind of boast? Not a boast that her father was a murdering brute, but that because he was a murdering brute, she gets to be something of a victim. A state that renders her special, and therefore, in the final analysis, she prefers having gotten the father she did rather than a benign one.

"Yes," I say, "I know about your father," and it really is not at all clear to me whether she is disappointed or relieved when I tell her that I have no need to discuss her father. That it is Herr Pro-fessor Falk and his family I wish to hear about. "And your mar-riage to him," I say.

She laughs at that and tells me, "We fought like wild boars. No, that is wrong. I fought like a boar and he fought like a mush-room. Once I hit him over the head with a frying pan."

The waitress is at our table, and Konstanze helps me decipher the menu. I get a bowl of cold borscht and an appetizer of chopped egg. "Most often," Konstanze says, "I get the gefilte fish, but today I will have the same as you."

Gefilte fish. She really does want to suffer for the sins of her father.

They were married just over one year when, utterly frustrated and at the end of her wits with him, Konstanze hit HF over the head with a frying pan* just like in the cartoons. She was driven to such an extreme because the frustration erupted with a bang. Mostly their fights were not really fights at all in the traditional sense, because fighting, like tango, takes two. Rather their fights were more like shadow-boxing matches with Konstanze throwing the punches, hurling the barbs and invectives, jabbing, while he just stood there mute. On that day, Konstanze had come home from university to find dirty dishes in the sink, no food in the flat, an unmade bed, and HF playing peek-a-boo with the baby, whose diaper was poop-laden. Konstanze went berserk over his uselessness. She shrieked and screamed and carried on, calling him names and insulting him to such an extreme in the hopes of getting a response out of him, but all he did was stand there, his expression one of pain; not the pain of his failure but the pain of not understanding why she was yelling at him.

> **What is with the head-whomping here? See Thomas Wolfe and Herr Haushofer.*

"It was his mother. His mother spoiled him. She did everything for him, so he could do nothing for himself," Konstanze says, but I'm not so sure that I agree with her assessment. I suspect it goes deeper than that, if it isn't rather the need to have his mother do things for him, things she wasn't always around to do. That he was, and is, perfectly capable of preparing a meal or making a bed, but he wants, oh so much he wants, his Mutti (or Mutti stand-in) to do it for him. "That was the one place where his mother was soft," Konstanze says. "With her sons. Especially with Heinrich."

"And what about with her husband?"

"About him I don't know much. I met him maybe two or three times. He was a man always with the women. Heinrich is very much his father."

Not long after he married his now wife for the second time, HF by chance ran into Konstanze in a bookstore on Ameliastrasse. She scrutinized him, up and down, and said, "You've got yourself a new lover, haven't you?" and he asked, "What makes you say that?" It was his sweater that gave him away to his first wife. "Your sweater," she said. "It's new, and it's not the sort of sweater a man would pick out for himself. It's too stylish for Maria's taste, and too expensive for Bettina's frugality. Your mother is dead, and I didn't buy it for you. So, you must have a new lover."

✻ *Maria = now wife!!!*

Maria. So that is the now wife's name. Maria. That fits. The long-suffering Maria. Saintly Maria. Blessed art thou among women. Maria, and then I tune back to what Konstanze is saying, because I sense something important. "It is my belief," she says, "that Frau Doktor Falk was forever much in love with him. She always referred to him as her husband, *mein Mann*, in German, as if he were at home waiting for her like a good boy instead of going off with this one and that one."

Boy. Not husband or man, but boy, and while I do have to account for English not being Konstanze's native tongue, it is nonetheless an interesting choice. In the final analysis, does it all come down to Mothers and Sons here? Did, indeed, the defeat of two world wars lost back-to-back render the men ineffectual?

An Amazon of a woman who waited forever for the man who deserted her to return, a powerhouse who doted ferociously on her sons, Frau Doktor Falk presents a paradox. Did she, without reservation, love these men in her life? Or did she perhaps, deep down, resent the hell out of them for being her Achilles' tendon?

Our food arrives. The borscht is thin. The chopped egg is, well, a chopped egg. Hard-boiled, chopped up on a plate. "Delicious, isn't it?" Konstanze seems to be enjoying her gruel, and then she says, "I will always be grateful to his mother. It was because of her generosity and encouragement that I was able to complete my studies. My own mother thought I should stay at home and take in sewing like she did." Her own mother thought she should be suitably punished for getting knocked up, for disgracing her family in that way, and yes, I get the absurdity there, that Konstanze should be shunned for getting pregnant before marrying, but Konstanze's father should simply get-out-of-jail-free and go along on his merry way. "Frau Doktor Falk never would have let me take in sewing. She believed women must go to university and have important work."

Just a few days prior to her son's leaving their home in Frankfurt to attend university in Freiburg, Frau Doktor Falk sat HF down for a mother-and-son talk. She told him that if he got a girl pregnant, he mustn't let that ruin his life. Or the girl's life, for that matter.

"So you see"—Konstanze blots her mouth with her napkin—"Frau Doktor Falk was most compassionate of our situation."

To me, it sounds as if Frau Doktor Falk was advocating an abortion, but whatever she was saying, she did put her money where her mouth was. She gave sufficient financial support to the young couple so that neither of them had to leave university. And she was bonkers for her little granddaughter who got her golden hair.

Konstanze reaches into her purse. "Here," she says, "let me show you a picture of Rebekka." She has her wallet out and shows me first the same picture of their daughter that HF showed me. "And this is Rebekka with her husband, Rudolf." Rudolf, it turns out, curiously enough, is a gray-haired gentleman. Rebekka has married a man old enough to be her father. "And here"—Konstanze hands me another picture—"is my son. From my second husband." The son is a boy with acne. "He's been circumcised," she tells me, to which I say, because what can one say to such a statement, "How nice." The next picture she shows me is of three little boys lined up in size order. "Our grandchildren," she smiles.

"Grandchildren? Whose grandchildren?"

"Mine," she says. "And Heinrich's. Rebekka's boys. This one is Georg, and the middle one is Werner and . . ." she is talking while I write.

GRANDCHILDREN???!!!!!!!!!! What?

The coffee is weak and tepid too, and because the restaurant is kosher, we get that awful nondairy artificial cream. Really, what I could use right now is a stiff shot of bourbon—grandchildren— and I ask Konstanze if that's available here, a shot of bourbon.

"Jews don't drink spirits." Konstanze is baffled by my request, and I really hate to burst that dream-Jew bubble of hers, but I tell her, "Yes. We do." As nicely as possible, because she is a decent person, I tell her, "We do what everyone else does. Good and bad." She nods her head, as if to humor me. She's not buying that Jews are merely human, which gives me an opening that I take. "How did Frau Doktor Falk feel about the Jews?"

Konstanze has no idea, to the best of her recollection the subject never came up, and she doesn't know what HF's father was doing exactly in those years either. "It might be difficult for you to understand," she says, "but our parents wouldn't speak of it. And my generation does not have much to say about it either. We're like those three monkeys—speak no evil, hear no evil, you know who I mean. We behave as if we make our guilt go away by ignoring the cause of it."

"That's not as difficult to understand as you seem to think," I tell her.

"But it makes a hard job for finding the truth," she says. "So as far as I know, the Falks had no political associations. Except maybe that business with Josef and the Werewolves, but even that, I don't really know."

A few months after the end of the war, Frau Doktor Falk was back at her parents' house in Saxony. HF was with her then, and Josef too, although that was when Josef had been lucky enough to find work on a nearby farm, so he often wasn't around. One afternoon, Frau Doktor Falk answered a knock on the door to find two officials there with papers for Josef's arrest on suspicion of being a Werewolf.* Four of his friends had already been arrested, all of whom were soon to be given lengthy prison sentences. Frau Doktor Falk told the officials the truth. "He's not here," she said. And then she lied, "He doesn't live here anymore, and I have no idea where he is. I have not seen him in many months." Allowing the Russians time to get in their car and drive away, Frau Doktor Falk hopped on her bicycle and pedaled furiously in a race against time to the farm, where she found her son tilling soil. "You have to leave," she told him. "A mistake has been made. They are accusing you and your friends of being Werewolves. You have to get to the West." She gave Josef the bicycle and warned him to stay off the main roads. It was a long walk from the farm back to the house, and Frau Doktor Falk wept the whole way, wept over what this war had done to her family, torn them apart, rendered them homeless and hungry and in danger, reduced them to people with nothing, trapped her in this hellhole without her husband, and not unlike the fictional Scarlett O'Hara, she vowed it would never be this way again.

*The Werewolves were a ragtag band of young men, boys really,

*who refused to accept Germany's defeat. They vowed to continue
fighting the enemy with terrorism and guerrilla warfare until they
achieved victory and honor was restored to the Fatherland.*

"That is the way Frau Doktor Falk told the story," Konstanze
says. "It is likely to be true enough."

"But was Josef really a Werewolf?" I ask. "Or was the accusation indeed false?"

Konstanze shrugs. "I do not know. Josef is a gentle man, and
broken in many ways. But back then, I would not swear for anybody."

"And what of Herr Professor Falk? What are his attitudes
about Jews?" I ask a dangerous question, one I immediately regret
asking. I'm scrambling for a way to take it back when Konstanze
concludes, "I think he is afraid of them. No. It is that he is afraid
of himself around them. He is afraid that he will say something
or do something that could be considered offensive. So he tries to
avoid them. He is sometimes a coward," which prompts me to
remember to ask her, "At university, was he in one of those frater-
nities that fight duels?"

"Never." Konstanze shudders. "Those groups had fascist over-
tones. Even if he had wanted to, I never would have allowed it."

Out on the sidewalk, as she and I prepare to part company, I
thank her for her time and candor, and ask, if need be, may I contact her again.

"Oh yes," she says. "Please do call me." We say our goodbyes,
and she starts to walk off, but stops, turning back to ask me, "You
are in love with him, are you not?"

I laugh, and I say I am not, but she sees through me as if I were the Visible Woman of high school biology class, as if all my inner workings were exposed, labeled for easy viewing.

"He's going to break your heart," she says. "Not deliberately. But he's going to do it all the same."

Face to face in my narrow bed, I break away from his kiss, and I say, "You're very sexy. For a man with grandchildren. Three of them, no less. Funny, you never mentioned them."

As if *oops! you caught me doing something mischievous and decidedly adorable*, he turns on the smile.

"Three grandsons," I say. I confess I'm getting a kick out of this. "Three grandsons. And why didn't you tell me that you have three grandsons?"

"Well," he says, earnest and sincere, "basically, I don't give two shits for them." A statement which decidedly is one for the *Nutball* section.

If it's done judiciously, of course, a historian may, and often must, interpret a supposed sentiment beyond the face value of it.

"Basically, I don't give two shits for them" (his three small grandsons). Is this to be believed? Why would a man who is positively ga-ga for his own children not give two shits for his grandchildren? First of all, I think he likes them more than he lets on. But perhaps not a whole lot more. For one thing, they are boys. And although they are part of his immediate family, they are not his children, the offspring of his sperm hooking up directly.* But mostly it pains him to think of those grandsons because it means thinking of himself as a grandfather—sweet, kindly, fruitless—and it is to assume he has reached an age

that could be considered old. If you did not know that he was born in 1943, to look at him you would likely guess he was born in '54 or '55. He knows this, that he looks much younger than he is, and he is glad of it, relieved. He fears growing old not because he fears death, but because there would be no reason to live if he were no longer desirable and potent.

*As high up on the evolutionary ladder as chimpanzees, but hardly exclusively to primates, it is quite common in nature for the alpha male to destroy all offspring that he did not sire personally. (Check Jane Goodall for study.)

"Do your grandchildren call you Grandpapa?" I ask.

"Absolutely not," he says.

"Do they know who you are? I mean, do they know that you are their grandfather?"

"Yes," he nods, but slowly. "I imagine they do."

"How? How do they know?" I ask, and he tells me, "Instinct, I should think." Then he wants to know, "What other secrets did Konstanze tell you?"

"A story about a sweater some lover gave you," I say.

"Yes." He remembers that business about the sweater, and he adds, "Konstanze gets more like my mother every day."

"Have I ever seen it? That sweater?"

"No," he tells me. "My now wife put it in the washing machine and ruined it. She's very clever that way. She acted sorry about ruining it, but she did it intentionally."

"Which one of them gave it to you? The Tick Girl?"

"No. One before her. I think I forgot to mention her. She was from Vienna and we used to meet halfway in Salzburg, but that got to be too much trouble, so I forgot about her."

"And what else have you forgotten?" I ask.

He laughs and says, "Plenty, I'm sure. But look who is talking. You," he says, "you tell me so little about yourself. I know almost nothing about you."

Astutely observed, and so very unexpected, my stomach bounces like a rubber ball, but I muster up nonchalance and say, "You never ask me anything." And I love him all the more for rarely asking me any kind of question and certainly not exerting the sort of effort it takes to pry.

"You are right," he says. "I don't ask you much. It's a cultural trait now, this kind of narcissism. We even have a word for it. *Nabelschau.* Navel vision. After the war, we got so much attention for being horrible. We were in the center of things, and where everyone is looking, you've got to look too."

"Sounds good to me," I say, and I slide downward. The other question I have for him can wait.

As he sits at the edge of the bed to put on his socks, I slide over to be near to him.

>   *HF has decreed this the most important rule of lovemaking: When the shoes come off, so must the socks. (File under Nutball.)*

And then I ask, because I do have to know, "Was your brother a Werewolf?"

After moment of pause, HF says, "Half brother. Did Konstanze tell you that too? She's not going to be happy until everyone is found guilty of something."

"She didn't say he was guilty of anything. She said he was accused, and that she didn't know if the accusation was just or not. So I'm asking you. Was he or wasn't he?"

"I don't know." HF says the question remains unanswered because it was never asked. Not by him or anyone else that he knows of.

"Ah, I see," I say, and I recite a piece of a childhood rhyme, "Ask me no more questions and I'll tell you no more lies," and as I finish it—I'll tell you no more lies—I am struck by the vastness of our common ground. There is no denying that *Ask me no more questions* is the rule of thumb that I too have lived by.

Chapter Ten

A mysterious longing

With the black silk scarf I keep draped over the bedpost, he blindfolds me, but not for sex. Still, when you are naked, when the breeze pauses to billow the curtains before gliding over your flesh, when you are naked like that and blindfolded with a black silk scarf, it's hard to care what it is about if it's not about sex. But I go along with him anyway. When he removes the blindfold, I see, on the table where I do my work and eat my dinner, three candles lit. Not birthday candles that go on a cake, but large candles in the shape of cylinders. The candles are white, and the flames are flickering yellow, casting dancing shadows on two boxes wrapped in lilac-print paper and tied with purple ribbons.

Ah Liebeliebeliebe. It is time we went to our little star. The constellation of Cancer (under which we both were born) contains

no stars brighter than those of the fourth magnitude, but in 125
B.C. the Greek astronomer Hipparchus discovered that the sun
was among the stars of Cancer at the summer solstice, which
marks the longest day of the year. I love you. (Letter #89 to the
author from HF)

Our birthdays are but eight days apart.

"Happy birthday." He kisses me, chastely. "Happy birthday, my
Hester," he repeats, and then tells me to make a wish, blow out
the candles, and open my gifts.

The larger of the two boxes contains a chain-link belt, gold-
tone, which he puts on me so that it drapes below my hips, as
if I ought to have a ruby snug in my belly button. He steps
back to study the effect, which pleases him. "Yes." He rubs his
hands together. "Yes, this is how I imagined it would look on
you."

The second gift is a necklace, a choker of solid silver, ham-
mered, that rests on my collar bone. There is, apparently, a theme
to these gifts. These are the sorts of accessories worn by Bathsheba
and Salome.

He likes the look of the necklace on me, as well. "It goes so
nicely with your black hair and dark eyes. It's exotic." Exotic
erotics. Like Bathsheba, like Salome. He believes that Jewish
women sizzle. This much I have figured out. "Oh, look. I'm getting all hard," he says, he laughs. He gets such a bang out of that,
out of his erections.

From another letter (#74), his salutation read:

xoxoxoxoxooooOOOps! Getting hard again.

Taking me by the hand, he leads me to the bed. And the earth moves. I am not exaggerating. Like the parting of the Red Sea, the burning bush, light, something of enormous proportion and significance. As if sex with him were a kind of baptism, a ritual dunking into the *mikvah* bath from which I emerge a changed woman.

And I am a changed woman, in more ways than one. Such as: that I love him as I do, how complete I feel in his arms. Complete, as if fitting in the last piece of a jigsaw puzzle, a solid blue piece set into place with a snap, making whole the sky above the barn.

Another change, previously noted but growing more and more acute day by day, is my awareness, consciousness, of my heritage. I have heard Jews such as myself—that is to say, marginal, by birth alone—say the same thing after a trip to Israel. That three days in Israel and bam! there is an urge to *daven*, an inclination to answer questions with questions, and the stirring of memory that had been dormant often for generations. I have no urge for piety, but from the periodic tweaks and twinges of some weeks ago, there is now a sensation with me always. Like a dream that won't entirely fade, a patina from another world clings. I walk the streets here as a Jew. I'm a Jew in a café, a Jew in the library, a Jew in the supermarket as surely as if I were branded with a yellow star. But, unlike loving him, this particular transmutation I don't announce, even though HF might, in fact, be pleased by it.

On the Jewish subject, he has gone whole hog from his absolute inability to mouth the word *Jew* to wallowing in it. Now he boldly ventures into all things Jewish. He wants to have talks about Jewish history and theology and about the German Jews. He wants to take me to related places where I don't want to go.

He wants to take me to monuments and shrines of commemoration and exhibits of Jewish art, as if I am his ticket in. As if he is on the right side of the fence because he is with me, as if being with me legitimizes his being there. I don't want to go to any of these places, and I did go only when he pulled a fast one, pretending that we were taking a walk to nowhere special. When we got there, which wasn't really a *there* at all, but rather an open space, he told me that this was where the largest synagogue in Germany once stood. "They tore it down to make a parking lot," he said. "They claimed they needed more parking for all the cars." By *they* he, of course, meant the Nazis. Now, no cars park in that open space. All that is there is a bronze plaque fixed on a block of granite.

There is much talk in Germany these days of the plans for the Holocaust memorial in Berlin. HF is all for it because he says it's right, how could we deny the Jews such a thing, and he refuses to consider otherwise. I am dead set against such a memorial. "Memorials memorialize nothing," I said. "A hunk of marble or bronze and soon enough there is pigeon shit all over it, and no one stops to look and those few that do are never those who ought to. A memorial will do nothing," I argued, "but allow some politician to pat himself on the back."

"Maybe," he said, "but it's still better than not having a memorial."

The truth is that no matter what they, the Germans, do, it will be the wrong thing to have done. Either way, these people can't

win, and somehow I feel that is justice. That's how it should be—
that nothing can make it right.

These people. My people. So new to me, and, frankly, it's
exhausting. So the hell with *these people* and *my people*. At this
moment in history, it is only HF and me, and he is taking me out
for lunch for my birthday.

I get dressed and deliberate whether to wear the gold-tone
chain-link belt or the silver choker. As lovely an ensemble as they
made when I was naked, they don't work together with clothes
on. Not that I would stand out in a Munich crowd if I weren't
dressed with panache.

A word about the clothes here: frumpy, boring, without distinct style except for the men wearing lederhosen with knee
socks and women in the dirndl skirts and puffy blouses. Initially I
assumed these men and women so absurdly attired were waiters
and waitresses and tour guides wearing Bavarian costume to
tickle the tourist trade. Practically on every street corner is a shop
selling such get-ups, all adorned with embroidered edelweiss. *Trachten Mode*, it's called, and it is pricey, and I laughed as I imagined
silly tourists, Americans most likely, buying this stuff, laying out a
pretty penny for it, only to get it home and ask themselves,
"What the fuck was I thinking when I bought this?" I imagined
the lederhosen and the puffy blouse in the back of the closet
alongside the sombrero from Mexico and the wooden shoes from
Holland and the caftan from Morocco. Only I had it all wrong.
"Most of us find these clothes very comical," HF explained. "But
Trachten Mode is what the die-hard Bavarians wear to parties and
to the opera and to Oktoberfest. When they want to look their
very best." Which is all well and good except when some man

dressed like a storybook elf shakes his head at me. "They are not accustomed to your way of dressing here," HF says. He is referring to the fact that my summer dresses are often skimpy. "They don't approve," he tells me, which is another thing that doesn't add up, because Germans love being naked. They sunbathe nude in the Englischer Garten, which is the same as sunbathing nude in Central Park. Old men, fat women, children sunbathe nude, sit naked in coed saunas, frolic *Freikörperkultur*, naked, through open fields, but I wear a dress showing a little cleavage and it is ogled with stern rebuke.

Okay, there's another example of my willful blindness. What I said about the clothes. Not about the *Trachten Mode*. That, in its full spectrum of ridiculousness, is for real. But what I said about the German women dressed exclusively in frumpwear, that's not so. I see plenty of women with style. It's just that when I do see one, I think, "Oh. She must be French or Italian or Slovenian." I'm doing it even now; as we pass a well-dressed woman on the street, I'm thinking to myself, "Definitely not German," because she wears her scarf draped with perfect *insouciance*. It's as if I refuse to allow them anything lovely.

As we turn the corner onto Franz-Josefstrasse, a drop of rain lands at my feet. I extend a hand, palm up, to feel for more. Or was that an aberrant drip? He, meanwhile, with a fear of getting his head wet that borders on pathological, has opened his umbrella.

He fears getting his head wet because he suffers from headaches. Severe headaches, which he believes are the by-product of wet hair.

P.S. My headache has diminished, but it is still lurking in the bones of my skull. (Postscript to letter #65 to the author from HF)

Although he has never consulted a physician about these headaches, he regularly visits the quack who endorses his wet-hair theory. She treats him with foot massages and recommends inhalation of eucalyptus oil in boiling water, which sounds like a New Age remedy, but more likely it is one of the Dark Age.

There is precedent, early documentation of his suffering similar afflictions, which were similarly treated with home remedies akin to leeches.

Liebe Frau Doktor Falk, He is doing nicely. The cold in his chest is all better, but he now has big red bumps on his head. I had those same things all through my youth. They cause no pain, and I am treating them with the fat from a groundhog. (Letter to HF's mother from his caretaker, June 1946)

We walk for five or six steps more and then he stops to collapse his umbrella. He puts it away in his briefcase because, although there are intermittent drops of rain posing danger, no one else on all of Franz-Josefstrasse has an umbrella out.

"Ah darling, you slay me," I tell him, and love rushes over me the way embarrassment does, in a flush.

This restaurant is the sort of place where ladies lunch. The chairs are dainty with curlicue legs and velvet seat cushions.

The tablecloths are linen and the napkins are folded like origami swans.

Yesterday we had lunch at one of those Bavarian pubs festooned with animal carcasses. Antlers and skins mounted on the walls, and the table next to ours was the *Stammtisch*, which is the table reserved for the regulars to sit and talk politics. These regulars, four of them, were old men. Eighty if they were a day, and I didn't need to calculate to know that they were of age back when.

When I see the old people here, I try to fathom them. What truly confounds me is the love that the people had for Adolf Hitler. And he was loved. Loved. Loved like a father or a favorite uncle or a dreamboat.

The 19th of April 1941, my niece Ulrike was born. At the hospital, it was suggested to her mother, my sister, that she hold back her labor so that her child would get born on the 20th of April and become a Führer-child, but as a doctor herself, she knew this was not possible. (From the memoir of Frau Doktor Falk)

Forget the message, and even if you could get past the fact that he was plug-ugly, you still had to contend with the shouting and shrieking and wild gesticulation and spittle spraying from his mouth, and he was flatulent to boot. Who could have loved him?

As early as 1926, Goebbels described his Führer as "the fulfillment of a mysterious longing." (Ernest K. Bramsted, Goebbels and National Socialist Propaganda 1925–1945, Michigan State University Press, 1965, p. 199)

What sort of people were inspired to love such a man? And what sort of women, and men too, desired to press their lips to his?

Having heard Hitler speak, also in 1926, a former aristocrat claimed the speech itself made no impression, but nonetheless he let go with "a liberating scream of the purest enthusiasm discharged under the unbearable tension as the audience rocked with applause." (Peter Merkl, Political Violence Under the Swastika, Princeton University Press, 1975, p. 106)

I mean, come on, really, we've all seen the mustache.

As if it were inborn proclivity, I sniffed the air between our table and the *Stammtisch*, as if I could determine which way the winds were blowing. "Nazis," I said under my breath, and HF said I ought not to rush to judgment. "I understand the tendency to do so, but for all we know, these men were part of the resistance. Just because they are old enough to be guilty doesn't automatically mean they are guilty. There was a resistance," he said, as if I'd never heard of such a thing.

My secretary Ilse was very intelligent, but she had been run over by a tram. A cripple didn't count for much in those years. Ilse hated them [National Socialists] for that. She was an angry woman. All close human contact was blocked by a glass wall. I sensed her Communist attitudes, but I avoided any political conversation with her because if I had known officially I would have had to let her go immediately because of the very strict rules. Ours was an office where the boss was a Nazi with a low number. I was able to ignore her careless remarks, which *increased with frequency and venom as the days marched on. So in fact the Nazis didn't harm her, but when the war was over and she tried to get to the other side, I heard that she got shot probably* by the Russians. (From the memoir of Frau Doktor Falk)*

> **Probably or probably not. I've not yet found evidence to support this claim either way.*

"Maybe their age doesn't guarantee their guilt," I said, "but it doesn't mean they're not guilty either. And statistically speaking, I'd put my money on their swastikas."

On August 19 [1934], some 95 per cent of those who had registered went to the polls, and 90 per cent, more than thirty-eight million of them, voted approval of Hitler's usurpation of complete power. Only four and a quarter million Germans had the courage—or the desire—to vote "No." (William L. Shirer, The Rise and Fall of the Third Reich, Simon & Schuster, 1960, pp. 229–30)

HF told me I was being too harsh in my blanket condemnation. "This is never to excuse the guilty, but most people didn't know what was happening," he said. "You have no idea how bad it was for the German people in those years. They worried about feeding their families. They worried about bombs dropping on them while they slept. They weren't thinking about the Jews. When I was a child, all they talked about was the bombings. Bombs raining on the cities. That's how they told fairy tales. Little Red Riding Hood was walking through the woods when a bomb fell on her head."

The First War didn't mean so much. There were no bombs then. At school we had a map with colored pins placed where we had victory. We wore wooden sandals, and we were saying farewell all the time. (From the memoir of Frau Doktor Falk)

"The bombings were not the be-all and end-all of the war stories." I got huffy, as if he had no right to terror. "And why are you defending them?" I asked. "You ought to be defending me."

"Defending you from what?" he wanted to know, but I could not manage an answer. I couldn't tell him I was thinking about how his people had wanted my people exterminated like ants, and about what I really fear, that if you hate, hate so viscerally, how can you, in the blink of an eye—and in the scheme of things, sixty years of history is merely a blip—simply stop? How can you one day want somebody dead and the next day say, "Oh, forget that. It was nothing." How I am afraid that this hatred, although outlawed and suppressed, was nonetheless passed along to the next generation, as surely as the blue eyes and a love of nature, and how I am afraid that what I'll find is that for which I am looking.

Rather than exploring this on any kind of personal level, I paraphrased for him a theory proposed by Thomas Kuhn about scientific progress: The only way in which new theories get accepted is that the adherents to the old theories die off.

"What new theories do you mean exactly?" he asked, and I said, "That Jews are just like everyone else."

"But you're not like everyone else," he said. "You're better than that."

Such are the matters with which I must contend, but not now.

Now, with HF, in this frilly restaurant, I prefer we keep our talk as airy as the lace curtains at these windows.

Other than the waiter, HF is the only man in the room. "Your presence is causing quite a stir," I tell him. "The rooster in the henhouse and the girls are all aflutter."

Oh, how he basks in the predicament of such a situation.

We drink prosecco, which is a kind of sparkling wine, and for me he has ordered a fruit salad. I take a plump berry between my fingers and feed it into his mouth. The two women at the next table watch us, and they smile at him, and I say, "Look at that. Those women smiling at you. Well, who can blame them? You are so handsome."

"Oh," he says. "You do puff me up. No woman ever said things like that to me. Except my mother. Sometimes I suspect it is part of a plan you have."

> *Hester Liebste, You are becoming more of a mystery to me everyday [sic]. You are very much an intellectual, emotional, even moral challenge. (I suspect that is part of your seduction strategy.) But to love you probably means not to analyze you at all (nor my own motives for that matter). I know there is something beyond all reasoning in my feelings for you, and I'm very glad you woke it. I'll give in if you want me to, Liebe. (Letter #9 to the author from HF)*

"What sort of plan?"

"Oh, I don't know," he says. "Puff me way up so that when you drop me, the fall will be that much greater."

"You don't trust me?" I ask, and he says, "Not entirely."

"You don't trust *me*?" I am slightly incredulous, but not entirely incredulous. If I were German, I might be inclined to watch my back as far as Jews are concerned. I might fear retribution, revenge. And he is on the money insofar as I do have a plan.

My plan: My plan is to puff him up. Way, way up. All the way to the sky, and he will need me to keep him there just as sure as a balloon needs helium to float.

After walking back to his office, we part company. Instead of going to the library or to my room, I decide to fritter away the rest of the day. I head for the old part of town.

On Sendlinger Strasse, I enter a small jewelry store. As I've come to expect, the shopkeeper is somewhat less than affable. She keeps her eyes hard on me and her arms crossed over her bosom, which I've concluded is the national stance. I am scanning the cases—a row of bangle bracelets, earrings set with pearls, thin chains from which hang small gold hearts and crosses—looking for something I might like when my eye clicks, like a camera's shutter, on a Star of David. Six points and otherwise unadorned, and not something I would have ever worn. It is the oddity of finding it here that induces me to ask to see it close up, but just like that, this bitch behind the counter shifts into nods and smiles and genuflections, and she throws in the chain for free.

With my Jewish star dangling from the chain and resting just above the swell of my breasts, I go to a café for a coffee, where my cup is refilled twice (!) without my having to gesticulate for it.

On the U-bahn, my Jewish star acts something like a rope of garlic in a crypt full of vampires. Not that anyone is actually backing off in terror. Nor am I in any danger, at least not physical danger. It's another kind of danger. A circuitous danger. Apparently, being a Jew here confers a kind of status, which is bizarre, but appears to be so. Jews have flip-flopped from persecuted to exalted. As if, like Konstanze, all the Germans are atoning for Nazi fathers. There is an obsequiousness to their smiles. I'm not sure if I like the effect or not. Power is always a mixed blessing, and the thing with flip-flopping is how easy it is to flip-flop back again.

It's more than I can bear, the weight of this star. It involves far too much responsibility for the likes of me. I unhook the clasp, and the Star of David slips into the waiting cup of my palm. And in that instant, as if I'd been wearing a yoke or an albatross, I am unburdened. I am just another woman on the U-bahn. But when I close my fingers tight, the star's six points dig into my flesh, a gentle enough, but adamant, reminder.

Chapter Eleven

His mother exaggerated

ith my notebook and a cluster of pens out on the table, I've been waiting ten minutes now in the appointed place—La Bohème, an apparently Italian restaurant on Türkenstrasse (I have no explanation for the international incongruities). I keep my eyes fixed on the door, although no one has come in since I arrived. It's likely that I am in the process of being stood up, when a woman seated at a table across the room stands and makes her way over to me. "Frau Doktor Rosenfeld?" she says.

"Yes?" I wonder who this is, and how this person might know me, and she says, "I thought that must be you." She proffers a hand and introduces herself, "Bettina Grasser," and I nearly swallow my teeth.

Here's the thing: HF has repeatedly described her to me as beautiful with a face fashioned after Roman works of art, and so

I'm thinking along the lines of Botticelli's Venus or Michelan-
gelo's, but her face is like Roman art only if you're picturing a
bust of Augustus Caesar with the hooked nose and fatty pockets
under the eyes as well as the jaw. Also HF said her hair is blond.
This woman has hair the color of rat fur, and although I otherwise wouldn't mention it, but because I was led so far astray, I
feel compelled to mention that she is homely like a crone. All
she's missing is the osteoporosis. And because I can't seem to
stop myself, I must note how her skin looks as if touched, it
would squish like marshlands. Her breasts, real big ones, have
drooped so significantly that her nipples are parallel to her navel.
She is in dire need of a good brassiere.

She is very tall, thin, and—breasts aside—angular, and maybe
Konstanze is the one who knows him the way his mother knew
him, but this is the one who looks like his mother looked. Only
more so, like his mother exaggerated.

Recovering from the shock of her—this is Bettina—enough to
say, "Yes, yes. Please sit down." I get up to pull out a seat for her.

He was right about one thing, though—she has no good bum.
Flat as the tabletop, and she's wearing pants.

Along with a good bra, she ought to invest in some new cosmetics. The thick, black eyeliner she wears is cracked and chipped
like old paint. Clumps of mascara blight her eyelashes, and her lipstick—a coral red decidedly not her color—is feathering.

> *He [Hitler] charmed everyone with tales of his youth, until he*
> *noticed lipstick on Eva's napkin. Did she know what it con-*
> *sisted of? Eva protested that she only used French lipstick made*
> *of the finest materials. With a pitying smile Hitler said, "If you*

women knew that lipstick, particularly from Paris, is manufac-
tured from the grease of waste water, you certainly wouldn't
color your lips anymore." (John Toland, Adolf Hitler, Double-
day, 1976, p. 740)

Some women might be relieved, delighted even, to find their
rival so hard on the eyes, but that would be the shortsighted
view. And yes, it could be said that there is something admirable
to HF's character in that he could, and did, fall in love with an
unattractive woman, and yet consider her beautiful. It even
speaks of a kind of depth, an emotional maturity, on his part, that
he is not one to fall for merely a pretty face. Fine. All well and
good. But, long after their love is supposedly dead and gone, that
he continues to describe her as beautiful, well, that is not well
and good. Too easily that could mean he is in love with her still.
Dizzy in love, and under a sort of Midsummer Night's spell,
because what other explanation could there be for this utter lack
of discernment? Nothing else makes sense.

Jealousy spreads through me the way blood pumps. The heart
is the point of origin and destination, but it courses through
every artery, vessel, and vein en route. There is no way to control
it, to direct it, or to stop it—short of death.

. . . love cannot exist without jealousy. . . . (Andreas Capel-
lanus, The Art of Courtly Love, Columbia University Press,
1960, p.102)

Moreover, I can't compete with her. I wouldn't know how.
Nonetheless, HF has cautioned that Bettina will try to compete
with me. "She will do whatever you do, and more so because you

are a Frau Doktor from New York. She is very impressed with New York, but envious too. She will try to prove herself more sophisticated than you." He meant this to be a warning of some sort, but I'm going to attempt using it to my advantage. While we are pondering what to drink, I make mention how martinis are in vogue in New York. "Everyone in New York is drinking martinis these days, but only the most fascinating people drink the martini in the afternoon." I wonder if she can tell how utterly fake I sound, or does posturing get lost in translation?

I order a martini with an olive for myself and a mineral water. It's an old ploy, that with the intent of remaining sober, I will only pretend to drink the martini, while she gets, if not drunk, then at least tipsy. I'm counting on the hooch to act as sodium pentothal.

She orders a martini *mit* two olives.

I could conclude this interview now before it's even begun and consider it a success in that I've learned plenty already, but I stay for one critical revelation more: the truth about the child, whose child she really is.

The child was three years old when Bettina first told HF that he was the biological father. This bit of news—coincidence, no doubt—was revealed to HF on the same day that Bettina's husband, the child's other and legal father, left her for good. HF, who would like to have fathered all children, insists Bettina would have no reason to lie about such a thing, but there are three obvious reasons: 1) to manipulate HF into marrying her, 2) to collect two stipends of child support (which indeed she does collect; HF gives her money for the child on the QT), and 3) it's a way to keep HF connected to her forever. Plus, he has said it himself, she's a notorious liar.

This morning, before he left me, HF said, "She will either tell you nothing or she will tell you lies."

It would seem he knows of what he speaks. "I do not think I will be of much assistance to you," she says to me. "I do not know Herr Professor Falk very well."

Toying with my drink, I smile at her and say, "You must know him to some degree. After all, you were married to him."

She takes a sip of her martini. "But only briefly. For two or three months. It was a mistake."

"Oh, I thought it was closer to a year."

"Yes. Maybe. Perhaps. Perhaps I try to wipe it away from my memory. Always he was a stranger to me."

"But you knew each other for a long time before you married?"

After another sip of the martini, she says, "Only professionally. From university."

"So how did you come to marry someone you barely knew?"

"It was, how do you call it, world-wind. Fast. We meet one day. Three days later, we are married."

"Whirlwind," I tell her. "But wasn't he still married to Maria then? Didn't he have to get divorced first?"

Before she answers, she goes for her drink. The pattern emerges: Like the poker player's tell, prior to lying, she drinks, as if the alcohol will fortify her, give her what she needs to prevaricate bold-faced. The bigger the lie, the longer the swallow. She empties the glass. "No. He was not married anymore when we met."

I signal the waiter to bring her a refill. We go through another round of thin answers until she's well into her third martini. Now she's far more talkative, although not talkative about herself. Instead, she wants to talk about Maria. The now wife. The then wife. "She is a mouse," Bettina fairly seethes. "She knows nothing to be a feminist."

"You are a feminist?" I ask.

"Definitely, yes."

✤ *Feminist. More shades of Mutti?*

I ask how she defines *feminist*, and she says, "Maria takes him back time and time again. She has no respect for herself. He had once an affair while we were married." A healthy gulp from the glass and she changes the story. "No. Not an affair. A flirting, but I did not accept it."

If this is indeed a way of life for her—drinking as preparation to lie—it is no wonder that she's got bags under her eyes the size of duck eggs. And is the lying pathological? Is she simply incapable of telling the truth? Or is she hiding something, and if so, what?

"Perhaps it is simply that Maria loves him," I venture, and as if stabbed, experiencing a brief but excruciating spasm of pain, she winces. Then she says, "Who could love him? No one could love him."

"You didn't love him?"

A guzzle of gin gives her strength to say, "No. I did not love him at all. And now I have a much better man. Better in all the ways."

I want to know exactly what she means by *better*. HF has told me that I am *better* than Bettina. "Younger, sexier, a published author, an intellectual. You are from New York, and of course you are Jewish. You are far better than she."

"So falling in love is a matter of credentials? That you simply love the *best* person you can get? What if someone better than me comes along? Is it a matter of trading up?" I asked him.

> . . . *jealousy is a true emotion whereby we greatly fear that the substance of our love may be weakened by some defect in serving the desires of our beloved, and it is an anxiety lest our love not be returned. (Andreas Capellanus, The Art of Courtly Love, Columbia University Press, 1960, p. 102)*

He considered that for a moment, and then he concluded, "There is no woman better than you."

Bettina's concept of *better* isn't all that different from his. Perhaps there is a national standard. "For one thing," she says, "my man is from Hamburg." She says this in a way that I am to understand Hamburg is a posh place to be from, as in New York to say you live on Gramercy Park, for example, lends you airs. "He is younger than Heinrich and he makes many more money. He is boss of a big and important business. And," she leans in close to confide, "he is a good lover." She polishes off the third martini and licks the glass dry. "Heinrich Falk does not know how to please a woman."

"Really?" I say. "That surprises me. Other women have said just the opposite."

"Who said that? Maria?" Bettina is still somewhat in control of herself, but she is also soused. I can see the inebriation in her eyes, how the whites have gone pink and her pupils can't focus. Her speech is slurred and thick. I ask her if she'd like to have one more martini. "That's the American businesswoman's lunch," I say. "Four martinis."

Yes. She will have the four-martini lunch, and I can only hope that she doesn't pass out on me.

Rather than wait for service, I slide my martini across the table to her, and then I inquire as to what business her husband is boss of.

With the not-quite-fresh drink in hand, she says, "An insurance company. He is boss of an insurance company. An international insurance company."

Less than fair beauty, notorious lying, and the feminist identity are not the only traits Bettina shares with the late Frau Doktor Falk. She is also supercilious, an aggrandizing snob. According to HF, Bettina's third husband is an insurance salesman.

I have only one more question for her. "The child," I say. "Your daughter. Is Heinrich Falk the father?"

Bottoms up, when she is done with the drink, she has lost all coordination. "What child?" she says. The glass falls to the floor and it shatters. "There is no child."

. . . there is a story from the country about a gentlewoman who was in the habit of getting up early in the morning. One day she did not get up at her usual time, which caused her neighbor to wonder if she were sick. The neighbor came to see her to find her still in bed and asked her again and again what was the matter. The gentlewoman was embarrassed that she slept so late, and did not know what to say except that she was so heavy with sleep that she could say no more. The neighbor pleaded for the love of God, she should tell her and promised, swore, and vowed that she would never reveal to anyone—not to her father, mother, sister, brother, husband, priest—what she might be told. After such assurances, the gentlewoman was at a loss as to what

to say, and for the heck of it, said that she had laid an egg. The neighbor was indeed surprised and she appeared to be shocked, and vowed to tell no one. Soon afterward, the neighbor left and met another neighbor who begged her to tell her where she had been, and was told that she was with the gentlewoman who was sick and had laid two eggs. She begged of her, and the other promised, that this must remain a secret. The other neighbor met yet a third biddy and in all secrecy told her that the gentlewoman had laid four eggs. That biddy met another and told her eight eggs; and in this way the number multiplied. The gentlewoman got up from bed, and all the townspeople were talking about how she had laid a basketful of eggs. (Le Ménagier de Paris [1393], ed. Baron Jérôme Pichon, Paris, 1846, Tome Premier, p. 180, author's translation)

Having helped Bettina into a taxi to take her home, I walk the couple of blocks to the university, all the while wondering why Bettina denied the existence of her daughter. I can understand covering up the father's identity, but denying the child entirely is extreme, even for a notorious liar. Why would she, why would anyone, deny having a child? And while I could simply chalk it up to a German ability to deny pretty much anything and everything, they, the Germans, usually have a good reason to deny the evidence. HF says the child is sweet and bright, so what is Bettina's problem?

The only explanation I can come up with—one that I know well—is that fearing she would reveal a salient or salacious detail, a detail that could trip her up, embarrass her, she went and buried the whole story. I once committed a similar subterfuge. My first year at college, I was dating a boy who said to me, "I'd love to meet your parents," to which I said, "My parents are dead." Although this is true now, and has been true for many years, it was not true then. But I said it, and then was sickened with dread that to say such a thing is like making a face that could stick, that my parents would die because I said they were dead. Rather than be reminded of what I had done, I simply refused to see that boy ever again.

At HF's office, I find him at his desk. He kisses me quickly, furtively, lest anybody be milling about in the halls. Smooching in the office of Herr Professor is, if not forbidden, decidedly indecent.

I take a seat across from him, and he asks, "How did it go?" and I come out with it. "She's ugly," I say.

> *Dearest Sir, I am letting your grace know that . . . Frau Elisabeth of Hehenlohe sent someone to question me about the kind of gentleman your grace is . . . and asked if I could find out if your grace had any desire or interest in her. . . . They also were concerned if your grace might be put off by the hump. . . . I said that I did not know whether your grace knew that she had a hump. But should your grace meet with her, do take note of the high coat she wears. (Letter to Erasmus von Limpurg from Anna Büschler, May 9, 1521; quoted by Steven Ozment, The Bürgermeister's Daughter, HarperPerennial, 1997, pp. 51–52)*

HF says, "What are you talking about?"

"Bettina. Bettina is ugly. You said she is beautiful, but she's not. She's not even plain. She's ugly."

He laughs. A great laugh, punctuated with a clap of his enormous hands. "Oh, Hester. You are funny."

I beg to differ. "I am not funny. The woman is ugly. Bettina is one of the ugliest women I have ever seen. But you always describe her as beautiful. You must still be in love with her."

He laughs again. "Not even a little bit. I have you. Why would I love her?" he asks, as if love were ever rational, because really, if love were rational, would I be here? "Maybe it's that she once was beautiful," he concludes. "It could be that I remember how she looked then, and not now."

It could be, but I don't think so. Perhaps it's her resemblance to his mother that has tainted his perception. Little boys, I have read, consider their mothers to be the cat's meow, and I suspect he clings to that delusion too. Certainly he has never said otherwise to me.

I never thought of my mother in terms of beauty, nor did I ever consider if my father was handsome or not. It was as if the strange could not be categorized in such known ways. I'm trying now to picture my mother when HF says, "I'm ready to go, if you'll just give me a minute."

He is packing up some books, making selections from the shelf behind the desk. His back is to me, and while he is reading titles, I remember my mother's face, etched with a supplicant's smile, eager to please, and telling me, ten, twenty, eighty times a day, *I love you, mine Hester.* As if she felt unworthy, as if life itself were all she was entitled to, to be alive and nothing else, she never once asked if I loved her. Now I can't remember if I ever said so. I can remember wishing that I didn't love her, and wishing the guilt of that would go away. "My mother was from Munich," I say.

"What?" HF turns to me. "I'm sorry. I didn't hear you. Did you say something?"

And then I can't say it again. I want to. I desperately want to tell him whose child I am. That I was their child, these victims, these soft people who were bullied and humiliated like that scrawny kid in the schoolyard routinely relieved of his dignity along with his lunch money. They were people chased out of their homes and their lives with rocks and sticks and eventually with guns and gas, and I want so much to tell him, how they came to America and tried and tried but no one befriended them, how lonely they must have been. I want to tell him how ashamed I was of them, of who they were and how they got that way. But I can't, and instead I say, "A drink. I could go for a drink."

Chapter Twelve · ·

Near-death experiences

क॰

I t began in Germany, with physics, with Munich's own Werner Heisenberg and his Uncertainty Principle: *The velocity and posi-tion of an atomic particle cannot be known simultaneously because the act of measuring one influences the other.* The anthropologists coined it the Observer Effect to illustrate how the social scien-tist, by the assumedly neutral act of observation, inadvertently alters the behavior and the life of the subject.

In other words, I did not intend for this to happen, but, appar-ently, it has happened all the same.

Simply put, he's been found out. We've been found out. She knows. Maria knows. Although she doesn't know with whom, and according to him she doesn't care with whom, she knows that he's up to his old tricks. And now, for reasons he cannot fathom, she has decided that she is no longer going to put up with it.

We're on the phone. Getting bad news over the telephone, without the reassurances of touch, amplifies the anxieties. Equally disturbing is the blasé tone he is affecting. He sounds as if he deems this catastrophe mildly amusing or maybe mildly annoying, but piffle either way, and certainly not the cataclysm that it is.

"She has been your wife for a total of fifteen years," I remind him. "With whom you have two children."

"Yeah, well, we haven't been very close lately anyway," he says. "We don't talk so much as we used to because the main thing in my life is you. You and the book you are writing, and I don't tell her about any of that. So lately I talk to her only of unimportant matters."

From my vantage point, there was never a whole lot in this marriage for Maria. As best as I can gather, he never treated her very carefully. He acknowledges that for her there were no romantic dinners. She got gifts of coffee-bean grinders (full-pot and cup size) and a digital alarm clock. All the niceties were reserved for his lovers. What he said was, "I never know if she has orgasms with me or not."

"Why don't you ask her?" I said, and he considered that for not more than a few seconds, and then decided, "No."

If I had been Maria's friend instead of her husband's mistress, I would have advised her, "Get rid of him. He's useless." I would have scolded her for putting up with him for so long. I would have told her to quit bucking for sainthood, and go have herself some fun.

"Now what? What's happens next?" I ask, but wishing I hadn't asked, because whatever comes next, I've got a hunch I'm not going to like it much.

"She wants me to move out," he tells me.

Oh, this is not happy news. Not any of it. Our love nest of cards is collapsing, and who knows where we'll land.

> *November 21, 1943*
> *My Dear Sister, We have lost everything. Our flat has been bombed to oblivion. When I returned there to see what I could recover, I found the ice box hanging from a water pipe. It has become difficult to detect the important from the unimportant because everything has become unimportant except survival.*
> *(Letter from Frau Doktor Falk)*

And I curse things for not staying put, as they were, the way I could trust them, but I, a historian, ought to know perfectly well that not much remains constant, and although we often wind up right where we began, a lot happens in between.

Maria has it all worked out neatly. A floor plan for the new arrangement. She will move her office into her (!) living room, and he can have the flat that was her office as his new home.

He may not be the least bit bothered at all this up-ending, but I am on edge, teetering on a precipice of doom. Of all the positions this puts me in, none are comforting. As best as I can figure, there are three ways this can play out: 1) His bravado is false, and he wants desperately to save his marriage. In the effort to do so, he will end the affair with me. 2) Should he decide to stay with me, still he will need to maintain his equilibrium. To do so would entail his getting himself a new wife, which would entail courtship and sex with yet another woman. I could not cope with that, with his dating. 3) Or, in a permutation of his loved ones, as if indeed we all are so easily rearranged like queens on the chessboard, he will want to make me his new wife, which is the most horrid of the possibilities. If I were his wife, who would be his mistress?

"I'm not going to be your wife," I warn him. "Don't get any ideas about trying to turn me into a wife."

He laughs. "Definitely not," he says. "You're not a wife type at all. For one thing, you hardly ever agree with my opinions."

> *Liebeliebeliebe, A woman's spikiness is all in the head and the mouth or the pen. The rest of her is soft and sweet. With men, it is the opposite. They are spiky all over, but mostly soft in the head. (Letter #71 to the author from HF and originally filed under Nutball but perhaps after further analysis not so nutball after all)*

He has put our love in harm's way. I accuse him of that, of playing fast and loose with what is sacred between us. "You fucked up," I say. "You fucked up big-time."

In some convoluted attempt to excuse himself, he tries explaining to me how this has nothing to do with his indiscretions, that he is doing what he has always done. It is Maria who has changed the rules of the board mid-game. The thing about Maria was how he always depended on her divine grace. He relied upon her patience. He counted on her eternal forgiveness, her willingness to wait it out. "Now," he says, as if she were a fallen angel, "she's not acting that way at all."

"She's acting human," I point out.

"Yes," he says. "But I had come to expect more from her, and I feel as if she has let me down. It's this new friend of hers." He makes more excuses for his own foolishness, for his going about with me as if he were impervious and his wife were a moron. "She made this new friend. I don't even know where, but this friend of hers put ideas in her head."

"That's crap," I say. "You have no one to blame but yourself. You were careless, reckless. What did you think would happen? I warned you to be more discreet."

"Oh, this is just great," he says. "My wife throws me out and my mistress is going to desert me."

"A mistress," I remind him, "is contingent on the presence of a wife."

With the idea that we are going someplace swank for our first dinner together in Munich, I'm dolled up like a Kewpie, in a black lace floor-length number, black suede sandals, my toenails and fingernails lacquered fire-engine red. My hair is in a French twist. I'm waiting for him downstairs in front of the hotel. He is coming by car.

Certainly I am able to open the passenger-side door myself, but I wait for him to get out of the car and walk around to open the door for me, because he so likes to do these things. He was raised, conditioned in the near-lost art of chivalry. These chivalrous acts define, for him, the role of the man.

Fashioned as an order of knights, the SS were trained in reno-vated, or copies of, castles that were called Ordensburgs. Later in the war, for a prescribed number of killings, they were *awarded the Ritter Kreuz.* And as if all of it were but another round of Dungeons & Dragons, all those who were awarded the Ritter Kreuz would get a tract of land, a manor, just as the knights did in the days of yore. These manors were all to be in the East, in what was intended to be the former Poland, the former Czechoslovakia, the former Russia. All the more reason to conquer these lands, because a whole lot of Nazis got the Ritter Kreuz.*

   *The Cross of the Knight.

He comes around to my side of the car, where he looks me up and down. "I'm so sorry," he says. "Obviously, I had a different plan. I thought we would have a short dinner and then drive to the lake." Having come directly from carrying cartons and boxes, all day, from one flat to the other, he is wearing jeans, a rumpled shirt, sneakers.

"That's fine," I say. "We'll do that. Give me a minute to change."

"No. Don't." He holds me back. "You look like a princess." He sports a five-o'clock shadow and dark sunglasses, and he tells me, "I stink really bad like an old fish."

Yes, he does stink, but that's okay. "I love it when you are stinky," I say. "It excites me."

The regulations of oFne tenth-century European monastery prescribed five baths for every monk per year. . . . One later commentator derided the Danish practice of bathing and combing the hair every Saturday, but did admit that this seemed to improve Danish chances with the womenfolk. (Robert Lacey and Danny Danziger, The Year 1000, Little, Brown, 1999, p. 121)

Along the way to the Starnbergersee, he is all lit up, as if moving into a new flat were a happening, like a moon landing. "The first thing I hung in my new wardrobe," he says, "is the denim jacket you got me. And I put up three bookshelves, and I got a bed at IKEA and two sets of sheets." The adventure is proving to be almost too much for him. "It's been rather fun. We've been joking and laughing all day. A project brings people together."

He is referring to Maria and himself. They are the ones who have been joking and laughing all day. The two daughters just sat and watched and made comments that ran the gamut from wry to snide to indifferent. "Kristina," he tells me, "very much approves of my moving out."

Kristina, his youngest daughter, age eight, holds a rather low opinion of her father. She is certain that he is a know-nothing and a big pest too. Whenever he nears her, she swats him away as if he were a horsefly or she holds her nose as if he were yeeuck! To the merriment of the others, she mocks him when he speaks and makes faces at him behind his back. That he hasn't been able to, thus far, win her over causes him great joy.

He whistles as he drives, and then he says, "I think you should move in with me." He parks the car by a *Gasthaus* at the side of the road, and I pretend I didn't hear what he said.

Over dinner, he again brings up the idea that I move in with him. "It makes perfect sense," he says. "Why pay for the hotel? You don't even like it there. And we could sleep together every night, and wake up together every morning. Won't that be something?"

Whatever the temptations may be, such a move is fraught with danger.

There's many a dragon that has to be slain before we can be together again. (Letter #84 to the author from HF)

"I don't know if that would be the wisest thing for us," I say.

"Oh please, Hester," he pleads with me. "We'll be so happy."

One thing he is not saying is something I happen to know: He has lived on his own only twice in his life, both times briefly and miserably. And then there is this:

Approximately two years ago or so, during one of those short takes of time when he was mistressless, Maria and their two daughters went on holiday without him. At first, the idea of solitude pleased him; he imagined evenings stretching out long and quiet and he could eat what and when he wanted and read and watch television in peace. But by the fourth day he had gone stir-crazy and perhaps another kind of crazy too, and that night, he claims out of sheer boredom, he wanked off with the intent to taste his own jizz. When that proved to be of some interest, he next urinated into a cup to learn the flavor of that too.

This is not a man who would've survived Walden.

The day after tomorrow, Maria and the two daughters are going on holiday to Greece. He schemes that with them gone, he can sneak me into his new flat, and no one's the wiser. He makes it sound as if he intends to hide me under a haystack or in the attic. And while that, living in secrecy, is a mixed bag of appealing and appalling, it has no bearing on my response. "No," I say. "I can't."

"Why, Hester? Why can't you? Are you afraid that I will have an affair with some other woman? Because I won't. It's different with you."

It isn't other women I am fearing. I fear losing what we have. I fear the unknown. "Think of how awful it would be if we had to discuss which of us is going to clean the bathroom," I say. "And what's for dinner? And what time will you be home from the office, dear? Not darling, but dear. Dear, and all that goes with it."

There are other questions too. Some for which we have the answers and some for which we do not. Such as, not where will I stay in Munich, but for how long will I stay in Munich? My time here was planned to be open-ended, but certainly not infinite. So much hangs in the balance.

"Will you at least think about it?" he asks of me. "You don't have to decide tonight."

I smile weakly, and I pop a piece of pretzel into my mouth.

The Starnbergersee is the lake where Ludwig II drowned or was drowned by political opponents who thought he spent far too much money on fancy castles and foppish clothing.

The sky is dark. There is a crescent moon and night noises, the hoot of an owl, the lake lapping against its edge. Artificial light here and there from restaurants and houses dotting the waterside provide a glow and shadows. We strip off our clothes. The cool air feels nice against my skin, and I ask, "Isn't there some law against swimming so soon after dinner?"

"Only for children," he says, and from off a rock that looks like the drawings of Plymouth Rock, he slides into the black water in a way so as not to get his hair wet. He swims a length in strong, even strokes and then turns around, treading water, and calls to me, "Well, come on."

"It's looks cold," I say.

"No. It's perfect. Come to me."

I have great misgivings about water. I am afraid of drowning. But after the fiasco on the mountain, I also shrink from his thinking that I am an unmitigated coward. So, I devise a plan to go in as far as my ankles and then insist it is much too cold for my blood. Feet first, I ease myself off from the rock, only there is no bottom to touch. I sink like a stone.

Underwater, and I am shrouded in turmoil. My eyes squeeze tight against the wet and the dark and my arms and legs flail against the void. I thrash and claw at the water, as if that way I could pull myself to the surface. But I can't even determine which way is up, and all I can think about is that I am going to die within the next few minutes. I am going to die in Munich. My lungs are going to fill with water from the Starnbergersee, and I will be dead. I can hear my heart pounding, a sound effect to drowning, and then, as if in a tidal wave, I break the surface. HF lifts me onto the rock, where there is land and air. I am saved.

With my knees drawn and tucked beneath my chin for warmth, I sit, and I take deep and even breaths. HF has his arm around my shoulder. "Hester, what happened? You sunk. You went all the way under. You frightened me."

"I frightened myself too," I say, and I chalk up yet another near-death experience. I'm keeping track of them, of all the times I have come near to dying since coming across the ocean. I have not included the near-death experiences that result from sex with HF. I include only those that are not wonderful.

Near-Death Experiences in Germany & Austria

1) Nearly run over by a bicycle on Leopoldstrasse

2) Nearly run over by a bicycle on Franz-Joseph-Strasse

3) Nearly run over by a trolley car at Münchener Freiheit

4) Nearly mobbed by crazed soccer fans

5) Nearly food-poisoned by hotel sisters (bad egg at breakfast)

6) Nearly run over by a bicycle on Wilhelmstrasse

7) Nearly fell fifty gazillion feet off a mountain

8) Nearly run over by a bicycle on Blumenstrasse

9) Nearly run over by a bicycle on Kaiserstrasse

And now, had HF not saved me, I would have drowned in the Starnbergersee.

I've got two choices: Pack up and go home to New York, where there are no lakes for swimming, or I can believe that he will keep me safe.

He holds me, and I am not so scared when he holds me. That ought to count for something, and so when he says, "Hester, please come live me," I rest my head against his chest, and I entrust myself to this philanderer, this rogue, this German, to see that no harm comes to me.

Chapter Thirteen

The view offers some trees

S omehow, my phone bill came to 346 D-marks, although I've called no one except HF at his office. But now that I'm leaving, I'm in a hurry to go, and so I'm not about to quibble. I fork over 350 DM more, and wait for my change. "You are returning to America, Frau Doktor?" the brown-haired sister asks while the blond one counts the money.

"Yes," I say. I'm hardly about to discuss my personal life with the Sisters Grim.

HF's car is parked out in front of the hotel. He makes several trips up and down the stairs with my suitcases, my books, and my computer. He won't allow me to carry any of it. I stand around and wait, useless, until it is time to say fare-thee-well to this little hotel with the sloped ceiling where I banged my head at least once a day. Even so, I'm a bit sad. The close of any chapter, even an objectionable one, is not without a modicum of sorrow, and certainly hours of jubilation were known in that room, and a slender willow of wistfulness ties me to it.

I tell HF how I am reminded of the month I spent at sleep-away camp in the Berkshire Mountains. "The August I was thirteen. I was miserable there. I disliked all sports, and that was how we spent our days. Volleyball, softball, tennis. I prayed for rain. The food was dreadful. The girls in my cabin were twits."

"What is that?" he asked. "Twits?"

"Silly, vacuous, superficial." I define *twit* as best I can given its singularity. "Twits. Every one of them. I shared a cabin with nine twits. All I wanted was for that month to end. And finally it did. And on that last day, I wept. I wept and wept and could not stop weeping."

"Why?" he asks. "Why did you cry?"

"Because," I explain, "I knew I was never going back there. I would never see those particular twits again. It was the most definitive end of something I had yet to encounter."

As he drives, I look out the window. I watch as the tenor of the streets changes from that of a busy city to that of the fringe where desolation encroaches. There are few shops and no restaurants or cafés. It is quiet here. I worry that living in the Olympic Village will be a little bit too much like living in a cul-de-sac in New Rochelle, a postwar place of conformity, a place where you have to commute to get anywhere from there.

In Frankfurt, he and his mother and his often absent father (who moved with them from Berlin if for no other reason than the further west he was, the safer he felt) lived in a spanking-new postwar high-rise. Very ooh-la-la with heat and plumbing and get this—an elevator. The design, the handiwork of the Social Democrats, was practically socio-realist, because they wanted Frankfurt to be a modern city. They were all for cars. But juxtaposed with the progress of these new steel-and-concrete buildings was the debris of war. And as a boy, HF and his friend Dieter roamed the ruins searching for treasure such as a packet of condoms. It was great fun, roaming the ruins. This friend, Dieter, was older than HF by perhaps two years and not of the same class. The friendship did not endure because Frau Doktor Falk did not approve of the boy, and perhaps he was something of a dullard. But back then, the boys had a time of it, exploring the remains of the old city, picking through the rubble. Adventurers and archaeologists they were. HF never found any condoms, but still they looked, because once, without him, Dieter had found one and told him, "The immediate effect was good."

The way a fork tapping crystal pings and resonates, a note of longing reverberates through me for the little hotel in Schwabing where at least the neighborhood was lively. Well, lively for Munich, that is. A small note of longing followed by a flood of ache for New York, for Ninth Avenue, for home.

Wie viel Heimat braucht der Mensch? Er braucht viel Heimat.* (German homily)
   *How much home does a man need? A fair bit of home.

This sense of loss is not much alleviated when he ushers me inside the apartment.

That it is one square room is not the depressing part.

I have, in the past, inhabited dwellings boxier and smaller than this one. While writing my dissertation, I lived in an apartment on 18th Street that was no more than a walk-in closet with an adjoining bathroom. However, there were features to that apartment: exposed brick walls, a working fireplace, personality, history providing the warmth of others having lived there before me. The walls had stories to tell.

This flat, as he calls it, has all the little extras of a white dinner plate.

"So what do you think?" he asks, and I scan the apartment again, panning the room the way a video camera would.

The walls are freshly painted unleaded white, the light fixtures are contemporary and without pizzazz, the window frames are made of aluminum. The bed and the bookshelves give off the smell of freshly cut wood.

My mother was always one to go with what was new. *Look always to ze moment, mine Hester. Zen look to ze future.* No dusty antiques in their house. Their sectional couch came straight from the factory, the coffee table was bought at Macy's, the carpet, bright yellow, went wall to wall. My bedroom was done up in all the latest styles: beanbag chairs, studio bed, modular desk and shelving. *Ze latest fashions.* Although in my parents' eyes my Ph.D. beatified me, my decision to study history was, no doubt, an act of rebellion. The past was the stuff of nightmares. *Do not be looking for ze regrets. Leaf ze past to ze dead.* But by delving into the American history, I did manage to leave their dead undisturbed. Rest in peace.

HF has often professed regrets that we didn't meet in the past, before, when he was a younger man.

My dear sweet Hester, I find myself wishing I'd met you twenty years ago or when I was eighteen. (Were you yet born?) I fear not pleasing you sometimes so deep the fear paralyzes me. (Letter #23 to the author from HF)

But, as I have pointed out to him, if we'd met when he was a younger man, I would have been either a child or a woman far too young and foolish to appreciate him.

Now he takes me in his arms and says, "I am so happy."

"Really?" I ask, because I can't help but feel I am here by default. It's not as if I won the game, but rather that the other team walked off the field. I try not to cry. It is so sad here, and no one knows where I am.

The inhabitants of our big apartment block in Berlin didn't take much notice of each other. We were drawn into ourselves. Even in the air-raid shelters this didn't change much. Everybody was tired and we would simply wait and hope for a quick "all clear" signal. There also lived in our building an elderly Jewish couple.* We found this out only because they had to stay in a different shelter during the alarms. I felt sorry for them even though they had more room** than we did because our shelter was very crowded. (From the memoir of Frau Doktor Falk)

> **On October 18, 1941, the first of the Berlin Jews were deported. One hundred and eighty-seven trains later, on June 16, 1943, Berlin was officially declared judenrein.*
>
> > ***If I've read this right, Frau Doktor Falk was a teeny bit miffed that the elderly Jewish couple got their own air-raid shelter, as if this were yet further evidence of Jewish greed.*

While HF prepares dinner, I unpack. He has emptied three shelves on a bookcase, two bureau drawers, and most of one closet for me. On the very top shelf of the closet is a jumble of his stuff. An old pair of sneakers, an electric drill, a few sweaters balled up and jammed in between some boxes, a tennis racquet. I wouldn't use that shelf for anything anyway, as it is well beyond my reach.

In the way of kitchen items, he has, in his possession here, three wineglasses, one water goblet, a coffee mug with a chipped handle, two knives, but no plates, bowls, or forks. Maria sent him packing without the basic necessities. Either she expects him to fend for himself completely or else to come to her for meals before returning to sleep in the doghouse.

We eat the bread and cheese, which he sliced and spread out on sheets of bond paper, which, despite similarities in color and materials, is not at all like paper plates.

> *At mealtime a very broad cloth is laid on the trestle table. . . .*
> *places are set along one side of the table only. On that side the*
> *cloth falls to the floor, doubling as a communal napkin. . . .*
> *Places are set with knives, spoons, and thick slices of day-old*
> *bread, which serve as plates for meat . . . and a thick chunk of*
> *bread with a hole in the middle serves as a salt shaker. (Joseph*
> *and Frances Gies, Life in a Medieval City, Thomas Y. Crowell,*
> *1969, p. 38)*

At one end of the table is a shoebox, which could, given the setup here, contain pudding or cake, but no, he tells me, "It's filled with old photographs. I found them when I was packing up at the other flat. I thought we'd look at them after we eat."

The one feature to this apartment that does cheer me is the balcony. It's modest, rectangular, and made of concrete. A pair of white plastic lawn chairs are placed side by side. In New York, a balcony is a luxury beyond my means.

I carry out the drinks—Campari and orange juice—and he's got the box of photographs. We sit in the white plastic chairs. The box rests on his lap.

The view offers some trees, a radio tower ahead, a couple of structures that look like smokestacks, but surely, given the Green power, are something else, and indeed, HF tells me that they are beacons of light illuminating the parking lot and the road to the Olympic stadium. If I squint, I can make out the barest outline of the Alps. Breathtaking the view is not, but it is pleasing enough, and it improves as the sun begins its descent below the horizon.

Reaching over into the shoebox on his lap is like reaching into a grab bag. The first prize is a picture of him and Konstanze. He is wearing a suit and she is dressed like Jackie Kennedy circa 1962, A-line dress, a string of pearls, and the *de rigueur* pillbox hat. They are holding hands, gazing into one another's eyes. Ah, young love. I toss it back in the box and take another one. Here he is a child of six or maybe seven. And even though it's a black-and-white studio portrait, the colors are evidenced in the tones. Hair so very blond and milky skin with a pinkish glow. He could have been an angel or Himmler's poster child, what they had hoped to manufacture by the thousands upon thousands.

Himmler was determined to breed out, within a hundred years, the dark German types (like himself and Hitler) by mating them exclusively with blonde women. . . . Certainly Himmler envisaged a huge operation but Lebensborn (Spring of Life) never realized anywhere near its full potential because of the overriding needs of the resettlement and extermination operations. (John Toland, Adolf Hitler, Doubleday, 1976, p. 764)

Indeed he was a charming child. Even then with the killer smile, but when I focus in on his eyes, I detect a film that is a configuration of uncertainty and hurt. I reach over and squeeze his hand.

We look at more pictures of his mother, a faded snapshot of the Nazi cousins, some of people he doesn't know or can't remember. "Oh, this one is interesting." He passes a photograph to me. HF at sixteen seated beside another boy in a café. HF is looking directly into the camera, exuding boyish charm. "There was a girl taking that picture," he says, "and I was after her."

"Yeah? So what else is new?"

The other boy in the picture is looking not at the camera, nor at the girl behind the camera. He is looking at HF, and it is a look I recognize. The boy is painfully in love, and HF, my darling, is devastatingly unaware of it. "He and I were on holiday, that boy. We were in Hamburg, and the night before this picture was taken, in our room, we kissed and touched each other. It was okay," he says, referring only to the sensations of kissing and touching. "You know, just two boys experimenting, trying things out. But after that, we went back to girls straight away."

"You don't really believe that, do you? Look at this. Look at this again." I return it to him, and I ask, "Whatever became of that boy?"

"I have no idea," HF says. "I think the next year at school, I fell in with a different crowd," and he goes quiet as if he is first realizing that something important was lost.

To change the subject he reaches back into the box and brings up a picture of his grandparents' house in Saxony, which appears to be stately and big for a house, but small for a castle. He shows me yet another one of his mother. Here she is standing in front of the United Nations building in New York. In the fading light of evening, I'm squinting to make out the details of a picture of Sabine (the ham-faced one) on a bicycle when the telephone rings. HF and I look at each other slightly petrified, as if we've been caught at something, as if we ought to be scrambling for our clothes, or racing to a closet to hide. On the third ring, he goes to answer it, and I can hear his end of the conversation, but because it's in German, I'm not eavesdropping.

In the few minutes he's been on the phone, night came. It's too dark for me to make out much of anything but the sky and the blinking light from the radio tower transmitting sound that I cannot hear. He comes back to the lawn chair and tells me, "That was Maria. They are in Crete. She just wanted me to know they've arrived safely."

And what of me? Have I arrived safely? Or is it too soon to tell?

LET'S GO GERMANY *and annex the Sudetenland while we're at it*

को

Day One: HF loads up the car with his suitcase, an atlas, a stack of road maps so well-worn that the paper has the texture of velvet, two towels, a bag of food (a bottle of water, three bananas, something he calls biscuits but I'd call cookies, and a giant-sized bar of Milka chocolate), and my things packed in two of the suitcases I'd unpacked only days before. My notebook is in my pocketbook along with a packet of fresh pens, my wallet, passport, and cosmetics. It is his brainchild, this road trip, but I am all for it.

> *Hester Liebste, We don't have a world of our own, but couldn't we just make a world of our own by going to all the relevant places together? Like Amsterdam, Berlin, Vienna, Budapest, Prag, Valley Forge, Golders Green, Jerusalem, and Jericho.*

We'd have a long way together, and we could make love and if you don't want to have a baby, we always have our book. (Letter #96 to the author from HF)

It was only yesterday that I said to him, "You know, I'm going to have to do some traveling soon. To visit Saxony and that town on the Baltic. And there is research that can be done only in Berlin."

"Why don't we go together?" he offered. "University is closed. We can go to Berlin and to Nossen and the Baltic. We can go to all the places of my past." Oh, to holiday where the sights are his life, monuments to his milestones, a journey across the landscape that is himself put him over the top. "I'll take you to where I was born, and you can see the schools I attended, and the church where I was christened." He pronounced *christened* with a long *i*, *Christ-ened*, but I didn't bother to correct him. It suits him better his way.

Already the heat is beastly. I roll down the window. When we reach the autobahn, he feeds a CD into the player's slot—something baroque—and hits the gas.

Within minutes of leaving Munich, we are in farm country. Cows by the dozens lollygag in pastures, and sheep too.

Some of the older farmhouses still retain the house and barn all in one building. HF tells me how it used to be, how the livestock—cows, sheep, pigs, and horses—got half of the ground floor for themselves, and the people—the farmer, his family, and the hired hands—slept upstairs. The animals and their dung generated heat, which rose up and warmed the sleeping quarters. If the smell got real bad, they put down carpets.

Before we get to Bamberg—a medieval town on the banks of the river Regnitz, and on our itinerary because he has written several papers and monographs on a variety of economic circumstances of Bamberg in the thirteenth and fourteenth centuries—he pulls the car into a parking lot, in a space between two tour buses.

There's a cloister here, he says, wherever here is, that he thinks I might like to see. We enter through the portal into a courtyard. We glance left, then right, and then he says, "Okay?"

"Okay what?"

"You've seen enough," he says, or he asks. I can't determine which.

This way of sightseeing—out of the car and take ten seconds to gander—is amusing and curious. I mean, why bother?

"This is an important place," he says. "You must see it."

"But I'm not seeing it. Not really."

"Yes, you are. You have seen it, and now you can ding it off the list. You can say you've been there." This is like a stopover flight in Reykjavik, a twenty-minute wait in the airport, and then claiming Iceland as yet another country visited.

Our hotel is outside the Bamberg town walls, and there is a tub in the bathroom. After a nice long soak, I wrap myself in a white towel that is not fluffy. They must not use fabric softener in Germany. All the towels I've used since I've been here are stiff. I go to HF where he is seated at the desk and lean over his shoulder. He's got a map spread out before him. "Do you want to see where we've been today?" His index finger on Munich, he traces the route north, pausing where we paused—Nürnberg and Fürth—and coming to rest at Bamberg.

It is dark when we go for dinner. At the entryway to the town, we stop, as if halted by guards. There, on the ancient stone wall, freshly spray-painted in red, are swastikas. Three of them of varying sizes. Ah, seek and ye shall find. I feel vindicated, which is probably not the finest response to a swastika.

HF breaks into the quiet and says, "You know, before it was a Nazi emblem, the swastika was a primitive religious ornament, often simply a good-luck charm."

"Oh yeah?" I say. "So this is the handiwork of a happy-go-lucky pagan? Is that what you're trying to tell me?"

"No," he says. His eyes traverse the wall, reading the graffiti. A few paces to the right, he finds what he is looking for. "See that?" He translates for me. "That one says 'Death to the Fascists,'" as if hate were an algebraic equation, and one could cancel the other out.

I take his hand in mine. Our footsteps reverberate on the cobblestones, making ripples in time. Every few steps we stop and kiss, as if he is trying to assure me of something.

> *Liebeliebeliebe, I have never before you kissed an American* girl, but my awareness has increased. Two years ago I held [sic] a rather important speech of [sic] the result of confiscation of foreign** wealth in the growth of XIVth century Bamberg. (Letter #12 to the author from HF)*
> **Read "Jewish."*

**Read "Jewish."
***Read "Jewish" and now it makes sense.

He is emboldened here—all this kissing in public. Even in the restaurant, he kisses me, and later when we sleep, I hold on to him as if for life itself.

Day Two: I wake to find him at the desk with yet another map—a street map of Bamberg—and a guidebook, planning our itinerary, choosing what we will see, figuring for how long to see it, and estimating distance and time between each site.

> He learned this mode of travel from his mother. Pop in on every castle, cathedral, and cloister, the mania for stopping at monuments long enough to speed-read the plaque at a glance, to ding the lot of it off the list, to content himself that he's been there and seen it. Frau Doktor Falk armed herself with maps and guidebooks cross-referenced, a list of all the obligatory sights in her pocket along with a pencil so that, once seen, she could cross it—the Eiffel Tower, the Parthenon, Buckingham Palace—off the list, as if a sightseeing list were the same as a list of chores. "Traveling is hard work," she told her son, and apparently he, good boy, learned from his Mutti.

Breakfast. Saint James Church. Michaelsberg Monastery. The tomb of Saint Otto (which is new, 1751, and therefore not really worth seeing, but we are in the vicinity). The Brewery Museum. Altenberg Castle. Lunch. Then the cathedral so big that it's named for two saints: Peter and George.

There he points out a statue, some guy on a horse, and I spy two carved figures set before the south choir parcloses, and I am drawn to them. Ecclesia is triumphant, crowned with a cathedral. The sister statue is Synagogue. She is blindfolded, her staff is broken, and the tablets of Moses have slipped from her exquisitely carved hand.

On the way out, he stops at the gift shop and buys me a postcard of Synagogue.

Day Three: En route to Marienbad, to where his father was born, we cross the border into the Sudetenland. Border towns, the areas which flank the dividing lines, are peculiar places. It's as if reasonable people, all too aware of annexations and invasions, aim to keep far away from lines drawn in the sand. So what you get at border towns is either an eerie desolation or something weird. Here it's weird. Fields of gnomes. Garden gnomes. Fields of red-capped garden gnomes like poppies. Huge lots filled with them, in all sizes, for sale. Take a gnome home.

We stop because I want a postcard of this, of gnomes as far as the eye can see, but there are no postcards. Only the gnomes themselves. "The Czechs are putting the German gnome makers out of business," HF tells me. "It's a real controversy," which is something I jot down in the section headed *Nutball Stuff He Says*, which prompts him to tease, "You're a regular little Stasi, aren't you? Writing down my words to use them against me."

In 1979, before the Iron Curtain fell, when East was East and West was West, and no one expected the twain would fuse, HF attended a conference in Leipzig. Only the lure of three fun-filled days of talks on "The Establishment of the Pension in Thirteenth-Century Frankish Society" could persuade him to go to the East. At this conference HF (surprise, surprise) took up with a woman who claimed she was a student, but right away he had his doubts about that because over lunch he made reference to the Merovingian king Clovis I, and she asked, "Who is that?" Whatever she was, she was no student of medieval history, that's for sure. Weeks later, as arranged, they met up in Marienbad, a place where neither of them needed official permission to go. And so Marienbad became their place until he tired of all her questions. All the time she was asking about computers, a subject on which he was as knowledgeable as she

*was on the laws of Aethelbert, which is to say not at all. He
was fairly certain that she was Stasi or maybe he wanted her
to be Stasi because there was a kind of romance to that, a love
affair with the enemy who is a spy to boot. Years later, after the
Germanies united, he got a letter from her asking him to meet
with her again. Not one to refuse a lady, he drove to Leipzig.
No check points, he was free as the wind if you don't factor a
wife and children into the equation. He took her to dinner
someplace nice, but she could not eat anything other than boiled
potatoes because of her stomach, which was ruined. Ulcers and
colitis and more ulcers. She could not have so much as butter
on the potatoes. "It was very sad," he said. After dinner, he gave
her what cash he had in his wallet, because she had no job
now. The reunification was not the economic boon the East
Germans had imagined. HF had just one question for her.
"What was your job then?" he asked. She drew her worn cardi-
gan sweater over her bosom as if to give herself cover, and she
said, "Computers."*

Marienbad, he tells me, was, in its day, the most splendid of
the baths. Goethe frequented there. But after the war, when it
again became part of Czechoslovakia, it went to ruins under the
Communists.

*It was in Marienbad, in 1823, when he was seventy-four, that
Goethe fell in love with Ulrike von Levetzow, an eighteen-year-
old girl (which adds up to her being some fifty-six years his
junior). Carrying on like a lovesick puppy, the old fool composed his "Marienbader Elegie" for his Ulrike, who wanted no
part of him.*

Perhaps Marienbad did go to ruin under the Communists, but now that the capitalists are back, it has been restored to its original splendor. Up on a hill, surrounding the colonnade flanked by fountains, gardens, and a statue of Goethe, are a half-dozen magnificent late-nineteenth-century hotels. The scene is not marred by cars or pedestrians. A ghost town of turn-of-the-century magnificence. If we were to see people, I'd expect the women to be wearing corsets, bustles, and hats decorated with dead birds, and the men would sport waxed mustaches.

Indeed, the postcards for sale (60 krone = 3 cents give or take) at the hotel desk reflect my imagination.

It is with surprise, but decidedly some relief, that a clean-shaven desk clerk appears at Reception. Yes, he has a room available. What he doesn't say, but what is certain, is that he's got a whole hotelful of rooms available, and the one we get causes my eyes to go wide as a field of daisies, and I giggle, almost nervously, as if I have inad-

vertently wandered into a fairy tale where I get to be Queen. Velvet bedspread, brocade-covered chairs, gilded frames, crystal chandeliers, and the bathtub could comfortably fit six.

Day Four: The curative waters stink from sulfur. I spit mine
out, but HF takes second helpings. During the hour when we are
scheduled for a medicinal whirlpool, we lock ourselves in our
room and make love instead. "I feel better already," I say.

Day Five: I spread the map out across my lap to orient myself.
I note that Dresden is but a hop, skip, and a jump from Terezín.

"Do you want to go there?" he asks, his voice rising as hope
does.

"No," I say. Unequivocally no. I do not want to go to Terezín. To
go there would take some doing on my part, more fortitude than
I've got. While I can't quite make-believe that theirs were victim-
less crimes, I don't want to see the evidence of the victims. Just as
I can watch a hawk in action but can't bear to consider the mouse
in its talons, I can look the Nazis in the eye, but never their prey.
In that same way, almost as if HF considers them to be the
unlucky victims of an earthquake or a flood, he has come to be at
home with weeping for the victims without quite fully acknowl-
edging who precisely did what. To point the finger of blame at
Hitler, Himmler, Goebbels is not the same as to blame people of
flesh and blood and bone. Collective guilt absolves the individual.
Of course, he would deny this take, but it's true all the same.

Nor is he alone in this kind of night-blindness. He has pointed
out to me plaques and monuments which read *Dedicated to the
Memory of the Victims of the Fascists*, which led me to ask, "Which

fascists might that be? Franco's fascists? Mussolini's fascists? It's as if you all want desperately to be forgiven for something you can't quite admit you've done."

Now he says to me, of Terezín, "This is your history too, Hester," to which I say, "Mine? No. Not mine."

"Of course it is. You are Jewish of German descent."

"German descent? What gives you that idea?" I snap, and he tells me, "Your name, of course. Your pretty German-Jewish name. Rosenfeld. Field of roses."

"Plenty of Jews have German names, and they are not German at all." I remind him that Jews were rarely allowed to stay put for any length of time. "They didn't often have much in the way of national ties."

"But your name is German, and it's a bought one too. We know because it's pretty."

"Bought?" I don't follow him.

He explains that initially only the nobility had surnames, but later, when further identity became necessary for all, it was decided that every family must have one. Most Christians could choose whatever name they wanted. Some took the name of the local lord, and others their father's Christian name. Often they went with their profession—Mullers, Schmidts, and the like. Others took names that were something like a crest, which was how they got to be Wolfs and Falks. But the Jews were assigned names, ugly names, like Knoblauch, which means "garlic," or Fleischhammel. Their only other option was to buy a name. A pretty name. Like Rosenfeld or Apfelbaum, but such an indulgence, paying for a pretty name, was only for the wealthy. "So you see," he says, "you had to have been German at some point and rather affluent."

"Perhaps." I give him that much. "At some point."

Another hour of driving, and he parks the car on a residential street nothing like I'd imagined Dresden to be. "This is Dresden?" I ask, and he says, "No. This is Terezín."

I am more than a little annoyed. "I told you I didn't want to go here," I say.

"But Hester, I think you should see it."

"Why?" I ask. "Why should I see it?"

He has no answer ready for me. All he can say is, "I want to see it. I want us to see it together."

Ghetto Terezín. Theresienstadt. Model relocation camp for privileged German Jews. The pit stop before Auschwitz. The last chance for air. Open to Red Cross inspection except for the Little Fortress, which was hidden from view. The fortress where we stand now, where executions were carried out. Evidence of torture remains. *Arbeit Macht Frei* to you too. I've seen enough.

But before we can leave, he insists we go to the cemetery where some nine thousand were buried during the ghetto's first year of operation. After that, the dead were not afforded such dignities. Instead they got cremated anonymously or shoveled into a pit with more dead bodies. I root around a tree for small rocks, collect four of them, and I place them at random on four headstones.

"What is that you're doing?" HF asks.

I point out all the other rocks and pebbles left on headstones, and I explain, "That's what Jews leave instead of flowers."

With a sense of purpose, he bends down and gets himself some stones and pebbles. I sit under the tree as he places the bits of rock on the headstones. He does this again and again, and I watch him as he keeps at it until he is far from my line of vision.

Although I can't see him, I assume he is thusly honoring each of the nine thousand headstones, because two hours pass before I see him again.

Crossing the border back into Germany is different from crossing into the Czech Republic. The Czechs wave you in, welcome, welcome. The Germans are checking passports, rummaging through luggage and cars as if the Czech-German border were the Bogotá-Miami line. After a while of this waiting, we notice there is a pattern here. Cars with German plates are waved through, no muss, no fuss. Cars with other tags—Czech, Hungarian, Polish, Italian—they're being strip-searched. We, German-plated, can expect clear sailing, and it almost happens that way until the border guard gets a look at me, and then we are treated like Rumanians.

Day Six: I ask about the cars dotting the road, those cute-as-a-button automobiles I keep seeing, and in such an array of colors and patterns, which isn't something you often get, a polka-dot car. "What kind of car is that?"

"A Trabant, but we call them Trabbis."

"Chubbies?"

"Trabbis." He tells me that this was the car the GDR manufactured in the GDR heyday. Trabbis run on a mixture of gasoline and oil, which pollutes the air worse than burning rubber, and they explode on impact. "Trabbis." He shakes his head in disgust. "We don't even let them into the West, and they had to wait ten years to get one."

HF makes more snide comments about the East, about the socio-realist architecture marring the landscape, about the air pollution, about the grime, about the Trabbis, about the political climate, the re-rise of fascism. "They complain there aren't enough jobs for them," he says. "Well, I have a job for them. They can put that wall back brick by brick."

We stop for gas, and at the convenience shop where I go to get a bottle of water, there is a rack of postcards. I buy one and bring it back to the car. "Look," I show HF, "Chubbies."

Dresden, the place where his paternal grandparents were from before they set up shop in Marienbad sometime around the turn of the last century, is a mess. More than fifty-five years after the bombing, and the place is still filthy and in ruins and under construction.

In the year 1945, on the night when February 13th rolled into the 14th, hundreds of American and British bomber planes ambushed the magnificent city of Dresden, leaving a firestorm in their wake. More than eighty percent of the city burned to a crisp and some 135,000 people died in one clip. The air raid was strictly punitive; there was no strategic military target in Dresden.

"It was an act of vengeance. That's all," HF says. "Vengeance," and I say, "Yes," but try as I might, I don't feel bad about that. I try to feel bad about it. I try to feel the terror of waking up to find yourself in the eye of a fireball, I try to feel sorrow for the children who died that night, for all those people who lost everything, life and limb, in the drop of a bomb, but I can't quite muster up sorrow. I experience intellectual acknowledgment of the horror, but visceral dispassion to the agony. It takes all my reserve not to say that it was vengeance well earned and who started it all anyway. Again, and hardly for the first time, I have to remind myself that HF suffered the effects of war—the hunger, the homelessness, the bombs dropping, the fires raging, the guns and hand grenades—and I did not.

There is no chance of finding his grandfather's house, so rather than engage in a mission of futility, we go and have a look at the Church of the Three Kings, where HF dismisses the nineteenth-century tower as new. What we are here to see is the fresco on the back of the church. Pre-Reformation, it depicts the *Totentanz*, the Dance of Death, Saint Vitus' dance, the twitching, spasmodic death throes connected with outbreaks of rheumatic fever. "Well, that's gruesome," I say, and I note to myself how this fresco, centuries old, has a greater effect on me than the devastation of a history far more recent. And again I justify: They started it.

Day Seven: Nossen, in the heartland of Saxony, is a small town, smaller even than I had imagined, and it is dark here despite the midday sun. The buildings are in a state of disrepair and the facades in desperate need of cleaning. It feels East, this town, East before the reunification. The shops are shabby. The merchandise is dated and the quality poor. The few cars we see are mostly Trabbis. As there can't be much of a tourist industry here, I have difficulty locating a postcard. I've tried at the hotel, at the tobacco shop, at a sad and dreary toy store, and at the post office. At the apothecary, I score.

Along the way to the house where his mother grew up, where she spent some of the years of chaos, and where HF sometimes stayed too, we pass the factories his maternal grandfather owned. Two paper mills on one side of the river and a tannery on the other. First confiscated for the war effort, then by the state, these factories are now closed and obviously have been closed for some time. They are dilapidated and forsaken; most of the windows are broken. When we peer inside, we see vast space, empty but for

Nossen vom Seminar aus

the remains of debris. "It's good that they are shut down," HF says. "Those factories must have polluted the river badly."

The grandeur of the house is better appreciated from a distance. Up close, it sags like a pair of overburdened shoulders. The yellow bricks are now mostly black from soot. It is a house busy with turrets and parapets, and big enough that the Socialist state subdivided it into ten apartments. The basement windows are so dirty that we can't see in, and there is no lock on the front door.

Rumors were chasing each other. The Russians were coming and the Americans too. Our hopes that the Americans would come first did not come true. They got only to Döbeln and left the rest to their eastern Allies. On the other side of the river were Russian soldiers with Mongolian blood. Women were not safe. Frau Schaeffer, who had been tortured by the Russians, went completely crazy but one barely had the strength to calm anybody else. We expected there would be shooting, and so before the Russians entered Nossen we went into the basement of the yellow house that had been well fortified by my father. We sat hunched over, paralyzed, and quiet. A hand grenade was thrown at the door of the house, and then from the basement windows, street level, we saw Russian boots marching. A symbol of fate. (From the memoir of Frau Doktor Falk)

Or rather there is a lock on the front door, but it's broken, and so we step inside. The hallway is littered with paper and bottles and shattered glass. A central staircase is made of mahogany, but the wood is splintered and scuffed, and any desire I might have had to explore this house further has been squelched by the stink of the place. It reeks of excrement and urine, and HF tells me, "There were only two loos in this house, which was enough for one family, but definitely not enough for ten families. Ten families sharing the two bathrooms and one kitchen. That was typical for the Socialists," he says.

Outside, when we can breathe again, I ask HF if he feels sad about this house, what has become of it.

He shrugs. "Maybe a little. I'm glad my mother never saw it in this condition. She was always proud of this house. It was so grand, you know."

The basement was cleared. We were taken upstairs. I had Heinrich in my arms. He was not yet two years old, but he did not cry. A Russian officer told me to polish his boots with the hem of my dress, which I did without blinking. Then he asked

for a drink of water. I brought it to him. He eyed me suspi-
ciously and poured the water out onto the floor. This happened
on the 6th of May, 1945. (From the memoir of Frau Doktor
Falk)

Then HF asks me, "Have you ever gone back to the house
where you grew up?"

"No," I tell him. "But I'm sure it would look the same as when
I left. The political climate in New Rochelle has always been rel-
atively stable."

At the top of the hill is the church where he was christened.
His family, his mother's family, had their own pew in this church.
A pew high up like box seats at the opera. This pew was one of
the things mentioned in his mother's "Account of Gratefulness," a
kind of sidebar to her memoir, a rather peculiar enumeration of
possessions and events that included a tulle ball gown, the especially soft leather her father's tannery produced, the occasion of
her presenting yellow roses to then Generalfeldmarschall von
Hindenburg.

—my heart beat as I approached him, this great man born to
be a myth—

Also she was grateful for the pleasure of dancing with tall
officers, for knitting socks from scratchy gray wool for the soldiers during the Great War, and for being chosen godmother to
one Katerina Gruen. The gratitude there stemmed from the
fact that this child's godfather was Wilhelm II, and although
no longer Kaiser, he was still a somebody. In the "Account of

Gratefulness" there is a footnote to the mention of Katerina Gruen.

In 1945, at the age of twenty-one, immediately before the Russians entered the town, she killed herself because of her father.

Having identified the family pew—there were only two box seats to choose from, one on each side of the altar—HF takes me by the hand and says, "Come, I'll show you where I used to play."

Down the hill, we turn the corner, and so does the weather. Out of nowhere come black clouds which split open with a rumble, and lightning cracks like a whip across the sky. We make a dash for a café, which is decorated in what was up-to-the-minute 1970s socio-realist. The tables and chairs are cheap, plastic the color of liverwurst, mass-produced possibly for all the cafés in the Eastern Bloc. Also there is speckled indoor/outdoor carpeting on the floor.

Except for one table, which is empty, all the others are occupied by old people. Very old people, and I fear we have wandered not into a café, but into a nursing home. This observation causes HF to laugh. "No," he tells me. "It's that there are no young people in this town. They've all left. There is nothing here for them."

If what he says is true, then when these people die off, the town will be deserted. Abandoned by human life. Just the buildings will remain. Monuments, and then ruins.

We order coffee, and another old woman comes in. There are no chairs remaining for her, but for one at our table, so she joins us, and I see that she has Parkinson's disease and no teeth. She orders ice cream. She and HF talk, and then he turns to me to translate.

"When the Socialists took over, she got a job in the uranium mines. She worked there, in the mines, until her teeth fell out and she suffered from shaking. But the Socialists gave her a pension, and she enjoys her life very much. Every day is a new adventure. Look how today she is sitting at a table with an American."

She is only sixty-six years old, but she looks eighty-seven, and I think about how miserable her life must have been, so miserable that sitting at a table with me constitutes a thrill. This is depressing.

HF must be having similar thoughts, because when I say to him, "Ask her if she knew your family," he shakes his head. "That would make me seem as if I were acting grand," he says. The likes of the uranium mines were never in his family's future or their past either, and I see that the sun is breaking through the clouds. I pay for our coffees and her ice cream, which may or may not seem as if I am acting grand, but still I think it is the right thing to do.

Having said our goodbyes, we go to where HF used to play. All alone as a little boy three, four, five years old, he roamed a wooded area rife with rock formations and bodies of water. Ponds, streams, and the river winds along to a point where rapids swirl and churn fast and furious. "You played here all by yourself?" I ask. "They let you come here alone? It's dangerous for a child here. You could've fallen from the rocks or drowned easily. Weren't they worried about you coming here?"

"No," he says. "You don't understand. When you are worried about finding food to eat and fuel for fire and are the Russians going to rape you or arrest you, nobody thought to worry about where a little boy played."

Certainly, my childhood was a cushion of rose petals compared to his. I never, ever knew what it was to go hungry or to be cold in the way that an extra sweater does nothing to alleviate the frost on the bones. So why am I feeling something I can identify only as envy? Is it that, while yes, his childhood was fraught with danger, it was also exciting? Am I romanticizing war and its aftermath? While contemplating that little absurdity, I look down and I see, profuse on the path where we walk, slugs. Fat, slimy slugs, inches long, and they're everywhere.

"Yes," he says. "After the rain, they come out. Slugs were a part of my childhood too."

Day Eight: We arrive at Spreewald, the Niagara Falls of Germany, the place where HF's parents married and honeymooned in October of 1942. The town itself is sentimental—the facades of guesthouses adorned with heart-shaped frescoes, ice cream parlors, beer gardens, kiosks selling postcards, film, and brightly colored

plastic pails and shovels for children, although there is no sand here.

The big draw to Spreewald is the labyrinth of canals under shaded boughs.

Lily pads sit still on the water's surface and they are in bloom, and canoes are for rent by the hour.

HF paddles. My heart is soaring and I'm not the least bit afraid of drowning because this water is shallow. "Like you," I tell him. "So pretty and warm and shallow." I love him madly.

We drift beneath the canopy of leaves. I lose all sense of time. In 1942, his parents were in a canoe, in a canal, in love, never-mindful as to what was happening around them. Never-mindful of what was yet to come, that such a moment would be shattered irrevocably by events of war and betrayals of the heart. I turn to look at HF, my love, and I consider just how unknowable the future is.

Flocks of swallows fly low to the ground as if playing chicken with oncoming cars. A sure sign, HF tells me, that it will soon rain, and so it does. The rain is thick, coming down in skeins instead of drops. When we arrive in the town of Zingst on the Baltic, HF swerves the car to avoid a troop of grown-up people riding bicycles in a line like goslings in the rain. Some of them are wearing plastic bags as hats. "No doubt my countrymen," he says, "having fun on holiday."

Day Nine: I wake to discover a note written on the back of the hotel's complimentary postcard, which HF left for me to find on his pillow. *Gone for a swim. Be back soon. Love.*

DIE OSTSEE

We have a view of the sea from our hotel room, and I rush to the window, which is as close to that body of water as I will get. I don't see him anywhere. I see only the Baltic, which is the color of storm clouds, the same gray as HF's eyes, but cold and harsh and without the twinkle. There are whitecaps on the waves, which are not high, but choppy and foreboding.

I pace the length of the room. The floor is carpeted in plush marine blue. A nautical motif dominates—a print of seagulls in flight, another of a lighthouse. The bedspread and matching curtains are patterned with yellow seashells. This is the new capitalism.

Swimming in the Baltic, to my mind, is a recipe for death. The Baltic has all the makings of a sea that claims lives often. There must be reams of men laid to rest on that floor. A mass grave. Back at the window, I try to brace myself for the sight of his body washing up on shore, but he returns from his swim refreshed, invigorated.

We're at the local church, built of stone in the early 1800s. According to the literature posted in the lobby, one of its ministers was a martyr. A disciple of Dietrich Bonhoeffer and his church of the resistance, this minister preached antitotalitarian sermons. His reward for basic human decency was to be ratted out by at least one of his parishioners. Arrested and sent to the camps, he managed to survive his sentence. After the war he returned to this town, to this church, where he died some years later, having, by then, pissed off the Communist Party too.

"So after the war, you might have heard him speak," I note.

"Probably I did," HF says. "They made us come to church every Sunday. But all I remember about church was that I did not want to be there. I was restless to go out and play. I was just a little boy."

The children's home, where HF spent months and years, is beyond the far side of the town center. The town is all of two blocks long and narrow as string. It's a town for tourists. Nothing more than eateries, ice cream stands, and souvenir shops which sell maps, postcards, candy, and seashells, and things made of seashells or encrusted with seashells, scented candles, cut-crystal figurines, and amber, which they call *Bernstein*.

Past the shops, the streets become cobblestoned and houses are shaped like boxes made of mortar with thatched roofs of straw.

Soon enough, we stop at one of these houses. "There," HF says. "That's it."

Zingst

Painted across the front of the house, over the arched doorway, in Gothic lettering, is *Blumenhaus*, and indeed the garden out front is in bloom. Roses, sunflowers, pansies, red poppies, black-eyed Susans, and daisies. It is not a formal garden. It grows wild with joy. "It's heavenly," I say. "You didn't tell me it was such a lovely place."

"I hated that house." He stands on the street facing it down, as if the house were a demon to be conquered. "I slept in a room on the top floor. The attic. And every morning I had to carry my pee pot down three flights of stairs. I lived in fear of spilling it. I hated that house. I hated that room. I hated that pee pot."

By the front door, beside an arbor of roses entwined through the lattice, is the bell. Not an electric bell, but a cast-iron one that hangs from a rod. HF gives it a clang.

> *Heinrich is healthy with pretty red cheeks. The Easter bunny*
> *plays a great role in his imagination as you can see from the*

drawings enclosed. He is quite proud of his drawing achieve-
ments. There was a wedding at the Koppls' house, and on the
eve he went there to make a racket.* Everyone got a piece of
cake but he preferred to make noise while the others were eat-
ing. (Letter from HF's caretaker, Frau Ingrid Betz, to his
mother, March 19, 1948)

　　*German custom of banging on pots and pans and breaking
　　pottery on the eve of a wedding.

A middle-aged man answers the door. He is wearing socks but
no shoes, and a white T-shirt is half tucked into his pants, half
hanging out. He sports a remarkably thick mustache, which fans
out like a broom over his mouth. It appears that we have roused
him from a nap.

HF and the man speak in German, and then the door closes on
us. Not slammed shut in anger, but closed firmly nonetheless. It is
clear that it is not going to open for us again. "Apparently," HF
explains, "the problem is that ever since the wall came down, a
steady stream of West Germans have come knocking on the door.
People like me coming back here looking for something. He's sick
to death of us traipsing through his house. He said there is nothing here for me. He's probably right. What could there be of
interest?"

"Who knows?" I say. "Maybe we would've found your little pee
pot in the attic."

Day Ten: From the map of the region, I read aloud the names
of towns that strike my fancy. Names that are fun to articulate.
"Hiddensee. Putbus. Heringsdorf," I read, and he says, "Herring
Village. That is an unpleasant name for a town."

The unpleasantly named town of Herring Village prompts me to reveal, "When I was four years old, I once ate a whole jar of pickled herring at six o'clock in the morning."

My father used to eat pickled herring then. My mother would buy it for my father, but she never ate any herself nor gave me any to eat either. It was stashed in the back of the refrigerator, as if it were hidden like hooch or forgotten like wheat germ. I have no idea what possessed me, on that morning, to open the jar of pickled herring instead of the box of Sugar Smacks, but I distinctly remember putting my hand in the jar and bringing the fish to my mouth. The scales had the color and movement of mercury, quicksilver shimmering and gliding. I remember thinking it was so delicious and eating more and more of it until there was only one piece left when my mother found me, and she screamed. "Oh mine Hester," she said. "You don't vant zat. Zat is not for American girls to eat." She made spitting gestures to let me know this was yechy, but also as if to ward off the evil eye. As if eating pickled herring were a harbinger of destruction. After that, my father must have been encouraged to give up this remnant of his past, because I don't recall ever seeing pickled herring in our house again, and unlike the memory of madeleines, the thought of eating pickled herring now makes me retch.

Day Eleven: Our hotel, a pension really, is in the Charlottenburg section of Berlin, a few blocks from the house where HF lived briefly with his mother, his father, and his father's mistress and her family. Old-world and intimate, the pension boasts a private collection of art that is not insignificant. I do wonder where they got it, or rather, how they got it, but I don't make inquiry because I am trying to cut back on the accusations.

Charlottenburg is decidedly an upscale area. The houses have been renovated, restored to their prewar bourgeois charm, and the streets are wide and tree-lined. HF does not consult the map. Like a homing pigeon, he effortlessly finds his way back to whence he came. But then he stops and says, "This is not it."

This is where his house should be, but a different house is there in its place. His house is gone, another piece of the past eradicated, like life forms extinct and never to return. "They must've torn it down completely," he says. "This one is the style from the 1950s." He stands there as if expecting a miracle, that the house will transform itself into what he remembered it to be, including how the roof was blown off.

"Well," he says finally, "I suppose it was too far gone to repair it."

At a kiosk, I buy two of the same postcard.

I give one of them to him, and I say, "So you can remember it as it was."

Later I had heard that the shopkeepers, remembering that the elderly Jewish couple from our building had been good customers once, secretly gave them food when they couldn't get any. I was glad of that afterwards. The destruction of the building they probably did not survive. There were no replacement flats to assign them to. (From the memoir of Frau Doktor Falk)

The hospital, where he was born in the air-raid shelter, is a massive and gloomy place. From the outside it looks like a turn-of-the-century insane asylum or a debtors' prison. Inside, however, it's been spruced up, freshly painted white walls and orange furniture in the waiting room.

The hospital too had been bombed, but remained open until 1947, when it closed for repairs and modernization. Alas, all records prior to its reopening in 1952 no longer exist. That there is no record of his birth is not news to him, yet HF seems to take it hard. He must have been hoping against the odds for irrefutable evidence, something to support his mother's testimony as to the date of his birth. It's got to disconcert him to rely on the memory or the whim of others for his own vital statistics. Historians, of all people, are well aware how faulty memory can be. We much prefer documentation. I imagine he feels the way a victim of amnesia does.

The hospital's air-raid shelter is now an underground parking garage.

There is no need for him to accompany me this afternoon. I try to persuade him to go visit a museum or while away the hours in a café, but he wants to tag along.

On the way, we pass a spread of posters tacked to a construction site and fencing. They read: *DEUTSCHLAND DEN DEUTSCHEN*. Germany for Germans. Even without the wall, there is a split personality to Berlin.

My efforts at the Zentrum für Berlin-Studien are not entirely futile. I do find the address for his mother when she was married to her first husband, and I am able to confirm that the Falks lived in the house that is now gone, and—my personal favorite—a 1941 address and phone number, Potsdam 46 29, for Klaus and one Margit Falk. Unless it was another Klaus Falk, Margit must've been the wife before Charlotte. However, I am unable to locate anything on the National Gas Board. The librarian suggests I try the Bundesarchiv and also the Landesarchiv. He writes the addresses on a piece of paper, and I am heading for the stacks to find HF when he finds me. "Oh Hester, there you are." He is all excited over something. "This is wonderful. Look." He takes several sheets of paper from his jacket pocket and spreads them out on a table. He has photocopied lists of Rosenfelds. "From the *Jewish Citizens Book for Berlin* and this one is from *Jewish Marriages*. I think we can learn something about your family."

I snatch the papers from the table and shove them in my pocketbook, crumpling them in the process. "We're here to learn about your family. Not mine." I speak tersely.

"But don't you think this is fascinating? Imagine, Hester, suppose our families were from the same place? Suppose our families crossed paths here in Berlin? Wouldn't that be something?"

"Oh, it would be something, all right. Think about what you are saying," I caution him.

—*1295 Berlin merchants are forbidden to supply Jews with wool.*

—*1349 Jews blamed for the region's Black Death. Those not murdered were expelled.*

—*1354 A few snuck back in.*

—*1510 Accused of desecrating a Host, Jews were murdered and again expelled.*

—*1571 Ditto on the murder and expulsion and sneaking back.*

—*1671 Edict inviting fifty rich Jewish families to Berlin to engage in trade without restriction. The catch: Each family was allowed one child only. Additional children were expelled.*

—*1879 Wilhelm Marr, Berlin journalist, founds the Anti-Semitic League. Slogan coined: The Jews are our misfortune (to be used later, as well).*

—*1933 Jewish doctors, dentists, opticians, and pharmacists are not to receive any payments from the state-run insurance agencies. Jewish judges must step down from the bench. State schools retire all Jewish teachers.*

—*1934 Jewish actors are forbidden to work in their field.*

—*1935 Jews forbidden entry to public pools. Marriages*

and sexual relations between Jews and Gentiles are forbidden.

—*1936 No Jewish children will be permitted into public day-care centers. Jewish journalists are forbidden to practice their profession.*

—*1937 Jews can no longer receive doctorates.*

—*1938 Jewish men must add "Israel" to their given names and Jewish women must add "Sarah" to theirs. Passports held by Jews must be stamped with a J.*

"I'm sorry," he says. "You are right, of course. I didn't think about it. Sometimes I forget about all that. Do you ever forget about it?"

We spend what remains of the day in bed, forgetting everything except the pleasure in the touch, the trust in the moment, losing ourselves to the way of the flesh, the sweetest way to forget.

Day Twelve: With the aid of the dazzlingly efficient librarian at the Bundesarchiv, I learn that the gas board where his parents worked, although called the National Gas Board, was, in fact, a private enterprise.

Set up by five big businesses—Berlin Gas Works, RWE (Rhinish Westphalian Energy), Junkers, GasAG, and Rauscher-Burkhardt—coal companies, gas companies, and a firm that manufactured stoves and refrigerators. All stood to profit with increased usage of energy. Rather than simple advertising, the promoting of one company or product, the propaganda devised was intended to appear scientific and official, to give the

impression of being something like public service announce-
ments rather than commercials.

But not everything adds up. Why, during the war years, would these companies then turn around and pay for advertising to encourage people to refrain from energy consumption? Even in support of the war effort, that is a bit much. I would have expected that their patriotism extended as far as to discontinue their initial efforts, but no further than that. And why, working not for the government, but for a private firm, wasn't his mother then evacuated from Berlin when all children and civilian women were sent away?

While I was off looking for dirt on his parents, HF was at the Jüdische Gemeinde Bibliothek looking, not for dirt, but again for my paternal ancestors or a stray uncle. Despite yesterday's acknowledgment that this is not a good idea, he was unable to resist. Now, he rushes across the hotel lobby, waving yet another list of Rosenfelds at me. This list comes from the *Jüdisches Adressbuch für Gross-Berlin*, the Jewish telephone directories. He's pushing me to look at his list the way you push a dog's nose into its accident on the carpet.

No doubt he's found it, my father's boyhood address spelled out. I could glance at it, commit it to memory even. Maybe I am a little bit curious, but nonetheless I say, "Would you please quit this hunt for Rosenfelds."

"Why don't you want to know?" he asks, and I wish I could explain to him what surely he would understand, that to know is to confront, to remember that which is best left behind. Too ingrained is the certainty that my parents' lives would render me pathetic. That he would pity me. The pitied are weak and at the mercy of the strong. I couldn't have that. It is preferable, all the way around, for him to think it was his people who lost the war.

"I'm an American," I say. "End of story."

"Maybe it is the end of the story," he argues, "but it is not the beginning."

"Let it go," I tell him.

He shakes his head. "I don't understand your lack of interest in this."

"Yes, you do," I say. "You understand all too well."

Like the Coney Island House of Mirrors, the distortions are what disconcert us most. It is beautiful here. The Wannsee Conference House is a lakeside villa; a lake where sailboats tack in the light summer breeze, and the water laps against the shore. Trees are everywhere. It is difficult to imagine that in such a setting, such a plan emerged. Then again, it is difficult to imagine that such a plan emerged at all.

At the front desk, HF gets us each a brochure, a blueprint of fourteen exhibit rooms laid out in chronological order. The Rise of National Socialism leads into the Prewar Period, followed by the War Against Poland, and so on until the Liberation before you exit. But I don't walk in order. I wander willy-nilly, looking mostly at the floor.

As if HF were my conscience, he catches up to me in Room 10, Auschwitz, and within nanoseconds of looking at the grotesque photographs—those of bodies heaped in piles like refuse, naked women lined up waiting to die, emaciated men—HF's face is wet with tears.

"Maybe you want to leave?" I ask him. "Frankly, there's nothing here we don't already know." In fact, I'm the one who wants to leave, because I don't know how to conjure images other than those before me. Can I make myself blind to what is right in front of my nose? Certainly, others have managed.

Only at the photographs of the Warsaw Uprising do my symptoms of distress abate. Buoyed by the strength of the resistance, I experience dignity. But then, with the next set of pictures, pictures of yet more victims, that dignity is dashed, put down the way the rebellion was. Witnessing the fear captured on film, I consider how some Israelis, so disdainful of these victims, refer to them as *sabonim*. Soap. Yes, I am ashamed of my shame, but there you have it.

Room 6 is dedicated to the Who's Who of Nazi Bigwigs, their headshots, their résumés, and the final note: suicide, execution, and those who lucked out with a slap on the wrist. In Room 6, I linger to look at them carefully, and I don't meet up with HF again until I meander into The Ghettos, where he is fixed on one photograph enlarged to poster size. It's a famous photograph, much like that other famous photograph, the one from *Life* magazine, of the Vietnamese girl running naked and screaming down the street, running from the bombs and the flames and the terror, and you know she'll never run fast enough. This photograph focuses on a little boy, five or six years old at most, his arms are raised too, in surrender to soldiers pointing rifles and bayonets at him, at this child. His mother and sisters are also in the picture, but it's the boy you look at. His face, his expression so frightened, frightened and bewildered as to what is happening and why. The same bewildered look that clouded my father's eyes. I cannot accept any identification with that frightened little boy. Or with my father, for that matter.

"I've read that he survived," HF says. "He is still alive. I wonder how he feels when he sees that picture."

"Humiliated," I say, and HF says, "Humiliated? Why would he feel humiliated? No. I'll bet he feels so proud."

"Proud of what? Of being one of the hunted?" I don't wait for his answer. I hurry off. HF comes after me, and takes me in his arms, holds me tight until I quit trying to get away.

Day Thirteen: The Schöneberger Rathaus is where John F. Kennedy gave his *Ich bin ein Berliner* speech. "I was here to see it." This memory causes HF's voice to warble with pride and stirring emotion. "I was visiting with my brother. He still lived in Berlin then. It was so inspiring."

I shrug. "I never liked that speech. I thought it was disrespectful," and he asks, "Disrespectful to whom?"

Think fast. "Well, to all the Americans who fought in that war specifically so that they would not be Germans."

HF refuses any tarnish to taint his hero, which I suppose I can understand given that, for him, heroes were in short supply. "Kennedy was wounded in that war."

"Yes, but he fought in the Pacific," I note, "and we didn't hear any *I am Japanese* speech, did we?"

"But still," he says, "think about what that meant to us. To my generation." He stares off at the spot where John Kennedy stood, and I get out my notebook.

He was a hero to us because he let us be part of the world again. For us, it was like when you are a child and you are sent to your room for punishment. And you sit there all alone until your mother tells you that you can come out now, you have been forgiven. We loved him for that. And we loved him because he was young. He represented us. A new generation. It was out with the old. I remember when I learned that he had died. I was at the movies. With a girl, to see A bout de souffle.* *It was already some years old, that film, but it was a favorite of my generation. We all wanted to be like Jean Paul Belmondo. When it was announced about Kennedy, I thought they had said that the president of Africa had died, and I remember being confused because there was no president of Africa. But I could not comprehend that it was the president of America who had died. I walked that girl home, and the asphalt was glittering from the cold. Over the years I have seen that film a few times on television, but I never saw that girl again.*

Breathless.

"How is it," I ask, "that virtually every memorable event in your life involves a girl?"

After lunch, we see, up close, the Brandenburg Gate and the Reichstag. I buy a postcard of Alexanderplatz, where there is a Burger King.

We go looking for Spandau Prison but we can't find it, because the British tore it down immediately after Rudolf Hess died. Now on that spot there is a Baumarkt, which is a store like Home Depot, and with that, we leave Berlin.

Chapter Fourteen

Home again

"It's good to be home," I say. Home, as if Munich were home, as if this monotone apartment were home, and as I hear myself say *home*, I'm sure I must have heard wrong.

HF, however, is beside himself. "Do you mean that, Hester? Do you feel like this is home? Do you think you could stay here with me always? We could get a bigger flat. One with an office for you to work and an extra bedroom for the baby."

"The baby? I thought we were done with that foolishness. I thought you'd given up."

"Oh no," he smiles. "To keep quiet about it for a while is just part of my strategy."

"Well, it didn't work," I say, grateful that this baby nonsense allows me to sidestep the question of home, as if Munich could be my home, as if America were simply a way station, a place to wait out the troubles before closing the circle and returning to place of origin. But I am an American, I tell myself, and I could no better live in Munich than my mother lived in New Rochelle. For more than twenty years, my mother lived in New Rochelle, but when it came to ways of the American suburb, my parents were like children. Naive and green and too enthusiastic and goofy. In a kind of role reversal, it was up to me to protect them, to guide them through the foreign territories. I've always maintained that you can't fit in where you don't belong. But the question is open: Do I belong in Munich or not? An argument can be made either way. There is the business of roots and heritage, and I do love HF. And I did say *It's good to be home.* But Munich? Germany? *My* home? And if I do come to live on foreign lands where I don't belong, can I rely on HF to watch over me?

Tired from the long drive, neither of us is up for going out to eat. But I am hungry, and HF is hungry too, only he won't say so. He rummages through the cabinets and comes up with a package of flatbreads. "Oh goody," I say, "cardboard," but I eat some nonetheless, and so does he.

We are making good use of the bed when the phone rings. "Let it go," I say, but HF is a family man. When you have children, you can't not answer the telephone. With children come worries that must be assuaged or else you're good for nothing.

Of course, I don't understand a word of what's being said, other than something about Berlin and automobile. HF is smiling and he laughs too, and I gather that there is no emergency. When he hangs up, he shakes his head at the wonder of it all and tells me, "That was Konstanze. Either she is using the powers of witchcraft or else she and Maria have spoken and put together all the pieces of the puzzle. Konstanze knows that you are here, and she wanted to tell me how happy she is that I have found someone I love."

"How does she know that? That you love me?"

"That is witchcraft for sure," he laughs. "Oh, I don't know. Maybe she is only fishing to find out. With Konstanze, it is difficult to determine when she fishes and when she has information."

"But I thought she and Maria were friends. Shouldn't she be annoyed with you on Maria's behalf?"

"Yes, but Konstanze will look at all the positions before she takes one. As I have said, she is much like my mother."

Then I tell him, "Konstanze warned me that you are going to break my heart."

"Yes," he says. "She would say that. Mostly, I suspect, this phone call of hers was meant for you. She wants you to know that you suit her. She wants to protect you, play Mama to you."

Was this call really meant to welcome me into the fold? Is Konstanze making room for me in the inner circle? HF says that is very possible. "She would like a Jew in the group. But to really be a part of it, you need to add another half sister to the brew. Think how happy you would make her if she got to be an auntie to a little Jewish baby."

Not that I will do it, but for the first time ever, I do not automatically say no to participating in his desire to repopulate the Jews, because the prospect of being included, welcomed, feels so nice, a sweetness that spreads like honey. Of course, I do not say yes to the Jewish half sister in the stewpot, but for fear of saying yes I put my lips to his.

After arranging an appointment for the following Monday with a professor of psychology who has studied the variety of psychological disorders afflicting children of war, I head out to the store, shopping list in hand: milk, bread, cheese, breakfast cereal, fruit, beer, wine, chocolate, coffee.

> *August and the middle of August is the time to sow hyssop. Easter cabbage is sown come the waning of the full moon; parsley too. . . . After the Day of Our Lady in September, peonies, snakeweed, lily bulbs, roses, and gooseberry bushes are planted. (Le Ménagier de Paris [1393], ed. Baron Jérôme Pichon, Paris, 1846, Tome Second, p. 65, author's translation)*

The essential provisions.

Also, I want to get a couple of forks and spoons and plates, because in this century, we, in the Western World, use these things routinely.

Along the concrete pathway, on the way to the shopping *Platz*, I try switching my perspective, aiming to see myself as, not a visitor, but a resident. As if to envision such a picture were a matter of prescriptive lenses or changing the channel on the television, and I instruct myself, "Imagine that you live here now. For always," and I come up with turning *sportlich*, making use of the Olympic Park, maybe taking up jogging or rowing on the lake or skiing in the Alps, whooshing down the slopes, a spray of pristine white snow in my wake. I imagine learning the language, and I contemplate a bigger flat.

Other things, too, that once were one way are now another. And vice versa. Gears shift. Places change. It used to be that HF came to me in the mornings before he went to work and in the afternoons prior to going home. Now, those times are reserved for his wife and daughters. Early in the morning, HF went and had breakfast with his family while I turned over and went back to sleep for another hour. Before coming home to have dinner with me, he will again visit with Maria and the girls.

More new developments include my discovery of which are the bicycle lanes and which lanes are for pedestrians. I now know to carry a tote bag with me at all times in case of an unplanned purchase. I have learned to say *Bitte* and *Danke* and to ask, "Do you speak English?" All in all, the climate here is warming. That, or I have become accustomed to the chill.

The Tengelmann is an uninspired supermarket. There are no beautiful foods here. In New York, I shopped for food in the way I considered to be European. That is, the greengrocer for fruit and vegetables, the baker for bread, the cheese store for cheese. Here, I'm shopping like an American all under one roof, and as I put the box of Post Toasties in my cart, it occurs to me that at this point in history, maybe it makes no discernible difference where you live, that the world has become so small, has overlapped and intertwined, so that one place is pretty much the same as the next.

On the far side of the chocolate aisle is a small housewares department, and while the offerings are pale, it's as if they were made to order for our flat. Stuff without a fleck of pizzazz.

Our flat. *Our* flat?

I buy, in sets of two, plates, bowls, water glasses, knives, forks, spoons, synthetic napkins, and a pair of coffee mugs: *ER* and *SIE*, which is German for HIS and HERS.

Back at the apartment, I put the perishables in the refrigerator. Everything else I set out on the table.

> *Table fountains spouted wines or fragrant waters. The more complex their pipings, the more varieties of drinks they served from their turrets, spigots, and sculpted terminals. Goblets or tankards made of glass or metal, or double cups—in which the cup's cover itself was another cup—were used for drinking. Medieval drinking bowls were sometimes footed, often had elaborate rim embellishments. Silver or gold spoons and a few sharp knives completed the table settings. (Madeline Pelner Cosman, Fabulous Feasts: Medieval Cookery and Ceremony, Braziller, 1976, p. 16)*

I am not setting the table for dinner, but rather I am putting these things—the cheap white plates, the HIS and HERS coffee mugs, the decidedly-not-crystal glasses—on display. Which is kind of dippy, how proud I am of them, as if they were lovely things, when they are not lovely at all. And perhaps that, their sheer homeliness, is the root of this groundswell of love for HF that is near to swallowing me whole.

I want HF to see these plates and forks and napkins and coffee mugs, to see them this way, spread out on the table like open arms, and so I leave them as they are because it is likely that today he will return to the flat before I do. My appointment is scheduled for 16:00, which is the same as four in the afternoon, and a half hour before then, I board the U-bahn (still no ticket, but I'm considering one) to meet with Frau Doktors Frisch and

Schmidt, HF's teaching assistants. Although I have met them twice before—our first lunch and at the fateful dinner—I barely remember them.

They are maybe a few years younger than me, but not years of significance, and they both are nearly done with their *Habilitationschriften*. Soon, they hope, soon they will be called, chosen, as professors in their own right.

"We are wishing for it." Frau Doktor Schmidt clasps her hands together in prayer. Frau Doktor Schmidt would look spectacular in a nun's habit, one of those severe habits, not the newfangled ones with shorter skirts and half a wimple. She could go the full nine yards with a habit of pure white. She has the physiognomy of a nun, one of those eerily angelic nuns, devout to the point of loony, the sort that have visions and stigmata. Her skin is very pale, the blue veins visible as if she were made of marble. She wears rimless glasses and not a dot of makeup. Thin, frail almost, she is very pretty and sexy in a way too.

Frau Doktor Frisch is round, built like the number eight. Her hair, a vivid red the color of a robin's breast, is cut short so that it covers her head as feathers would. And with the way her nose comes to a point she does look like a plump bird of the sort who helped Cinderella pick lentils from the ashes.

I first ask them if there are many women teaching assistants in their department, and Frau Doktor Frisch says no. "It is just the two of us. All the others are men."

"So, tell me," I ask, "how is it, do you think, that Herr Professor Falk wound up with the only two female teaching assistants?"

"Oh, Herr Professor Falk likes to have the women around him," Frau Doktor Frisch says, but Frau Doktor Schmidt disagrees. "No. He *needs* to have the women around him." The three of us laugh, but she is quick to add, "Do not misunderstand, Frau Doktor Rosenfeld. Herr Professor Falk is never improper."

> *The general coarseness of medieval manners was smoothed by certain graces of feudal courtesy. . . . Titles were innumerable, in a hundred grades of dignity; and by a charming custom each dignitary was addressed by his title and his Christian name, or the name of his estate. (Will Durant, The Age of Faith, Simon & Schuster, 1950, p. 839)*

Frau Doktor Frisch nods strongly in support of that, and I, growing dizzy with the *Herr Frau Professor Doktor*, say, "Please, call me Hester."

"Hester. Then please, I am Sigrid."

We wait for Frau Doktor Schmidt to cast her lot with our informality. The way mercury rises, from her neck up to her hairline, she is blushing furiously, an alarming shade of purple, as if this business of using first names is daring, as if we are baring our breasts for one another, and she stammers, "Yes. Thank you. Ulli. My name is Ulli."

So we are Ulli, Sigrid, and Hester, three women sitting around a table drinking wine and gabbing, which is a very different scenario from the Frau Doktors sitting around a table. Now, as intimates, we can get to the good stuff. "We are the only women with so many men," Sigrid says, "and still there is not one man at university who is attractive to us. Except Herr Professor Falk. He is handsome, but he is not a possibility."

"Yes, he is handsome," Ulli agrees, and she lights up her third cigarette in ten minutes. It's a bit disconcerting, the one who looks like a nun smoking like the Marlboro Man, but it causes me to like her even more than I do already. "Herr Professor Falk is very handsome, but all his smiling and teasing the girls is for a show. I think he is married very much."

"There has been some talk," Sigrid leans in and stage-whispers. "You know," she says to Ulli. "That woman. She is not a professor, but she works with university management or some such thing. There has been talk that perhaps she and Professor Falk were making an affair once, but I think it was a false story."

Aha! Bettina, no doubt.

"Yes. I also heard that same rumor. Even more, I heard that they were one time married," Ulli says, "but I do not believe any of it either."

"Why not?" I ask, stuffing the guilt that results from my deceit, the omission that I know the story, into some other pocket, where it will likely find me later. For now, I'm keen to hear the gossip and related theories. "Why didn't you believe it? Why isn't it possible that they were once married or even having an affair?"

"Because she is entirely without charm," Sigrid says, and she sure got that right.

"He is charming," Ulli adds. "It was good luck for us to be his assistants. He is very important. But also he is very nice. Many of the other professors are madmen. Like warlords. So arrogant. But Herr Professor Falk never loses his temper. He is always kind. And he respects us. He respects our work."

"Are you a little bit in love with him?" I ask them both, teasing, not really expecting an answer bearing any resemblance to the truth, but they chime with laughter and in unison say, "Oh, yes."

Ulli nudges Sigrid with her elbow and says, "Tell Hester about the event with the *Strümpfhosen*."

"The what?" I ask.

"*Strümpfhosen*." Ulli translates, "The pantystockings?"

"Pantyhose," I tell her, and Sigrid tells her story.

> It was maybe one year ago, I was in Herr Professor Falk's office to discuss some difficulties I was having with my research. I am writing on the professions of the midwife and the wet nurse for the feudal manor, and I had found two pieces of information that were in direct opposition to each other in regards to how the wet nurse was selected. But that doesn't matter to this story, except that it was the reason I was with him in his office. Professor Falk went over all of it very carefully with me, and he helped me decide which was more likely to be valid. Then, when I was getting up to leave, I got caught on a splinter on the chair which gave me the runner* on my Strümpfhosen all the way from my ankle to beyond my knee. I was so embarrassed. I felt so clumsy, and then Herr Professor Falk said to me, "Men consider those runners to be very attractive. We imagine climbing them." And I went directly home and, like a schoolgirl, I made the runners in all my Strümpfhosen.
>
> *A run.

"He has the gift," Ulli tells me, "for making women feel desired, but, it is too bad, he is never seriously making the pass. You call it that? The pass?"

"Yes. We call it that."

"I wish he would give lessons of his talent. My boyfriend," Ulli complains, "he never says the nice things."

And then we talk some more about men in general, and we giggle like three girlfriends, and maybe we are three girlfriends, and then Sigrid says, "I have heard that the Jewish men are very good lovers. Is this true?"

I pause to consider this, first to consider what's up with this question, but really it is no different from asking about the reputation of French men as good lovers or British as not. Then I consider which of the men in my past were Jewish, and it hits me that none of them were. It wasn't a conscious decision, but the oh-so-clever unconscious, no doubt, avoided them like the Black Death. "I wouldn't know," I tell her. "I never had a Jewish boyfriend."

"Why not?" Sigrid asks, while Ulli grows conspicuously nervous and shifts her gaze to a potted plant near the door.

I shrug. "I guess opposites attract."

"And who is opposite then from a Jew?"

"A German." I entertain the theory as I say it, but it is a theory that carries conviction. It is as if Germans and Jews were two sides of a coin, heads and tails. Front and back. Day and night. Up and down, Montagues and Capulets, and in our three-dimensional sphere, you can't have one without the other. Germans and Jews are inexorably bound together now, our histories are braided, the ethnic version of the Venn diagram. You can't discuss the Jews and not factor the Germans into the equation. Go ahead, out loud say *German* and see if the associative word that springs to mind isn't *Jew*. We need each other, not to survive, but to help define ourselves.

"You must all the time be hitting at the men with sticks here," Sigrid says. "Jewish women are the most wanted ones in Germany. It makes the man very important if he has a Jewish girlfriend."

"Well, I don't know about any of that." I play coy. "I haven't really been meeting men. I'm with someone here."

As if I'd been holding out on her, Ulli turns back to us and asks me, "You have a lover here? In Munich?"

"Yes." I admit that much, but I am fully prepared to lie if they ask for further identifying features.

"Are you going to live here then? I am all for that," Sigrid says. "I think it is a very good thing that Jewish people are coming to live again in Germany. If we have no Jewish people here, then the Nazis have won."

Sigrid gives me something to think about. By the time my mother left Munich there were only 637 Jews remaining in the city. Her departure left them with 636.

Then Sigrid gives me yet something else to think about. "Maybe we all go out together some night? With our boyfriends," Sigrid says. With our boyfriends. Could HF and I go out into the world, his world, together? Sigrid says she knows of a klezmer concert coming up, and she offers to get tickets for all of us.

"Klezmer?" I say.

"Oh yes," she tells me, "it is the craze here."

First the trendy kosher restaurant. Now klezmer music is all the rage. What next? The yarmulke as this year's fashion answer to the beret? Is there no end to the insanity? "To be truthful," I say, "I don't much care for klezmer music." To be truly truthful, I have never heard klezmer music, and I have no idea whether I would care for it or not.

Another truly truthful thing: To give in to this philo-Semitism is sorely tempting. To be exalted could be great fun. A lark, to be lady of the manor. Sigrid as my handmaiden, wearing a white cap, the fringe of her red hair peeking out, saying "Yes, m'lady" and dashing about the castle to do my bidding, whatever that is. I might find it comfy up there on the pedestal, but, ah, I know, ultimately dangerous. The position of the exalted is not a stable one. As with up and down, bubbles burst, idols fall, mortals can't fly, and the dialectic dictates that where there is a *for*, an *against* will follow.

Sigrid lowers her eyes. "I must make the confession to you. I am a philo-Semite," and I squelch the desire to quip, "No shit."

"Yes," she says. "Perhaps I am too excited. You are the first Jew I know to talk with," and Ulli breaks in, "Sigrid!" she says, her tone one of chastisement. The two of them face off and exchange words in German, and then Sigrid turns to me. "Ulli says I must not use the word *Jew*. That I must say *Jewish person*. Please, tell me. Is this correct? Is *Jew* offensive?"

"Only if you mean it to be," I say. "But generally, I think not."

"Oh, thank goodness." Sigrid's hand goes to her heart, as if to steady herself in the relief. "Please. I never mean to offend. Forgive me for what I do not know."

It is that, the innocence, which, granted, is only a split hair away from ignorance, that causes me to like her enormously. This philo-Semite who has never talked with a Jew until me must have a kind of faith like a belief in fairies. "There's nothing to forgive," I tell her, and I clasp my hand over hers as assurance.

"It is settled then. We will not go to a klezmer concert. We will do something else," Sigrid says, and Ulli suggests going to the cinema and a beer garden. "The all six of us. That would be fun."

Could be.

We need, of course, to work out an agreeable time with the men, and I'll need to work out more than that. I have no idea if HF will be open to a group date with his teaching assistants or not. How much of his private affairs is he willing to make public? But for now, we make a date for Saturday, just the three of us—under six eyes, Ulli calls that, the three of us—to go shopping and for lunch, and I am so pleased, elated even, to have made friends all on my own. Certainly, friends can make a place more like a home, the way hanging curtains can or buying dinner plates and coffee mugs can make a place like home too.

Chapter Fifteen

Potsdam 46 29

I could've taken the S-bahn—a commuter rail system—but when HF insisted on taking me by car, I didn't say no twice. Buckled in, my hand on his knee, Tina Turner on the radio singing "What's Love Got to Do. with It," we turn onto a *Bundesstrasse*, which is a major thoroughfare, but not an autobahn. There I see the sign, pointing north: Dachau 7km.

"I had no idea Dachau was that close to Munich," I say. The proximity makes the *we didn't know* routine another notch less credible.

"Oh yes. It's only a few stops on the S-bahn. We can go anytime. I think we should go." Synagogues, memorials, museums, Terezín was plenty, and now he's dying to take me to Dachau. If I am going to live here, I can't be facing down Nazis every day.

"Why would I want to go to Dachau?"

I mean my question to be rhetorical, but perhaps rhetorical doesn't translate, because he answers me. "To see it," he says.

"Dachau was built in 1933, the first camp built by the Nazis, as a prison for political dissidents. Communists and resistants to National Socialism. Many of our fathers wound up there."

"But not your father," I say, and he says, "No. Not my father," and that puts an end to that discussion, which was my intent.

As we turn off the main road, and into a residential area of private houses, he details the arrangement for this afternoon. He will drop me off at his brother's house and wait for me at a nearby pub.

"You're not going to come in with me?" I ask.

"No," he says. "My brother won't speak candidly to you if I am there."

"But you'll come in to say hello." I assume he'll want to say hello to his brother, but I am wrong.

"The sight of my brother depresses me," he says. "You don't need me there for anything. My brother's English is good. Our mother made sure of that. She was something of a visionary. She knew that English would become the important language. But his wife, I don't think she has any English."

Before I step out of the car, HF stops me. "Hester," he says, "I told you a lie concerning my brother."

I prepare myself for something, but I don't know what and certainly not the revelation that comes. "Remember," he says, "when I told you that my brother pats the bums of the neighborhood children? Well, maybe he does. I don't know. But really it's the bums of my daughters he pats."

"Maybe you should tell him not to do that," I suggest, and he nods his head. "Yes, I should. I know I should. But I never know how to say it to him."

And then I lighten the mood and ask, "He's not going to try to pat my bum, is he?"

"Definitely not," he laughs. "You are far too intimidating."

Josef Haushofer. Born in Berlin (1930) to Charlotte and Georg Haushofer. Conscripted into the Volkssturm* (January 1945). Received his Ph.D. in History of the Theater from then new Freie Universität in Berlin (1956). Married Gisela (née?) in 1957. No children. Attempted and failed to find work as an actor. Hired on (with mother's intervention and string-pulling) in public relations department of the Siemens Corporation in Munich (1964). Retired (1993).

*The very-last-ditch war effort when children and senior citizens were called into active duty.

The Haushofer house looks as if it leapt off the page of a Beatrix Potter tale. A cottage, albeit a large cottage, and it is made of fieldstone. Ivy clings to much of the facade. In stark contrast to the earth tones of the house, the garden is agog with reds and yellows and purple—roses, pansies, peonies, dahlias, larkspur, foxglove, and a plethora of snapdragon. Two amusing topiaries flank the steps leading to the door—rabbits, both. One on its hind legs and the other on all fours. It would seem someone here has a sense of humor.

Frau Haushofer, or a woman I assume is Frau Haushofer, opens the door and ushers me inside to the living room. She says nothing and she does not smile, but I don't sense that she is being unfriendly exactly. Rather, I get the feeling that this is a woman who has never smiled. She exudes sadness. I'd be surprised if the funny bunnies were her idea.

Her husband rises from the couch to greet me. He is very tall, taller than HF by three or four inches, at least, and that he is hunched over does nothing to diminish the height of him. Also, it does not seem as if he hunches over because of age—he appears quite sturdy—nor to make himself smaller, but rather as if hunching over will keep him hidden from the world. That he goes on stage, performs in those amateur theatrical productions, is not at all in opposition to this inkling of mine, that this is a man who wants no one to see him. On stage, he gets to be someone else.

All in all, the Haushofers strike me as a lugubrious couple, and if I had that sort of imagination, I could be fearing they will lock me up in the pantry to later make a meal of me.

There is nothing much to indicate that HF and Josef Haushofer are half brothers, other than the fact that they are both tall and thin. Josef resembles, as best as I can tell from photographs alone, their mother. Small deep-set eyes and a beaked nose, but their mother did not apparently impart any of her charisma onto this first son. He is awkward, ill at ease, and I see it is up to me to get the ball rolling.

"Your garden is beautiful," I say. "Do you do all the work yourself?"

"My wife does most of it, but I do some too."

I try to make sense of this sad woman and this broken man making a splendid garden that explodes in sunshine. Yes, Konstanze had it right. He is a broken man. I recognize the signs. My father was one too. But what are we if not a bundle of contradictions? "And the rabbits," I say, "the topiaries, who did those?"

"I did," he says, shyly, almost as if he is expecting to be chastised for impudence, and I tell him, "They are so delightful. I adore them," and he asks, "Do you like rabbits, Frau Doktor Rosenfeld?"

I know about his rabbits, and I am quite curious to see them for myself. "Oh yes," I say, "I like all animals," and he invites me out into the backyard, where there are two squares of grass edged with white picket fencing. Seven rabbits are in one square and the other holds a dozen or so guinea pigs. Both pens are divided with partitions of chicken wire. Lest Herr Doktor Haushofer wind up with a cornucopia of small mammals, he keeps the boys on one side of the chicken wire and girls on the other. The sun dapples through the leaves of the trees, and the animals are bathing in the warmth, and some are nibbling grass.

We go first to the guinea pigs, and he singles out each one for introduction. The large calico is Fritzie and the smaller calico is Fritzie's sister Sissy. The all-black one is Albert, and then I lose track as to which one is Franz and which is Wolfgang and which is Johann.

At the rabbit pen, he reaches down and lifts out a chubby gray bunny. "This is Gretel," he tells me, and he holds her in his arms, and with one hand strokes the rabbit's ears. "I confess that she is my favorite, but," he hastily adds, "I love them all the same much. Rabbits," he tells me, "have no natural defenses. They are helpless against predators. It is up to us to protect them."

Before returning Gretel to the pen, he places his lips on the rabbit's head, kissing her softly, and my heart squeezes tight, constricts with a kind of anguish, and a kind of love too, for this man.

Now I must see where the guinea pigs and rabbits sleep and where they stay indoors when it rains. He has built a garden apartment complex. It's extraordinary, and maybe a little loopy on his part too, because while I'm sure the guinea pigs appreciate having a warm, dry place to sleep, I don't know how much they appreciate that their little huts are painted in *trompe l'oeil* brick, and the same goes for the rabbits. Over the entrance to one of the rabbit houses is a black ribbon, draped, and a small wreath of flowers. "We had a death in the family," he explains, and I say, "Oh, I'm so sorry. Was it sudden?"

"It's always sudden, even when it's expected." And then he says, "But you came to speak with me of my brother. We will go inside."

He waits until I take a seat on the couch, and then he goes to a desk and brings back some papers and pictures. "I made preparations for you," he says. He sits on a chair across from me, and as if she had been signaled by a butler's silent bell, Frau Haushofer appears with a tray. She sets out coffee cups, but only for two. She is not joining us. Also she sets out a coffeepot, creamer, sugar bowl, and a plate of little cakes.

Herr Doktor Haushofer pours the coffee, and I help myself to one of the cakes. It looks as if it is made with nuts, and when I pop it in my mouth, it crumbles, stale and dry as Styrofoam. If I'd been alone or with friends, I would've spit it out into a napkin, but here I wash it down with a swig of coffee and smile.

The photograph on the top of the pile shows a gangly boy, twelve or thirteen, knee deep in a stream. By his side is Klaus Falk. The two of them are holding fishing poles. The boy is grinning, his happiness spills from the picture. "That is me with Uncle Falk. He taught me fishing. I always called him Uncle Falk. Even after he and my mother married."

Josef Haushofer has another, earlier memory of Klaus Falk, sitting at the table in the Haushofer flat and picking up the telephone. "This is Berlin 23 84 28. Connect me please to Potsdam 46 29."

Hurriedly, I flip back some pages to corroborate the number. Bingo! Potsdam 46 29.

"I still recall those numbers after all these years," Josef is saying. "I do not know who he was calling, but I do remember committing the Potsdam number to memory. The Berlin number, of course, was my mother's. That must have been in 1940 or '41."

He doesn't know who Uncle Falk was calling? Could that naiveté be for real? How about that he was calling his wife, who was waiting at home, dinner on the table, to tell her he was working late, not to wait up for him? There's a reasonable hypothesis if I know my Falk men.

Often Josef and his mother would, by coincidence, meet up with Uncle Falk when they went boating or for walks through the park or to a café. He and his mother would set out alone, just the two of them. But having arrived at their destination, his mother would say, "Oh look. There's Uncle Falk," and Uncle Falk would say, "Well, isn't this a pleasant surprise. Do you mind if I join you?" This charade went on for a few years. Then in 1942, his mother tried to ease him into the idea that she was going to marry again, and she asked her son, "Who do you think would be good for me to marry?" Josef thought for a moment and then said, "Otto Lintz from Dessau." Otto Lintz from Dessau had teeth the color of yellow mustard. "Not Uncle Falk?" she asked, and Josef said, "Uncle Falk is already part of our family," which his mother interpreted as her son's consent. From August 1942

through the end of June 1943, Josef and his mother and her new
husband Klaus Falk lived together in Berlin.

I look up from my notebook and say, "August?"

"Yes. They married in August 1942."

Not according to the certificate of marriage I saw. That has
them tying the knot in October.

But nor is it likely that Josef Haushofer is mistaken. Not a man
who can recall phone numbers from sixty-one years before.
Something is awry.

✳ *August? October? Frau Doktor living in sin?*

"So they married in October," I say, trying to catch him in a
cover-up, but I fail.

"No," he says. "August. Those were very happy days," he tells
me, and perhaps I look skeptical or confused here too, because
how happy could war years be, and certainly they weren't the
least bit happy for some. "I was very happy," he explains. "I had a
real family now. I was very fond of my Uncle Falk. I loved him.
He taught me fishing. I told you that already?"

I don't say yes, but nod, urging him to never mind repetition,
to continue.

"Every night I remember finding a pair of his wet socks hanging over the steam pipes to dry. Each night he washed the socks
he wore that day."

Sock washing? Like philandering, further behavior passed
down like an heirloom, a pocket watch or a pipe, from father to
son for how many generations?

While I'm writing, Herr Doktor Haushofer pauses to drink his coffee, which is mostly cream and sugar. I look up in time to see some dribbling down his chin and onto the front of his white shirt. As if to hide what he has done, he covers the wet spot that is faintly brown with his hand. His eyes glaze over as if he is lost in thought, or simply lost.

"I'm always doing that," I say. "Spilling things on myself."

"Really?" he seems genuinely surprised, as if dribbling coffee were territory exclusive to the feeble-minded. "My wife knows a way to get the stain out. Perhaps before you leave, she will give you the recipe."

> . . . to remove a stain of oil or other grease, the recipe is this: Collect urine and heat it until it is mildly warm, and let the spot soak in it for two days. Then gently squeeze the cloth, but do not wring it. If the stain remains . . . soak it again in urine mixed with ox gall. . . . (Le Ménagier de Paris [1393], ed. Baron Jérôme Pichon, Paris, 1846, Tome Second, p. 65, author's translation)

"So," I say, "Where were we? Ah, socks. Herr Uncle Falk washed his socks every day."

"Yes, yes. The wet socks, they were a great comfort to me." Josef Haushofer visibly warms with the memory. "They meant a father was in the home. Then in August of 1943, all the children were sent away from Berlin. Heinrich was only weeks old when we went to live at a children's home on the Baltic. There were as many as thirty children in that small house. I was the eldest, and so it was my job to be the butler, and I peeled the potatoes. All the children had to work."

✳ *Butler? Training for future in the theater?*

I want to go back some weeks or so before the evacuation, to verify HF's date of birth. "So you were at home with your mother and stepfather when your brother was born?" I ask.

"No," he tells me. "I was away camping. When I got back home, the door to the flat was locked and nobody was there. I was frightened because these were war times. Who knew what dreadful thing could have happened? So I sat there in front of the flat for a long time not knowing what to do when a neighbor saw me. She did not know where my mother had gone to, but she let me come inside and use her telephone. I called my mother's office and from there I was told that my mother was at hospital and that I had a brother."

"Camping?" I ask. "You went camping in 1943? Wasn't that dangerous?"

"We didn't think if it were dangerous or not. It was an adventure. Often we went camping with the Hah Yott," he says, something that sounds like that. Like *Hah Yott*.

"Hah Yott?" I want to know. "What is that?"

"Hah Yott." Then he stops, and looks out the window to his garden, and I fear that he is lost to me again, but then he says, "Hah Yott was Hitler Youth. It did not mean anything. For us children it had no political associations, but it was like Boy Scouting. A nature club."

I'd really rather not, and I wish I didn't have to, but I do have to and so I ask, "And what about the Werewolves? Was that a nature club too?"

"No," he says. "That was something else."

As best as I've been able to ascertain, they weren't anything deadly, these Werewolves. An outlet for youthful romanticism that never amounted to much more than mischief-making and fanciful talk.

It's not like I'm asking if he was SS or a camp guard, but still, it is unpleasant. "And were you one?" I ask. "Were you a Werewolf?"

But I get no answer, and I see Frau Haushofer is standing beside me. Soundlessly and without warning, she has entered the room, and she says, "It is time for you to leave, Frau Doktor Rosenfeld. It is time for my husband to make his nap. Now."

So she does have some English after all, and I feel the sting of rebuke: Be careful where you tread.

Chapter Sixteen

What is done

M
ost of my day is spent at the university library
photocopying articles and monographs that HF
has written or coauthored. Although I cannot read
any of the pages for detail of content, it is evident that there has
been an emphasis on the economics of the Middle Ages. That he
went from the nunnery to the bordello to taxation and confisca-
tion to the development of the merchant class to the price of
beans. More of his mother's influence, no doubt.

*When the Socialists took over, factory owners were put in jail
for irregularities and their business would be shut down. Then
they wouldn't be able to pay their taxes and the factories were
given to the people. No one in my family wanted jail, so we
gave over our factories first thing. Because of the Socialists, my
family suffered hardships. I have always been opposed to*

socialism of any type. (From the memoir of Frau Doktor Falk)

His mother, he has mentioned more than once, was a great fan of Maggie Thatcher.

When I am done, the sheaf of papers in my bag, I head over to his office only to find he is not there. Instead, I find him at our flat, seated at the table, holding a heat lamp to the left side of his head. A circle, five inches in diameter, glows red. "I have a dreadful headache because I went for a haircut," he says to explain the reason for the heat lamp and the genesis of the pain. He is still talking as I go for my notebook, flipping quickly to the *Nutball* section because I know a good one is coming.

First they gave it a washing and then they gave me a man to cut the hair, which can't be good.

Ah, my love does not disappoint.

"What are you writing down?" he asks, and I tell him, "About your haircut. And your headache. Why don't you take an aspirin?"

"Aspirins don't work," he says, and he switches off the heat lamp, which I suspect doesn't work either.

"Well," I suggest, "how about a nice bloodletting, then? Or, with a red cloth, tie a stalk of crosswort to your forehead."

"Very funny, my Hester. Seriously, though, when are you going to let me read all that you've written?"

"You can read it whenever you want to," I tell him. "There are no secrets here. Although I haven't actually written anything yet. It's nothing but notes. But feel free." I toss the notebook at him, and he catches it with both hands.

In the middle of the night I wake and grope for him in the bed, but he's not here. I sit up and see that he is at his desk, the goose-neck reading lamp illuminating the open page of my notebook. "Hey, darling," I say, soft, half asleep, patting the empty space beside me. "What are you doing? Come to bed."

"I think we need to talk about this." He holds my notebook up as if it were a courtroom exhibit. "You got some things wrong."

"Sure. Okay. We'll talk later."

I say that we'll talk later, and he agrees to talk later, but it seems he can't wait for later. "For example," he says, "you got a number of facts wrong."

"No doubt I did," I say.

"For example, you say my mother studied economics, but she studied engineering. Engineering was even more remarkable for a woman. Even today, it is rare for a woman to study engineering."

"Noted," I say. "Now come to bed."

"And I would never have said *Mutti* for *Mummy*. If you are the least bit upper-crust you say *Mama*. *Mutti* is someone who cooks cauliflower. And you can't make soap from mortar. My mother never wrote that."

"Soap from mortar?" What is he talking about? Oh, oh. I remember. The pamphlet. "Oh, darling. That was a joke. What time is it?" I lean over to look at the clock on the nightstand. 3:36. "It's three-thirty in the morning," I tell him, but he isn't concerned with the time. Instead, he is hell-bent on lecturing me on how I didn't present an accurate history of the Sudetenland.

"An accurate history of the Sudetenland is a book unto itself," I say. "And you are reading notes. Notes. Not a finished book. Not even a rough draft of a book. Notes."

"Yes, and why do you make so many notes on the Middle Ages? The Middle Ages have nothing to do with my family."

"Well, they've got plenty to do with you, don't they? Anyway, they were just things that struck me as interesting or amusing. Things that seemed relevant still in some way. It's just stuff I wrote down."

"And you did not always sufficiently document your sources." His tone is smug, professorial.

Again, I repeat, "This is not a finished book. You are reading notes."

"But still you will use these notes, and much of what you have here worries me. For one thing, do you have to mention about my daughter's nipples? I don't want to hurt my family."

"No. I do not have to mention your daughter's nipples. I don't want to hurt your family either. We can go over all the things that worry you and take them one by one. But can't we do that later? In the morning. After sunrise."

"Yes. Certainly. But I think you should be aware that some of your perceptions are tainted. Like how you make the comparison between Goebbels and me. That was a man who killed his own children."

It is obvious that this conversation is not going to take place later. He needs to have it now, and so I get up and put water on to boil for coffee. "There is no comparison with Goebbels and you," I say. "Where are you getting that from?"

He flips through the pages, and then says, "Oh. My mistake.

It's what you say about Martin Bormann having all those children. But still, you are comparing me to a big Nazi. And you are making way too much of all the Nazi business. All of it. What do they have to do with anything? The Werewolves were not serious. They were a bunch of boys who wanted to play war."

"I think I make that clear. If it's not clear enough, I will clarify it further." I spoon instant coffee into my mug and ask him, "Do you want any?"

He shakes his head no, which is a good thing, as he is already wired and racing. He does not need any coffee. "You are focusing on the Third Reich. All those quotes. You are looking for Nazis under every cabbage. It seems as if you want every member of my family to have been one. And not only is that not true, but you know perfectly well it is bad scholarship to twist the facts to fit the theory."

I take my coffee cup with me and get back into bed, but I sit up, cross-legged, and I try to explain that I am not twisting any facts, but if I am going to be writing about a war baby, I have to write about the war. I have to write about the environment in which he was raised, and the people who did the raising. "How can I look at what you've become without looking at what you came from?"

"Yes, but you emphasize the Nazis. You take things out of context. You don't really get into all the good things my family did."

"Like what?" I ask. My tone is terse. "What good things did they do?"

"I don't mean those sorts of good things, but how my mother really helped women. What she taught them about home economy was important. And she was a role model."

"I do mention that," I say.

"You have to be careful with this, Hester. You have to be careful how you present things. You don't want anyone thinking that you are one of those greedy Jews."

"Excuse me." I place my coffee cup on the nightstand. "What did you say? Repeat that."

"I said, you don't want people to think you are one of those greedy Jews. I . . ."

"Greedy Jews," I cut him off.

He realizes what he has said, but perhaps not what he has done. "Come now, Hester. That's not fair. English is not my first language. Sometimes I don't choose the best words. You're not greedy. There is nothing greedy about you. What I meant was that you don't want to be like that Goldhagen."

Goldhagen. Daniel Jonah Goldhagen, author of the controversial *Hitler's Willing Executioners*. Harvard professor of government and social studies who pointed the finger at the whole lot of them, who said that, one way or another, pretty much each and every German was guilty. "So," I keep my voice level, as if I were calm, but I am seething with fury, which is the only response that can keep the hurt, the horrible, horrible hurt, at bay. "Goldhagen is a greedy Jew, but I am not a greedy Jew. Is that what you are saying?"

"Yes. Yes. I don't mean it the way it sounds, but I'm talking about how Goldhagen wanted everyone to be guilty. He needed everyone to be guilty. And whether they were or not, he made them guilty for his own purposes."

"I see."

"Good."

"No," I counter. "Not good. Not good at all."

No more than you can undo what's been done, once a thing has been said, it cannot be unsaid. And what's been said is there in the air between us like a permanent frost.

The sun is coming up, and the bed is swathed in a blue light, which will not reach his desk for a few minutes yet. For now, he remains in the shadow, until he gets up and comes toward me. "Hester," he says, "I love you," and he moves to take me in his arms.

The way a hedgehog curls into a ball of quills, I too pull inside myself, my head bent and tucked between my shoulders. It is not my life for which I am fearing. Rather I fear what I might do, what I might say, and I am all too aware of the effect words can have.

I go first to his closet. Down on my knees, I push his shoes off to one side and I run my hand along the floor. On the shelves, I root around in the shirts and sweaters which had been folded neatly and stacked. Then I turn my attention to his chest of drawers, where I rifle through his underwear. I toss socks rolled into balls over my shoulder until now the floor is littered with them, as if the aftermath of a hailstorm. From his desk and his cabinet, I unload files and papers and leave them on the bed. I turn this flat upside down and inside out, as if it were a pocket to be emptied of coins, lint, and perhaps an old tissue wrapped around a half-eaten piece of hard candy. I stand in the middle of the room stumped. The only place I haven't looked is in the closet that is ostensibly mine, on that top shelf, the shelf I am unable to reach unless I stand on a chair.

And there I find it. The box the size of a shirt box, wrapped in brown paper, tied with string, unopened. The cancellation date is still legible. 10.6.91. The tenth of June. Some months after his father died.

I sit at the table, staring at the box in front of me, and I consider the enormity of what I intend to do.

It is flat-out wrong, indeed it is dishonorable, to open what is not mine to open, but I don't owe him my honor. Not now. Besides, you can love a person and not honor him. I've done it all my life.

⚹ *Honor thy father and thy mother.*

And I cut the string, and that is done, and it cannot be undone.

The box is filled with photographs and papers and one watch. A pocket watch, gold, on a chain. The crystal is cracked, but I wind it and do not need to hold it to my ear to hear the tick, tick, tick. I place the watch on the table beside me, as if I need to keep my eye on the time.

But I'm in no hurry. I poke, sift, pick, choose, study, gauge what I can. Some of the photographs are duplicates of those I've seen before—HF as a boy, one of his parents together, the studio portrait of his father. I look at one of his father with an adolescent Josef standing on what seems to be a pier, and another of Herr and Frau Doktors Falk with the infant HF in his mother's arms. Snapshots of happy times. For them. Most of these pictures are of people of whom I've heard nothing or can't connect the face to a name. Maybe a paternal grandmother, neighbors, family friends. I don't know, and I don't much care.

I turn up a photocopy of Klaus Falk's certificate of death, his driver's license, his passport. There are some aged newspaper clippings, the paper yellowed and brittle. There is a child's rendering of an Easter Bunny, crayon on paper, and although it is unsigned, I assume HF to have been the artist.

No longer sifting through the papers, I methodically take each item out of the box and shake it as if the evidence will fall free. Evidence that incriminates, that is what I am after. I want proof that I can hold in my hand. Evidence. I want his father or his mother, or better yet, both of them to have done evil. I want them to be guilty of something beyond minding their own business. I need for them to be guilty of something unspeakable. And I want the proof of it.

So I keep looking. Maybe there's a clue in these newspaper clippings, and I stare at words which I don't understand, as if there's a coded message in them which will reveal itself to me. As if I'm expecting to see a swastika emerge in a pattern. It has to be here. I must find it. Somewhere in this box there is dirt or blood. It has to be. So I'm still looking, listening to the tick, tick, tick of the watch, when I hear his key in the door.

HF bounds towards me, big smile, arms open, as if everything were hunky-dory, and then he stops. At a standstill, he takes in the state of the flat. "Hester, what happened here? Are you all right?" he asks, concerned, as if I were not responsible, but perhaps a tornado or a bomb made this mess. Then his gaze fixes on the box, on the brown paper and the string, and all that is out before me. In the quiet, the watch ticks loudly.

"You had no right to open that," he says, and I quite agree. "That's true. I had no right to open it."

"Then why did you?" He takes the seat across from me. We are separated by the table and his inheritance in the middle of it.

"Because I don't owe you any courtesy, that's why."

✳ *Once a thing has been done, it cannot be undone.*

"Hester, we need to talk about this. About all of it."

"Yes," I say. "All of it."

We are at opposite ends of the table, he and I, as if we are in negotiations, and he asks me, "What did you find?"

"Nothing. Yet," I add.

"What are you looking for?" he wants to know. "What are you hoping to find?"

"Symmetry," I say. "A way for it to balance out."

"For what? I don't understand. Because of what I said? I was tired, Hester. And upset. I wasn't thinking, and my English wasn't with me. Please, can't we forget it?"

"No. I can't forget it, and I am going to find your parents guilty."

"Why?" he asks. "Why do you want such a thing?"

"Because you never asked them if they were. You're a historian. Why didn't you ask?"

"Because our conflict with our parents was generational. Not personal."

"Exactly." I bang my fist on the table. "You weep over what *they* did, this *they* in the abstract, but you don't want to know who *they* were."

"Maybe I didn't ask because I knew it meant listening to all sorts of lies and legends, which I didn't want to hear or to challenge. They were still my parents, Hester. My father and my mother. My mother," he repeats.

This time, I do not whisper. I take no chance that my words will go unheard. I enunciate clearly and with resonance, as if this admission were the first step of twelve. "My mother was from Munich." I tell him how she was born in Munich, how from 1933 onward she and her family waited patiently for all the nonsense to pass, and then how my grandfather eventually realized the nonsense wasn't going to pass, it was only going to get worse and worse, and how, in the face of that realization, he scraped together every *Pfennig* possible to secure his daughter, my mother, a ticket out.

"And your father?" HF asks.

"Berlin," I tell him, and he says, "Those Rosenfelds I found. The lists when we were in Berlin, your father was one of them."

"Probably."

"It's the same then, with you and me. You didn't ask either."

"No," I tell him. "It is not the same. Your parents were of a people who made history happen. Mine were the by-product."

"I'm sorry," he says, and I say, "No. I'm the one who should be sorry. I loved my parents, but I was so ashamed of them."

"You were ashamed of your parents?" He says this as if I had no right to that, as if the Germans got dibs on shame, and I remind him, "You were never ashamed of your mother. You were proud of her. You were proud of her strength, her power, her position in the world. I saw my parents as weak. Objects of ridicule. The laughingstock on two continents."

"Hester, I don't understand. How is this possible? They were victims. Nothing was their fault."

"Victims. That's right. They were victims." I spit the word.

"And victims are pathetic. We feel bad for them. But we don't admire them."

"Of course we do. We admire them for having survived. How is it that you are not understanding their heroism?" he wonders. "How brave it was to leave home to make a new life in a new world. You should admire their courage."

"You make them sound like adventurers. You know it wasn't like that. They fled because they were prey."

Is it possible to make him understand how, at school, when we opened our history books to those pictures, I winced? Those pictures of that time. Just like they always show that picture of the boy with his arms raised, there's another one that you can't escape, one that is used everywhere, in all the books on the subject. It's the one taken on the day of the Anschluss of the old man scrubbing the city sidewalk with a toothbrush while a pair of Brownshirts stand over him laughing. Can I make HF understand how, for years, I thought that was my grandfather in the picture? Not even when I learned that it was taken in Vienna was I able to really let go of the belief that it was my grandfather who was the butt of the Brownshirts' idea of a joke. Every time I considered where my parents came from, I was confronted with how they were taunted, ridiculed, denied their humanity. And it wasn't always all that different for them in America, albeit on a substantially less significant scale. There, in the land of refuge, they were labeled as sad stories, poor things, and while decent people expressed compassion, no one wanted to be close to that, no one wanted to align with the meek and the dispossessed. As if vulnerability were contagious, my parents lived in social quarantine. And that was on a good day. On the bad days, they were scoffed at, their accents mocked, their weakness exploited. They used to flick spitballs at my father, his students, my classmates. While he tried to teach them the miracles of chemistry, they flicked saliva-soaked beads of paper at his head. And while spitballs aren't bullets, they are ammunition of derision aimed at the weak and the weird. My parents never fought back.

"Oh Hester," he says, and here come the waterworks.

"I don't want your pity," I tell him, and I'll give him this: He doesn't deny offering it. "Where do we go from here?" he asks.

And as if it were an answer to anything, I tell him, "I love you. I really, really do love you."

"And I love you." His voice is pitched with light, buoyant with optimism that this is simply a rough patch. As if we'd had an argument over money or who does the dishes or where to holiday this season. A lovers' quarrel easily smoothed over with a kiss. As if we could, just like that, put all this nasty business of betrayal behind us. "We must come to accept that there are some things we will never know." He makes disavowal sound as simple as a waltz. "Can we live with that?" He reaches across the table to take my hand, but I'm too far away.

"No," I tell him. "We can't live with that. If I were to stay here, I would keep looking. No matter how much I might want to stop, it wouldn't be possible. I would continue to look and look."

"And what if you continued to find nothing?" he asks, and I say, "Then I would look some more. I would tear your life apart, turn it upside down. Never resting, but searching, always searching. It wouldn't matter if I never found anything. I would always be looking. I don't want it to be this way. But it is. It's what we were left with."

"We do not have to accept this legacy. We can represent the

future," he says. "We are a new generation. We should be able to forgive the past. We can make this right again. Please, Hester," he beseeches of me, "will you forgive?"

But there is no point to asking me for forgiveness. I am in no position to forgive any of it, because I was not among the suffering. I shake my head no. "I can't," I say. And again the tick, tick, tick of the pocket watch is the only sound. Tick, tick, tick, our history passes between us, like an ocean between continents, and it is wide and deep and cold and I am drowning in a sorrow that I know is infinite, a sadness that will go on forever and ever the way time does, and the ocean too.

Chapter Seventeen

The ends of the earth

T his late-November afternoon is bleak and cold, and
gusts of wind send dead leaves rushing along the
streets, and the people too. I, however, am snug in
the warmth of the New York Public Library, the grand one with
the stone lions out front.

In the Map Room, at a sturdy wooden table, I'm sketching a
copy of the crude map placed alongside my notebook. Brouwer
Street, Broad Street, Pearl Street, Maidens' Path, all narrow and
crooked. In July 1654 when Jacob Barsimon—the first Jew to
make New Amsterdam his home—walked these streets, they
were muddy and crowded with pigs, sheep, and chickens. One
month later—August 1654—twenty-seven Jews more arrived in
the city, but it is Jacob Barsimon and that time in July which con-
cern me; that one month, those four weeks when he was the lone
Jew on the continent. I imagine him to look like Harpo Marx,

and I'm going with that image when I'm startled by a familiar voice. "Hester. Hester Rosenfeld."

I turn to find Peter Bourne, Renaissance scholar and renowned lecher, standing at my left. "Peter," I say. "Nice suit."

"Armani," he informs me, although surely I did not ask. Pulling up the chair next to mine, he sits and says, "No one has seen you. For ages. There was rumor that you'd fallen off the ends of the earth."

Speaking as if he were a slow child, I say, "The earth is round, Peter. We can't fall off."

Despite what many of us were taught in grade school, the crews of the Nina, the Pinta, and the Santa Maria did not fear falling off the ends of the earth. From the time of Innocent III (1198), the teachings of Aristotle had made a comeback, and so while there was absolute certainty that Heaven was directly overhead and that Hell churned beneath our feet, it was widely accepted that the earth was shaped like an egg. Still, it took Fernando de Magallanes to make something of it, to go full circle.

"So where then," Peter wants to know, "have you been hiding?"

I shrug. "In the root cellar? Maybe behind a false wall?"

Peter Bourne seems to think this is my way of flirting, because he leans in close to me and whispers, "That sounds dark."

"On the contrary," I say. "It was enlightening." I close my notebook, slip the map back into its protective folder, and gather together, like rosebuds, my pencils, but before I can stand up to put on my coat, Peter stops me. "You never did tell me," he says. "How it worked out. Your medieval project. Was he of any assistance? Heinrich Falk."

I'm not surprised the effect it has on me, hearing his name spoken aloud. Not surprised, but it is anguish all the same to feel as if my heart were once again in his hand, his huge hand, as if his fingers were closing softly around it and the gentle pressure were something like a kiss, an excruciatingly sweet kiss.

"I've returned to the colonies," I say to Peter. "Landed square in New Amsterdam," and I say no more other than, "It was good to see you. Give my best to your wife."

Outside, it is growing dark, a dusk that tints the city, my city, a translucent, but deep, purple, the convergence of the onset of winter and night.

> *Although the earth rotates on its axis turning day into night as it revolves around the sun so that days become weeks and weeks become years, time goes forward only and not around and around. Oh, stories of the past can be reinterpreted, rethought, and revised, but no matter four hundred years ago or merely some months before, history remains fixed in time and space as if it were bits of debris trapped in amber.*

Amber, in some parts of the world, is called *Bernstein*.